Isolation

Alex Kane

PublishAmerica
Baltimore

© 2004 by Alex Kane
All rights reserved. No part of this book may be reproduced, stored in a retrieval system or transmitted in any form or by any means without the prior written permission of the publishers, except by a reviewer who may quote brief passages in a review to be printed in a newspaper, magazine or journal.

First printing

ISBN: 1-4137-1933-3
PUBLISHED BY PUBLISHAMERICA, LLLP
www.publishamerica.com
Baltimore

Printed in the United States of America

For Jason

Special thanks goes to Mary Shamley, Erik Vermeiren, and my family. Your encouragement and support has been invaluable, thank you all for giving me the gift of your time.

I am eternally indebted to the wonderful staff at PublishAmerica, who gave me this amazing opportunity and patiently guided me through the publishing process. Thanks so much.

Prologue

Live, as though the day were here.
             - Nietzche

Toronto, Ontario
June, 1980

The piercing sound of a ringing telephone startled Daniel Bradley from a deep, dreamless sleep. A groan escaped his dry lips as he reached for the phone with his right hand. Once he grasped it, choking off its third ring, he opened his eyes to read the clock radio. His stomach lurched at the time.

Three-thirty in the morning. Nothing good came from a ringing telephone in the middle of the night.

"Hello," he grunted into the receiver.

"Daniel, it's Kate. I'm sorry to wake you so late but something's happened to Mom. She was just rushed to the hospital and it doesn't look good. It doesn't look good at all!"

His older sister's nervous, thin voice shook him from the foggy vestiges of heavy sleep. He reached out blindly, turned on the lamp on the wood nightstand and winced from the searing light.

"Just a second, slow down." He tried not to let panic creep into his voice, that would send Kate into hysterics. "What happened?"

"I think she had a heart attack. I heard a noise downstairs about an hour ago, and came down to see what it was. I went in her bedroom to check on her and she was on the floor. She said she had chest pain, and couldn't catch her breath. I called for an ambulance but by the time they got here she was unconscious!" she exclaimed, caught her breath and continued. "They left just a few moments ago, their taking her to St. Evans Memorial Hospital. I'm on my way. I called the girls and they're meeting me there but...."

She hesitated and sniffed a few times. He knew she wasn't sure what to say next, but he knew precisely what she wanted.

"I could call you later and let you know how she is, but…uh…it would be better if you could meet us at the hospital too. I know it's a long trip for you, but it would mean a lot to all us. It would mean a lot to me." Her voice quivered, she started to cry.

His pulse hammered in his temples but the rest of his body felt numb. He swallowed hard but could not force the huge lump down that had rooted in his throat.

"Daniel?"

He couldn't find his voice, and lowered his head in painful indecision.

"Daniel, I know this is difficult for you but we should all be together right now. Mom hasn't been well for some time, and this…could be it. No matter what happens though, we need to go through it together, be a family for once. Come home, it's time you came home," she pleaded and he nodded to himself. She was right, it was time. Almost twenty years had passed since he had returned to his hometown. He couldn't avoid it any longer. Every inch of his mind screamed resistance, but guilt was a powerful motivator. His sisters needed him, but more importantly, his mother needed him.

"I'm on my way," he said slowly, with the deep, full voice that defined his presence within a classroom. An authoritative voice that commanded respect and reverence from his students. A stranger's voice to his family. He seemed to have surprised his sister, for she didn't say anything for a few seconds.

"Good. I'm so glad Daniel. I'll see you at the hospital in a few hours then." She hung up.

He stared absently at the telephone for a long time.

* * * * *

He had just finished packing his suitcase when the telephone rang again. He assumed it was one of his other two sisters, calling to confirm that he was indeed making the trip home.

"Hello," he answered.

"Daniel, it's me." The familiar female voice shocked him, he almost dropped the phone. "Kate called me. She told me about your mother and I'm so sorry."

"Kate called you?" he gasped, wondering why Kate would call his ex-girlfriend to tell her about his mother's medical crises at such a late hour. "I don't understand. Doesn't she know that we're not together any more?"

"Our relationship doesn't matter right now. Kate is a dear friend of mine and she called because she thought I should know what was going on. I'm glad she did. I'm going to Aldon with you, I'm packing as we speak."

"I don't think so!" he burst out incredulously, deeply annoyed with Kate for putting him into such an awkward situation. Returning to Aldon would be hard enough; but to do it with Rachel, of all people, was unthinkable. "I wouldn't feel comfortable with that at all."

"I don't care how you feel about it. I'm going to see your mother, and that's that. I have every right to go to the hospital to see her." Her voice raised to an angry pitch. He had offended her.

"If you don't take me, I'll drive there myself. I swear to God I will, Daniel. And when I get there I'll…"

"Fine! I don't have time for this," he cut her off. She was notorious for long-winded speeches peppered with profanity when she felt she had been wronged. He didn't have the time or energy for that nonsense. He knew that since she had her mind made up, she would go on her own anyway, so he might as well indulge her to save himself future agony.

"I'll pick you up in twenty minutes. You better be ready and on your front step," he snapped.

"This *isn't* about you, you know. This isn't a last-ditch attempt to see you or change your mind about us. I know that's what you're thinking but you're wrong. I want to see your mother and that's all. Understand?"

"Of course," he replied dryly.

"Good, I'll see you in a bit." She hung up before he could say another word.

In a bewildered daze, Daniel stumbled to the connecting bathroom to brush his teeth and pack a few toiletries. He caught his reflection in the mirror above the faucet and stopped. At thirty-two, he was pleased that the wrinkles of time hadn't caught up to him yet. His face was smooth, tanned and flawless. His hair, black and thick was stylishly cut short. He knew he looked athletic and young, one might even guess that he was in his mid twenties. He was an avid jogger, which kept him fit, and was a solitary pursuit that he engaged in each morning at daybreak. Running kept him trim and strong, invigorated his mind for the day ahead, and was a great outlet for stress. Which he had more than enough of.

It bothered him to know that his father had passed away at the age of thirty-six, and had looked at least a decade older. Joe Bradley had always had an old, wearied look about him despite his young age. His skin had appeared deeply wrinkled and rough, stubbled with coarse facial hair. His hands had been square, thick masses of hard callouses, with the fingers of his right hand a sickly yellow from a lifetime of smoking. Daniel looked down at his own soft, well-manicured hands and knew things could have turned out much differently for him.

* * * * *

He left his condo shortly after four, and drove down the empty city streets in his slick black BMW. Usually, these roads were a bustling mass of frantic energy, but at this hour, there wasn't another car in sight. Cool rain fell gently, giving the city a romantic, dewy look. He parked at the curb in front of Rachel's townhouse and impatiently considered honking when she wasn't in sight.

Within seconds, the front door opened, and she came running down the concrete steps with a large duffel bag and thermos clutched in her hands.

"I made coffee," she announced after throwing open the passenger door. She handed him the plaid thermos and threw her bag in the back seat. When she was finally settled in, he handed the thermos back to her.

"Pour me a cup," he ordered, put the vehicle in gear and looked over at her. A stab of pain struck him in the chest so hard that it nearly took his breath away. He had forgotten how beautiful she was. He had been awe-struck by her long wavy dark hair, impish smile and sparkling bright eyes, the first time he had laid eyes on her. Now, almost twenty years later, he still found her incredibly stunning. What he found was her most attractive attribute, was the fact that she wore little make-up and hardly paid attention to her looks. She always wore loose, comfortable clothing with soft neutral colors that accentuated the natural auburn highlights in her hair. She never wore jewelry or unnecessary accessories, though she could well afford to bask in those luxuries. Rachel was a natural beauty in a world of material goddesses.

"What are you going to do about work?" she questioned as she buckled up her seatbelt.

"I'm not teaching any summer courses so I don't have to worry about that. I'll just call my assistant later and tell him that I had to leave town because of a family emergency," he answered uneasily, knowing that that would send curious tongues wagging. There would be many questions when he returned, questions he didn't want to answer. Questions he simply wouldn't answer, no matter how much his colleagues pried.

"Good ol' Rick will take care of things for you won't he?" Rachel grinned slyly. It was a long-running joke between them. She had always maintained that Rick, his loyal assistant, leaned towards the same sex. And while Daniel knew this was probably true, she used to push the jest further by claiming that it was obvious to everyone else that Rick had a huge crush on his employer. Daniel still did not find this amusing, and would not dignify it with a response.

She knew enough to leave the subject alone, and handed him a cup of steaming hot black coffee. "I was wondering if there even was a hospital in Aldon. You always made it out to be so small."

"When I was a kid, the town population was fifteen hundred. It's too small to have its own hospital but there is one in the neighboring town, Tarlington. It's thirty-five miles south of Aldon."

"How long of a drive do we have?"

"Three and a half hours but if the highway is quiet, I might be able to make it in three."

It was pouring rain now, the windshield wipers pumped hard to allow him a margin of visibility. He sipped his coffee quietly, enjoying its warmth. Rachel leaned back in her seat and gazed out the passenger window. A tape of Madame Butterfly played but was barely audible over the sound of rain pelting against the car roof.

"So, how have things been?" she attempted at conversation; knowing that Daniel, unlike her, was comfortable in complete silence. He could drive the whole way there and not talk to her once, a social faux pas that she found to be incredibly rude.

"Fine, all things considered," he replied dully. "And you?"

"I'm still teaching and running the studio. Same old, same old." She shrugged.

"Huh," he grumbled with little interest.

"You writing another book?"

"Yep." He nodded and wouldn't elaborate further. She didn't push him, knowing he hated discussing a work in progress. She changed the subject again.

"Has your mom been ill for a while or is this a complete surprise?"

He felt the familiar twinge of guilt creep coldly up his spine. He hadn't spoken to his mother in over a month. And the last time he had talked to her, before that, was at Christmas. She had left plenty of phone messages for him that Rick relayed, but he just never found the time to call her back. The truth was, he didn't know if she had been sick or not.

"I'm not sure," he muttered.

She shot him a dark look. "You don't know?"

"It's been a while since we last talked, we've both been busy," he responded with indignation.

"Sure." She folded her arms across her chest and looked back out the window. "It's funny to me that you are by far the smartest person I have ever met, but clearly the stupidest too."

He bit his tongue and told himself not to let her get under his skin. Not tonight. She was the only one who talked to him as if he were a socially inept moron, and pushed the boundaries he purposely set up to distance himself from others. Everyone else accepted his withdrawn, introverted nature, respected it and gave him the space he needed. Not Rachel though.

"Can I ask you something? I know it's not my place to say this but I didn't have the courage to when we were together but now I do. Especially with your mom being sick, it seems like the right time to say this."

She shifted her weight and turned to face him. He clenched the steering wheel with frustration. Here we go. A confrontation, or worse, an interrogation had been exactly what he had been afraid of. But they weren't a couple any more, so he didn't have to listen to it.

"No, you can't ask me anything. If you hadn't noticed, I'm not in the greatest frame of mind here. I just want to drink my coffee and drive in peace."

"I want to know what happened to you!" she pressed.

He gritted his teeth in exasperation. She knew exactly what buttons to push to get him going. That was the beauty of long-term relationships, you end up knowing a person disturbingly well. Knowing someone's flaws, likes, dislikes, pet peeves, hopes, dreams and fears was power in its simplest form.

"Why do you *insist* on talking?"

"You weren't always like this, Daniel. When we first met, you were very different. Shy still, but innocent and naïve in a sweet, simple way. You didn't hide in books then, you read and studied because you wanted to. You loved learning, you loved a lot of things. You didn't have this haunted, angry look on your face all the time. You didn't push everyone away and isolate yourself like a recluse. You were happy back then. I fell in love with that person, and I miss him. I really, *really* miss him....and I know your mother misses him too." Her voice wavered. "It's too late for us, I've finally accepted that but I think you need to let your mother back into your life. Before it's too late. Before she's gone, and you're completely alone."

ISOLATION

A wash of nausea overcame him at that thought. What if she *did* die? What if his mom didn't pull through this, what then? He couldn't even bear to think about it. It didn't seem possible that *his* mother *could* die.

He gave this some serious thought, wondering if the time really had come to be completely honest. His silence irritated Rachel, who slumped back into her seat with an odd expression of melancholy and exasperation. Ten minutes later, he turned unto the main highway out of the city, and startled himself by saying, "You're right. I hate to say it but you are. There *is* something I've kept from you. I saw something horrible happen when I was fourteen. Only I was there, and I...I swore to myself that I'd never talk to anyone about it."

Rachel looked skeptical, she was probably thinking that he was just pulling her leg to make her words sound foolish. He reached over and grabbed her arm reassuringly.

"I'm not joking. I'm going to tell you what happened not just because you need to hear it, but because I need to get it off my chest. I didn't know how badly until now. But don't say anything, kay, just listen and let me tell it my own way. The only way you'll understand, is if you know the whole story."

Her lips widened to a sad, gentle smile. She had been waiting years for this moment, and of course it would happen after she had completely given up on him.

Daniel started to talk, and the years fell smoothly from his lips. "It all started in 1961. When my parents were called into a meeting with my principal at Aldon Elementary school..."

Part One

Chapter One

    The young couple walked up the steps of Aldon Elementary School on a crisp November morning. Once inside the double doors, they walked in silence down the barren hall and found the small administration office.

    Joe Bradley was not at all pleased that he had to neglect work for the morning to attend a pointless meeting with his son's principal. That was his wife's job. But Maria had stubbornly demanded that he come with her, despite his protests, because the principal had stated over the telephone that they both needed to hear what he had to say. Joe doubted that it was about anything important, and felt it was a huge waste of time.

    "We're the Bradley's, we have an appointment with Mister Kensington," Maria said quietly to the elderly receptionist when they approached her desk.

    "Principal Kensington is expecting you. Go on in." The plump, ill-dressed woman waved them off without looking up from her noisy typewriter.

    "Come in." Jacob Kensington appeared in his doorway. He was slim, tall middle-aged, and wore a wrinkled brown jacket and faded tie. "Please, call me Jacob." He shook their hands enthusiastically.

    "It's nice to finally meet you, Mister Bradley." He urged them into his small, cluttered office. "Please sit down."

    He sat behind his desk and they sat down across from him. Jacob could detect the faint but distinct scent of manure that wafted in with them. He was surprised by their appearance. He knew very little about them. Just that they had four children, ran a small dairy farm outside of town and were in their mid-thirties. He thought that Joe looked much older than that. Although Maria's hair was starting to gray, she was still a pretty sight with enviable clear complexion, bright blue eyes and a trim, healthy frame.

    Joe was of solid build, and looked like a typical farmer with jean overalls, work boots and heavy, plaid jacket. His hair was straggly underneath his cap and although scruffy in appearance, he was handsome in that rugged, masculine way. They looked like hard-workers; people who knew how to get their hands dirty and didn't know any other way to live. Looking at the attractive couple before him, it was evident to Jacob where Danny got his strong good looks from.

"Don't worry, Danny is not in any kind of trouble. I just need to confirm a few things. Our records state that he was home schooled. By you, I assume?" Jacob looked at Maria.

"Yes." She nodded. "We went over all this when he registered here a few months ago."

"Yes, but we need to be sure that this information is one hundred percent correct. You taught him up until this year? He received no other form of education?"

"Yes, that's correct." She looked over at Joe who looked bored and surly.

"And you taught him to read, write, do arithmetic and so on."

"I taught him the basics. What my mother taught me, I was home schooled myself. Danny learned a lot on his own through books. He reads an awful lot. I work at the Aldon library part-time and Danny likes to come in on my shifts to read. He says it's more quiet there than at home," she replied.

"What kinds of books does he like?"

"Well, everything I guess. I encourage him to broaden his mind and have never restricted anything from him. He sometimes reads three or four books a week," she boasted.

"Why did you send him to public school now, Mrs. Bradley? Is there some reason why you felt he required more formal education?" Jacob leaned back in his chair, it creaked noisily under his weight.

"Danny is so shy, he can barely even look someone in the eye. We thought a few years in a school with other kids would open him up. We wanted him to make some friends, be more social. Plus, there were subjects I thought he needed to run the farm that I couldn't teach him."

"How does he like school so far?" Jacob asked.

"He hates it," Joe spoke up finally. He and Maria had discussed pulling him out and home schooling him again because he had been so miserable lately. He planned on taking Danny out of school permanently next year anyway, so that he could work on the farm full-time.

"Alright. I'm going to be honest with you and what I'm about to tell you might come as a surprise." Jacob took a deep breath in and exhaled excitedly. "Danny's class had a spelling bee a month ago, and he did extraordinarily well in it, garnering first place. It was then that his teacher noticed that he was much further advanced in English then his peers. She brought this to my attention, and we decided to test him on various subjects to see what level he was at. We thought that he might be able to skip a grade. We tested him in science, math, English, geography, history and algebra. He received perfect scores so we decided to give him tests at a secondary level."

"He never mentioned any of this to me." Maria frowned.

"In short, he surpassed all our expectations."

"What exactly are you saying?" Joe sat up straight.

"To put it bluntly, your son is incredibly intelligent for his age." Mr. Kensington grabbed a handkerchief from his pocket and wiped his moist brow. "Whatever material you teach him he retains. He's got some sort of photographic memory or something. He's at least at a secondary school level intellectually, possibly grade eleven."

"You think he should skip *three* grades?" Joe frowned skeptically at the principal.

"Yes, at least. However, he does lack in certain areas. Math is his weakest subject, but he is much stronger in it then any of his classmates. Now, the secondary school here in town is a good school but they are not capable of giving Danny what he really needs."

"What does he need?" Maria urged.

"Top-notch education that will push and challenge his intellect."

"I still don't understand. What exactly are you trying to say here?" Joe asked, becoming rather irritated with Jacob's evasiveness.

"There is a private school out west that works with gifted children to help them reach their potential. It is the best in North America as a matter of fact. It's near Rowland, 'Steinem Academy for Gifted Children' which would be perfect for Danny. I've arranged for their director of admissions to come here to speak with you today."

"Wait a minute here, don't you think you're getting a bit ahead of yourself here?" Joe growled. "What made you think we'd be sending him to a private school?"

"The school was founded fifteen years ago for children with extremely high capabilities to have an environment to learn in with a more structured curriculum. It's a co-ed college preparatory private school dedicated to educating talented and gifted students who require smaller classes and a rigorous curriculum to help them reach their academic potential," Jacob read this information off the school brochure and handed it to them across the desk. "It has a lovely campus outside the picturesque town of Rowland. The school is in the mountains, practically in isolation. It's really something to see."

"Rowland is a six-hour drive!" Joe proclaimed to no one in particular.

"Are you absolutely certain about his intellect? Could there have been some sort of error? Is there some other tests he could take?" Maria asked. She always knew her son was bright but this was too much to take in.

The door opened behind them and they turned to see the secretary poke her head in. "Mrs. Temple has arrived. Should I send her in?"

"Yes, please." His face flushed with relief. "Clarice Temple, she wears two hats at the academy. Director of Admissions and Guidance Counselor."

"Look, this is all getting to be a bit much." Joe slammed his fist down. "We never agreed to this."

"I understand that this is a lot to absorb but what I am telling you is true. Your son is exceptionally intelligent and does not belong in elementary school. Clarice will enlighten you more on the subject." He stood up and patted his tie down as she walked in. Clarice was in her late forties, thin, with graying hair pulled back into a tight neat bun. She wore immaculately applied make-up and an expensive black pant-suit with matching high heels. She had a strong, intimidating presence that instantly put them all on edge. After the pleasantries, she sat down and pulled out a file folder from her leather briefcase.

"So from what I understand, your son, Daniel Leonard Bradley was home schooled from the age of three until this year. Is that correct?" Clarice shifted through her papers.

"Yes, I taught him." Maria nodded, suddenly feeling very inadequate next to a woman so well-groomed, confident, and in a position of authority.

"Why did you decide to send him to a public school at this time?" Clarice asked pointedly.

"I thought…we thought," She gestured to her husband, "That he was having trouble interacting with other people. He spent so much of his time reading and working around the farm alone that we started to worry. He doesn't have any friends, even now that he's at school. He's painfully shy. We thought by bringing him here that he'd open up a little but so far he hasn't."

Clarice stared hard at her causing Maria to squirm under her formidable gaze.

"Now tell me the real reason you sent him please," Clarice demanded.

Jacob's eyes widened at her boldness. Maria blushed a deep crimson.

"I don't mean to be rude, Mrs. Bradley, but I can tell when someone is not being completely truthful. I would just like to understand why you sent your son to a public school instead of continuing to teach him at home."

Maria was stunned. How could this woman know that she wasn't being completely honest? The truth was, she wanted her son to be educated so that he could do a better job at running the business side of the farm than his father. Joe had not received any formal education, and though he was the hardest worker you could find, he relied far too much on old methods in getting things done. He wasn't willing to change his routine, or do anything different than what his father and grandfather had done. He was old school and proud of it. The farm suffered because of this, she knew there was much more money to be made. Joe also drank a little too much of what profit they did make, making it that much harder to make ends meet. He wasn't an alcoholic, merely bordering that slippery, destructive edge. She would never in a million years tell him what she thought of his excessive drinking, or speak disrespectfully about his work methods. It wasn't her place.

"Well, Danny surpassed me in all subjects last year. He asked me questions I couldn't answer, knew things I didn't know a thing about. There were subjects that I didn't have a thorough education in myself. Subjects that would benefit him when he took over the farm; math, science and chemistry, stuff like that." Her voice faded. It was true. A few years ago she *had* realized that her ten-year-old son was smarter than her. She had been home-schooled by her own militant mother for fifteen years. She spent most of her those years living in fear of displeasing the woman.

Even at a young age, Maria had been dedicated and diligent in her studies. She would have done anything to receive a kind word from her mother, to impress her with her cleverness. Her mother had spent many grueling hours grilling her on various subjects, but unfortunately she didn't catch on to things easily. She wasn't like Danny. He retained everything quickly and effortlessly, and for that she was envious. How her mother would have praised her, would have boasted about what a bright little girl she had. It would have set her apart, made her special. Instead, Maria was but another child to feed in a house of ten. She was told to feel grateful that she received any individual attention at all.

"I want to ask you…" Clarice started, but Joe immediately interrupted her.

"I don't mean to insult you, lady, but we won't be sending Danny to your fancy school, so we might as well not waste your time. Thanks for the offer, but we're not sending him anywhere."

"I see." Clarice turned to Jacob. "I was under the impression that you had already spoken to the family."

Jacob blushed. "I didn't want to discuss it over the phone and they couldn't make it in until today."

"Some people have to work you know," Joe mumbled.

"I thought it would be best if you told them about the academy, since you have first-hand information about it," Jacob added feebly.

Clarice frowned at him, sighed and turned to the couple. "Usually there is a proper application process. This is unusual indeed."

She pushed her papers aside and leaned forward. "Mister Kensington sent me some of Daniel's test scores and a history and English report that he had completed. I was intrigued by it and saw great potential. I spoke to his teacher, Miss Kendall, and she praised your son's abilities but suggested that smaller class sizes would more beneficial for him. He would still have to go through an extensive evaluation process to see if he is capable of functioning in the type of rigorous educational environment that the academy offers. I have several tests for him to complete and would like to personally meet and interview him. If that all goes well, you could come up and visit the school."

"We could never afford a private school," Maria admitted.

"Yes, there is a financial issue that needs to be discussed. The cost of room, board, tuition and books is quite high but I assure you it is well worth it. This type of school is usually only an option for the very affluent but I have this offer for you. The government would cover the tuition and half of the room and board expenses. You'd only be responsible to cover in full, the cost of the books and school uniform."

"Why would they do that?" Joe cut in, stinging from the snide at their income level.

"Think of it as a loan. Daniel would be expected to pay it back in the future with small monthly installments when he is through college and employed for five years. The government naturally wants to assist individuals with uniquely high capabilities when possible."

"Sounds too good to be true." Joe stood up and grabbed Maria's arm. "Come on, I've heard enough."

"Wait!" Maria pulled away from him. "I want to know more about this."

"This is ridiculous!" Joe snapped. "The boy ain't going nowhere and that's that."

Clarice ignored him, realizing that he was not a man who changed his mind easily and turned to Maria. "Think of the future Danny could have with the education he would receive. All of our students thus far have been accepted to elite universities and colleges, and because of their exceptional marks, have received full scholarships."

"Full scholarships?" Maria repeated. "Can we have time to think about it?"

"Maria!" Joe barked.

"I just want to think about it," she whispered. Joe fumed out of the office, slamming the door behind him.

"I'll contact you in a few days." Clarice smiled thinly handing her a file folder of information about the school. "We have one opening. There is a long waiting list but we have a made an exception for your son. You will need to decide within the next week whether we should proceed with the evaluation process."

"Okay, thanks so much." Maria stood up.

"Can I have your permission to meet Daniel today and ask him a few questions?" Clarice stood up as well.

"Sure, thanks again for your time." Maria smiled and started to walk away.

"Remember...do what's best for your son." Clarice called out to her, stopping Maria in her tracks. "If his test results are any indication, Daniel is truly a gifted little boy. I'd hate so see anything or *anyone* hold him back."

Maria stood still for a few seconds, with many thoughts racing through her muddled mind. The woman was right. A good parent wouldn't let an opportunity like this go by. She decided in that moment that absolutely *nothing* would hold her son back. That he would indeed go to that school.

No matter what.

* * * * *

With their battered Ford truck, they pulled into their long driveway, five miles outside of town. Maria stared upon the crumbling farmhouse and wanted to cry at the degeneration of their farm. Everything was falling apart, but there was no money for anything to be fixed properly or replaced. Time and money were their adversaries.

"I can't believe the school sent information away about our son without our permission! The least they could do is let us know that they were testing Danny to see how advanced he was, but they didn't even do that. They bring in that woman without preparing us, dump everything on our laps and expect us to jump at the opportunity. I don't know, it just don't feel right," Joe went on, and when his wife didn't respond, he became agitated.

"He's my son, Maria, I'm not sending him away. What kind of parent sends his child away for four years?" He parked the truck abruptly.

"Aren't you proud? Even a little bit? If what their saying is true, then Danny is special. Gifted in ways most people only dream about. Did it ever occur to you to be happy for him? To be happy that he has the potential to be…whatever he wanted. That he probably won't have to live like this!" She flicked her wrist around.

Joe's face hardened, his body stiffened. "There's nothing wrong with the way we live Maria." His voice was cold.

"I know, but with this education comes opportunities. If he took them, he would never have to struggle or worry about money. Isn't that what every parent wants for their child? For them to do well?"

"The best thing for him, is to be here on the farm with his family, where he belongs!"

"I want to give him the chance that we never got. To be educated, to have the power of knowledge and choices."

"Maria, I thought we wanted him to take over the farm! That was the plan for Christ's sake! Did you forget that he's our only son?"

She didn't answer so he continued. "I don't care how smart Danny is, he's staying here! I'm his father and it's my decision!"

"Well, he's my son too so it's part *my* decision!" Her voice trembled with anger. "Don't try to talk me out of it. I want the best for my son and if that means sending him away for a few years than I'll do it. We have to do this, because he'll hate us later if we don't," she reasoned.

Joe turned away. He opened the truck door, slid out and forcefully slammed it shut. She watched him go in the house and clenched her fists in determination. She wasn't going to let him get his way this time. Not about this.

They fought hard for four long days on the issue, but not in front of the other children. Everyone in the household knew that they were fighting but had no idea what about. In the end, Maria was victorious simply because Joe tired of her endless crying, nagging and baleful looks across the room. She wouldn't give it up, and every moment that they were alone, she tied into him. She could articulate her side of the argument much better than he, and would leave him speechless and rattled. He didn't deal well with stress and tension to begin with, so her strong will wore him down and his resolve eventually disintegrated. They were bickering in the shed, so the children wouldn't hear, the night he gave in. She was giving him the third degree, yet again, when he hollered impulsively. "Alright, Fine! Let him go then! Will that shut you up, woman?"

"Yes! Yes it will! Oh thank you, Joe, you have no idea what this means to me!" She ran to him, hugged him and raced into the house before he could say another word. Euphoric, she made a call to the academy that very night and began the process to send her son away to school.

While Maria made the necessary arrangements, Joe sat wearily on the concrete step outside of the shed. The moon was full and the sky was clear and bright. If not for the freezing temperatures, it was a beautiful night to sit out. He inhaled a cigarette slowly, and looked out at the endless acres of land that he had hoped one day would belong to his son. Apparently, his hopes for his family and his farm didn't particularly matter. According to his wife, his son was meant for a much better life than this.

Farming ran in his veins just like it had his ancestors; he knew every square inch of the hundred acres surrounding his two-story brick house that his grandfather, Leo, had built with his own two hands. His father had left this to him, just as Leo had left it to him. He lived and breathed this land, it was a part of him and he a part of it. He wanted this life for Daniel; he wanted to give it to him when he was old enough to appreciate what it was worth. It was literally all he had to give to his children. But apparently, it just wasn't good enough.

Joe flung the cigarette butt on the ground and sighed. He looked down at his eleven-year-old yellow lab, Sam, who sat faithfully beside him. The dog had been his constant companion for eleven solid years, and Joe truly believed that the mangy mutt understood him much better than his own wife. At least Sam wouldn't argue with him, question or belittle him. Sam was loyal to the bone, and knew his place in the world. Joe envied the simplicity of a canine's life, and wished everyone could be as unfailingly devoted and complying as a good dog was to his master.

"If only life were that simple, eh, Sam." Joe petted the runny nosed beast.

* * * * *

January 2, 1962

"You'll need lots of underwear and socks, I really don't have the faintest idea how often they do laundry up there so it's good to have plenty just in case. I really should have thought to ask that when we toured the place. But I'm sure they do it often. It looked like a nice school so surely they would be mindful of such things as clean clothes," Maria spoke rapidly as she packed

Danny's suitcases. The two battered pieces were plopped open on the bed, they both looked as if they had seen better days.

Danny was sitting at his desk on the other end of his small bedroom. His back was turned to her and she could almost see the steam rising from his head. He was furious. He didn't want to go and no matter how often they discussed the issue, the conclusion was always the same. Now he was pulling the silent treatment, hoping that that would prove to his parents how serious he was about not wanting to go. Maria desperately wanted to make his last night at home pleasant, but that was not to be.

"You're going to have so many friends, you'll be surrounded by nice boys and girls that are just like you. It's going to be great, I know it. You'll have access to the school library which is twice the size of Aldon's. You'll be able to read tons of books and learn about things we've never even heard of. The next time we see you, you'll be able to tell us about all the fun and exciting things you've been doing. It's going to be great Danny, you just have to give it a chance." She closed the suitcases and snapped them shut.

Seeing him sitting slouched over his desk, not even responding to her was so unlike him. He was usually such a sweet, kind child and it broke her heart to see him so unhappy.

She walked around the bed and knelt down beside her son. "I know this will be wonderful for you Danny, it's everything I ever could have wanted for you."

"But it's not what *I* want." Danny blurted out, breaking his two-day silence.

She sighed and put one hand on his arm. "You may not realize it now, but it's a blessing. I really think it is. Going to this school will change your life."

"That's just it. I don't *want* anything to change." Danny turned to her, grief-stricken. "Don't make me go, I don't want to go! Please, Mom, I want to stay here with you!"

A small part of her wanted to give in, to keep her beautiful baby close to home because it would make things so much simpler. But this type of life was not his destiny. She had come to believe her son was meant for greater things. She stood up and embraced him. "Some day you'll understand that I'm only doing this because I love you."

Moments later, she walked down the creaky stairs with a large lump in her throat. Daniel's fury would be easier to take if her husband would back her up, but he had taken the by-stander approach. His neutral stance on the issue enraged her, because she knew Danny looked up to his father and placed him on a pedestal. If he would only support the idea of him leaving and motivate the boy to go, Danny wouldn't be so troubled and miserable.

She found Joe in the kitchen, drinking a beer at the table. He was reading an old newspaper, still wearing his overalls and dirty cap. Maria couldn't remember the last time she had seen her husband cleanly shaven without a hat on.

"Danny's upset," she stated, and sat on the other side of the table. "Maybe you should talk to him."

Joe snapped the newspaper shut and narrowed his eyes at her. "He doesn't want to go. Whatever I say isn't going to change his mind."

"Yes, it will. You have no idea how much influence you have on him. He's confused right now because you won't acknowledge that he's leaving. You won't talk about the school at all, how do you think that makes him feel?"

"This was all your idea, you talk to him!" Joe stood up and Maria quickly stood up in front of him, to block him out of leaving the kitchen.

"Don't do this, Joe. You're angry at me, don't take it out on Danny. He needs you."

Joe pointed his finger at his wife. "You wanted him to go to this fancy school and pushed me into letting him go when I was dead-set against it. Now you want me to go up there to save your ass. To make him feel better about going and I won't do it. You're responsible for this mess, don't come crying to me because it ain't going the way you wanted." He grabbed her shoulders and pushed her aside.

"I just want what's best for him!" she cried out as he headed out the front door. He let the door slam shut behind him, indicating that the discussion was over. She desperately wanted to shake some sense into him. She had hoped a small of him, like her, was proud and honored that their son was accepted into such a prestigious school. But she should have known such things mattered little to Joe. She also should have known that the issue was far from settled.

* * * * *

A soft knock on the bedroom door startled Danny from his thoughts. He looked up from his book and shifted his weight so that he could sit up in bed. "Come in."

His fourteen-year-old sister, Katie, poked her face in. "Hi."

"Hi."

She stepped in the room and shut the door gently behind her. She was barefoot, and wore an ankle-length white nightdress, and her hair loose. She had beautiful thick locks like her mother; that cascaded down her back and were the envy of her two younger sisters. Usually though, her hair was thrown into a sloppy, loose braid. She was very pretty, rail-thin with a smattering of freckles across her cheeks and nose.

"Maddy wants a story." She eyed the book in his hands "Dickens again? Don't you ever get sick of reading the same books over and over?"

"No," he mumbled. She looked over at his suitcases and grimaced.

"So you're really going. I can't believe it." She shook her head in amazement.

"I can't either." He placed a bookmark on the page he was on, closed the hardcover novel and put it on the wood nightstand beside him. He sat up straight and crossed his long legs.

"Maybe it won't be that bad. It could be a good thing you know." She forced a smile.

"There is nothing good about living in a boarding school out in the middle of nowhere with a bunch of stuck-up city kids," he snapped.

"You don't know that they're stuck-up."

"The kids in Aldon were all snobs, I'm sure the rich ones in Rowland will be even worse. This is so stupid. I don't want to go, so why are Mom and Dad forcing me to!" He crossed his arms and put on a serious pout.

"I don't know. They've been acting kind of strange though, don't you think?"

"Their fighting about me. Mom wants me to go and Dad doesn't."

"Yeah, but I think it's more than that…" She hesitated then shrugged. "I don't know. Never mind. You better get over there and tell Maddy a story before she starts screaming." She started back towards the door.

"Yeah, alright."

It struck him then that it would be several months before he would be able to tell his little sisters a bed-time story again. His stomach turned. He couldn't even imagine a life outside this house, and the thought of leaving made him sick with fear.

* * * * *

The next morning at dawn, he stood on the deteriorated porch steps and hugged his mother and sisters good-bye. They huddled tight as a unit, shivering from the frigid cold for almost a full minute.

ISOLATION

"You be a good boy, and I'll call you tonight," Maria whispered through her tears. Her voice was barely audible, she had to force herself not to sob uncontrollably.

"I don't want to go, Mom! Please don't make me!" Danny pleaded with tears in his eyes, but Maria disentangled him and led him firmly to the truck.

His father sat in the cab, with Sam, watching the spectacle with a cigarette hanging from his lips. Danny reluctantly got in the truck, put his two suitcases beside the panting dog and wiped his eyes. Crying would not get him far with his father. Joe put the truck in gear and they pulled out of the driveway. Danny waved frantically to his mother and siblings; and watched them through the back window until they became little dark specks amidst the vast white landscape.

Joe took another long drag from his cigarette, and they drove quietly for a few moments. Both shivered numbly, the rattling heater in the cab was practically useless but it filled the empty silence between them. Joe dug into his coat pocket, produced a pack of cigarettes and held it out for his son. Danny eyed them, looked up to his father who nodded in encouragement and took one from the pack. Joe tossed him a box of matches and watched him light up the cigarette. He took one inhale, and was reduced to a fit of violent, painful coughs. When he caught his breath he glanced sheepishly at Sam, who stared down at him blankly, and kept smoking clumsily.

"Don't tell your mother," Joe quipped. They smoked in silence and then tossed their butts out the window.

"How come you never asked if I wanted to go to this school? Don't I have the right to an opinion here?" Danny finally asked, looking around the large dog to see his father.

"You're too young to have an opinion," Joe answered simply, his eyes never wavering from the icy road.

"Why don't you two care that I don't want to go!" Danny raged with burning frustration.

Without responding, Joe pulled out another cigarette and lit it up. As he smoked, Danny turned and looked vehemently out the window.

They drove the rest of the way in silence.

Chapter Two

Daniel Bradley raced down the hall towards his algebra class, his least favorite of all the subjects. The wide halls were bare and poorly lit. His padded foot-steps broke the eerie silence in the over-sized tomb-like institution.

He was late again, the third time this week and would most likely be punished for it. But it didn't matter. Their form of detention consisted of doing extra homework and that was nothing to him, he had nothing better to do than schoolwork anyway. He had lived here just over two months and liked it less with each passing day. Everything was still strangely new and memories of his family weighed heavily on his mind. Homesickness plagued him every waking hour. It was a dull sick ache that crushed his appetite and left him feeling lethargic and ill.

The worst thing though, was that his birthday had passed by uneventfully on February second. His mother had called him that night, but his father was allegedly not around to speak to him. All day he had half expected his family to show up with a birthday cake and presents in an attempt to surprise him. But they didn't, and no one in the school even acknowledged the occasion.

He hated it here. The campus was beautiful but too widespread and cold to make him feel welcome. The instructors were friendly but strict, and his fellow students were polite yet distant. They were either talented in the arts or excelled academically like him. He was most interested in their talents but learned quickly that when they spoke outside their scope of knowledge, they were quite average indeed. He rarely talked to any of them anyway, he kept to himself and walked around as if cocooned in an isolated bubble.

He was brought in rather late; most of the students came here when they were at the age of ten and formed their 'cliques' then. All of them had planned on coming here, their parents had gone through the application process when they were very young to get them on the waiting list. They had actually hoped that this was where they would spend their adolescent years.

He looked down at his clothes and scowled. Boys were required to wear black pants, white dress shirts with ties and navy v-neck sweaters with the school crest on the upper left side. They were reprimanded heavily if their shoes were not properly polished or if their ties were tied incorrectly. Daniel hated the stupid tie and always had a disheveled, sullen look about him. He didn't realize, however, how attractive he looked to the girls. That his rumpled appearance accentuated his good looks. The years of hard labor around the farm had produced thick neck and leg muscles, defined biceps and broad shoulders. He was rather tall for his age, almost six feet, much taller than the other boys. He was terribly embarrassed by his size, his growth spurt last year was most unwelcome for it was yet another feature that set him apart. He had short, dark hair that his mother had cut punctually every three weeks, and was fortunate to have a flawless golden complexion. He was oblivious to his looks though, and felt self-conscious and awkward most of the time.

The girls' uniform consisted of a navy, knee length kilt, white, starched blouses and navy cardigans when the weather was cool. They had the option of wearing their long hair up in tight buns, braids or pony tails. Their hair was never to be loose or straggly, that was forbidden. All the students were taught early to always look their best, that good grooming habits were essential for success.

Classes started at eight thirty, and there were seven periods until three thirty.

Daniel had trouble making it to his first period, his motivation was low and he had a habit of sleeping in. He approached the classroom door and stood before it for a moment. A part of him wanted to run away and hide, to flee from this awful place and go back to the comfort and security of home. He didn't belong here, he couldn't talk to the other students and was intimidated by the aggressive teachers. Frustrated tears welled up in his eyes. He felt like he was being punished for being smart. He didn't believe he was as bright as his fellow students either, they were so confident and sure of themselves. Most of them were from wealthy families and that alone bred a certain amount of esteem and self-importance.

He lowered his head dejectedly and opened the classroom door.

*****

Each student met once a month with Clarice Temple in her office for a counseling session. This was the time for a student to state a grievance or open up about a personal problem. She had a thorough education in psychology and felt a happy student with a clear mind was a productive one.

She would also discuss their progress and set goals, both personal and academic for the next month. She was tough to please and most of the students found these sessions exhausting and obtrusive. Her aggressive manner intimidated them, and most would not willingly confide much to her.

She noticed that Daniel was having a particularly tough time adjusting and made a point to have a session with him once a week.

When he first walked into her small but cozy office he immediately noticed that all her walls were shelves clad with leather-bound books. There were hundreds of them, of all different genres in pristine condition. His opinion of her changed slightly. He couldn't totally dislike anyone who loved literature as much as he did.

She always kept her heavy curtain shades drawn and the only source of light came from a small lamp on her thick oak desk. A large framed picture of rain falling on a translucent pond hung behind her on the wall. Daniel found the painted picture calming. The whole office, with its dim lighting and countless books, felt comforting and peaceful. It reminded him of a library, which was a sanctuary to an avid book reader.

Despite her gruff approach, Daniel eventually came to enjoy these sessions and liked to banter lightly with her. At first they talked only about their mutual interests; their favorite books and authors. They differed on their taste in literature though; she enjoyed primarily female authors like Louisa May Alcott, Virginia Woolf, Jane Austen, Charlotte Bronte, and Emily Dickinson, but also liked Ernest Hemingway and poetry by John Keats. He preferred the likes of J.R.R. Tolkien, Mary Shelly, Jonathon Swift, Charles Dickens, H.G. Wells, Bram Stoker, Mark Twain and Shakespeare. He liked horror novels and comic books too, genres she was not familiar with.

In the upcoming weeks, she continued to urge Daniel to open up more and asked him what he thought about most. He reluctantly admitted, after several sessions, that he was terribly homesick and furious that his life had turned upside down. He didn't understand why his parents sent him here, and confessed to feeling angry and confused most of the time.

"My father always told me that I'd take over the farm, so why am I here?" he asked one rainy Friday afternoon.

"Why do you want to go home so bad, Daniel? What's the real reason that you feel so homesick?" she questioned.

He stared at her blankly so she rephrased the question. "Do you miss being on the farm, the routine you had there or do you miss your family?"

"Both, I guess."

"Do you want to be a farmer when you grow up or is that something that your father wants for you?" She raised a hand in defense. "Don't get me wrong. Farming is an honorable profession, but I don't think you are aware of the opportunities that are available to you. Now if you graduate from this school and decide to still go back home and farm there would be nothing wrong with that. That is your choice, but I would hate for you to go through the motions here and not take advantage of the many things we have to offer you. Not everyone is fortunate enough to have so many options."

Daniel shrugged.

"I realize there is an adjustment period, but you've been here a few months and it's time you tried to make an effort to fit in here," she stated with a frown. "I know you miss your family very much, but why don't you make the most of your time here and make your parents proud?"

He *still* wouldn't answer and she felt the edge of frustration creep into her voice.

"You can't change the fact that you're here, Daniel, so you might as well make the best of it. Do you want to be miserable for the next four years?"

"I just don't fit in at all, Miss Temple, I'm not smart like everyone else," he replied sincerely.

She smiled at his modesty. "Really. Your mother told me you had a fondness for a certain author in particular. Tell me where you've heard this before. 'Arise, fair sun, and kiss the envious moon. Who is already sick and pale with grief, that thou her maid art more fair than she."

Daniel looked at the floor.

"Can you tell me where you've read that paragraph before and who wrote it?"

"O Romeo, Romeo! Wherefore art thou, Romeo." Daniel rolled his eyes.

"Shakespeare, of course, wrote the most popular love story of all time, and that is the oh so romantic orchard scene."

"Do you think many fourteen-year-old boys would know that?"

"Yes. It's taught in school," he nodded.

"Okay, so that was an easy one. How about this, can you tell me what a colloquy is?"

"We're having one right now. We're also having a confabulation," he answered.

"Yes, we are," she chuckled to herself; they were indeed having both a discussion and a conversation. "Can you tell me what convoluted means?"

"Are you *trying* to ask me convoluted questions?" he asked seriously.

She laughed then, and it was a pure, unrestrained sound. "Alright, can you tell me what years the American Revolution was fought?"

"Seventeen hundred and seventy-five to seventeen hundred and eighty-three. Look, I know where you're going with this."

"Good, can you explain to me..."

"I'm not answering any more of your stupid questions," he cut her off with a scowl.

"Why? We could go on and on like this all day. What does that prove to you?" she threw out her hands.

"Nothing. You don't have to be a genius to regurgitate information," he argued.

"A genius is a person that retains what others forget. That is what makes them special, they have the capacity to learn vast amounts of information and store it away in their brain for future use. The average person uses very little of their brain, and it's a tragedy really." she looked directly into his eyes and continued. "What's more of a tragedy is when those who have a gift disregard it and never try to see what might become of it. Everyone is creative to some degree; everyone has the potential to be intelligent, productive creatures. But few have the discipline, diligence and patience to be more than average. You were born more than average, Daniel. I've worked with gifted kids for many years so I know that you belong here,"

She smiled. "And I agree with you, you're not a genius. You just have the potential to do much more then you think."

"I think you have me mixed up with someone else," Daniel said flatly.

Miss Temple hesitated before speaking, cleared her throat and leaned forward. "You were born with a gift, Daniel. When you realize how special it is...I do believe you'll be able to accomplish anything you set your mind to. I want to help you see that."

"And I just want to go home," Daniel muttered and looked at his watch.

"I'm going to be late for my next class." he stood up, walked to the door and stopped in the doorway. He turned around to look at her.

"I have a question for *you*, Miss Temple. Do you know what the term 'folie de grandeur' means?"

"Yes, Daniel, I know what that means," she nodded.

"Good," he hesitated, as if he were about to say something else and then walked swiftly out of her office.

She took a long, thoughtful sip of coffee. 'Folie de grandeur' was French for 'delusion of greatness'.

ISOLATION

* * * * *

Clarice stared down at his student records and sighed in exasperation. She had a problem on her hands. Daniel excelled in all subjects and did extraordinarily well in all his tests and quizzes. He absorbed information easily but had little to no motivation. He was required to do two hours of homework per night, which he never did, and his assignments were rarely completed. He was tardy, lethargic and obstinate with his instructors.

She knew he spent most of his time reading fictional novels, he had free access to the school library but never checked out books that were relevant to his courses.

He moped about lifelessly, and had little inclination to participate in school events or befriend the other students. Clarice worried that if the other students found out how well Daniel was doing academically, without trying, that they too would adopt his slothful ways. Either that, or resent him because he *could* get away with minimal effort.

She pushed his records away from her and exhaled loudly. She had never come across anyone like Daniel Bradley. Most of her students were ambitious and driven. They enjoyed the attention and praise that their talents drew and worked hard to maintain their level of excellence while Daniel either didn't realize his potential, or simply didn't care.

* * * * *

"I'm afraid you can't check those out." The school librarian frowned at Daniel, who had placed five fictional novels on her desk.

"Why not?"

"Miss Temple has informed me you are only to check out the books on this list." The elderly woman produced a sheet of paper from a desk drawer.

"These are the only books you can check out and they are relevant to the courses you are taking this semester."

"Let me see." Daniel snatched the list from her hands and read them over. "I'm not allowed to check out anything but these? Why would she do that?"

"Ssh!" she hushed him with a glare, her face wrinkled within itself in distaste. "Keep your voice down. You'll have to work this out with Miss Temple, there is nothing I can do for you." She pushed his books to the side.

"Fine, that's just fine!" He stormed loudly out of the library and went straight to the administration office. He stood before her secretary and demanded to see Miss Temple immediately.

"Do you have an appointment?" she asked, looking over her calendar.

"No, but it's very important." Daniel's voice was firm. She sent him in.

"How can you take away my library privileges? What kind of school restricts a student from reading!" he exclaimed the moment he walked through her door.

Clarice closed the binder that she was working in and sat back in her chair. "It's for your own good. You were reading material that was not relevant to your course load and it was taking time away from your required assignments. Ten percent of your final grade depends on class participation and regular attendance. Twenty five percent of your final grade depends on assignments. You have to maintain an eighty percent average in all your courses and you will never achieve that unless you start making changes. You're also not participating in the many extracurricular activities that we offer here."

"If I complete all my assignments, answer some questions in class and make it to my classes on time, will you give me back my library privileges?"

Clarice sighed and leaned forward. "Your missing the point here, Daniel. I certainly advocate reading in your leisure time but you need to get all your homework done first. I also think you should start challenging yourself in other areas and improve your social skills. Learn to play an instrument and join the choir. You could join the debate or chess team, something along that line. By joining various teams, you have the opportunity to expand your horizons and meet other students as well."

"Isn't that for me to decide? If I do well in my courses I should be able to do whatever I want with the rest of my time," he argued.

Clarice crossed her arms. "If you learn anything from this educational experience, I want you to learn that sometimes you have to make yourself do things that must be done whether you want to or not. That is what distinguishes the successful from the average, their perseverance to put in that extra mile."

"I just want to read! I want to read whatever book I choose and that's it! I don't think that's asking a lot! What's the big deal?"

"Tell you what, after you read the books I listed this semester you can read whatever you want. *If* you join the chess team," she added.

"I don't even know how to play chess!"

"You'll learn."

"So I have to read a ton of books and play chess to have access to the library. Is that all?" he asked sarcastically.

"No. I know you read fast so after you read the books, you will be tested on the material to see if you actually comprehended what you read. If you get eighty percent or higher, your library restriction will be waived."

Daniel's eyes narrowed on her own and she could see his whole body stiffen. A few seconds passed before he spoke. "Fine. I'll do it. It isn't right, but I'll take your stupid test. If I pass it, though, you have to promise me that you'll *never* take away access to the library from me again."

"Okay, but I'm not trying to make your life difficult here. I'm trying to help you. Perhaps one day you'll understand that," she articulated while folding her hands primly on her desk.

He walked out of her office without responding. She was pleased with herself and felt she handled the sticky situation well. She highly doubted he would even read the books, it would be too much work. She predicted that he would focus on his studies with the extra time he now had, and would make some friends in the chess club. She would then reward his good behavior by re-instating his privileges. It seemed so simple but she had clearly underestimated him.

Three weeks later the dean, John Wilkens, approached her desk with a stack of papers. John had been the dean since the school opened and was an incredibly intelligent man hidden under a morbidly obese frame. Although heavily overweight, he had plenty of energy and immersed himself completely in his job. He was involved in every aspect of the school, and worked hard to uphold the academy's high standards.

"Mrs. Beal brought this to my attention this morning. Daniel Bradley took that test of yours yesterday and passed it with a near perfect score."

He dropped the papers on her desk "Ninety percent. The kid is amazing! He skimmed over twenty books in fourteen days on top of his usual homework and practically memorized every word. He's got some sort of photographic memory or something."

Clarice let her head fall back and couldn't help but laugh.

"Can you imagine, Clarice, what he could do if he actually tried in his schoolwork?" John plopped down on the chair across from her. "That boy could do wonders for this school."

"Yes, but first we have to get him to believe in himself. He has no idea how intelligent he is. He's so miserable and homesick that he doesn't seem to care anyway."

"We have to find a way to motivate him, there's got to be a way," John stated with a shiny gleam in his eye.

"Well, he's joined the chess team even if it is unwillingly. Perhaps some social interaction will make a difference," Clarice suggested.

"I don't care what you do, but find a way to reach him, Clarice. Help him find some confidence; break open his shell and show him his potential."

They discussed the issue for twenty minutes, and after John left her office, Clarice pondered upon new ways to reach her troubled, but talented pupil.

This was a boy who could easily be at the top of his class, if only he would apply himself. She became excited at the prospect of the challenge before her. After twenty years counseling gifted children in exalted private schools, she had finally discovered one of the best of the brightest.

Chapter Three

"Do you even *know* how to play chess?" Thirteen-year-old Rachel Sheldon mocked with leering eyes. Daniel had been staring intently at the chess board in front of him for over five minutes and had yet to make a move.

Twelve other games were going on quietly around them in the large auditorium.

Daniel shifted his focus away from the game and replied. "I read a book on it, but my parents didn't have a chess board. I've only played a couple of times at my neighbors house."

"You read a book on chess?" she scoffed. "How droll."

"What do you mean?"

"Well, if you don't have the board and pieces, than what's the point of learning how to play?"

"I don't know." Daniel shrugged.

"So, how do you like this place so far?" she asked, changing the topic.

Daniel hesitated. "I haven't decided yet." He turned back to the board and tried to remember the strategies that the book had outlined.

Rachel, he soon learned, enjoyed the sound of her own voice and proceeded to tell him all about herself. Her mother taught piano lessons in her home and had a degree in music history. Her father was a doctor, a surgeon to be exact and they lived in a large estate in Toronto. It came as no surprise to anyone that she carried not only her mother's musical genes, but the Sheldon superior intellect as well. At the age of three, she taught herself to play by listening to the radio and played back full songs accurately by ear. She was confident and assertive, and Daniel could tell that she worked hard to come across as mature and intellectual. When she quit bragging about her musical accomplishments and family, she finally turned the topic back to chess.

"There's twenty-five of us that meet here every Tuesday afternoon at three-thirty. We had twenty-six, but Harold is not allowed to be on the chess team anymore because he failed a mid-term last fall. We've been taking turns sitting out, but now that you're here, we can all play at once. We have an all-day tournament on the second Saturday of every month. It's kind of a big deal here."

Daniel had not realized that his roommate, Harold Spencer, had played on the chess team. He knew that he was having trouble with his courses, so it came as no surprise that he had failed a mid-term and hadn't mentioned it.

"You guys are going to cream me," Daniel groaned.

"Well, you probably won't want to play with Todd or Justin right away. They're amazing chess players and very competitive. The rest of us are just average and you'll learn quickly." She smiled encouragingly.

"Todd and Justin?" Daniel looked over at the boys who were playing across the room. Todd and Justin Steward were teenage twin brothers from a wealthy family in Ottawa. Their family was heavily involved in politics and owned a great deal of property throughout the province. Amazingly, both heirs to the Steward fortune were math whizzes. Although they were identical twins, Todd was at least thirty pounds heavier with an unruly mop of thick, flaming red hair. Justin's hair was a shade lighter, his hair was straight and cropped short. He was the more attractive of the two, and more intelligent but had a quick temper that flared often. Todd was a big lug who looked like a bully but loyally worshiped his brother, and only acted out when he was encouraged to by him. They were inseparable, an odd little pair. Daniel decided, without having a conversation with either of them that he disliked them both. They carried a distinct air of arrogance.

"It's good that you've joined the chess team. You've kept pretty much to yourself and no one knows a thing about you," Rachel acknowledged, breaking his train of thought.

"What?" He blinked twice. "What do you mean, what do you want to know?"

"Where are you from? Do you have any brothers or sisters?"

His stomach rolled at the thought of his family. "I have three sisters. Katie, Madeline and Eve." His voice cracked, he lowered his head in embarrassment. It was indescribable how much he missed those girls; he had never been apart from them since the day they were born. It didn't seem right that there was so much distance between them, that he wasn't a part of their daily lives.

Rachel reached across the table, grabbed his hand and squeezed tightly. "The homesickness will fade, it gets better you know."

Daniel blinked rapidly and could not respond. He didn't like knowing that his emotions were that visible to everyone else.

"I've heard people talk," she whispered quietly, leaning forward as if she were telling him a secret. "Some think you're the brightest one here and that's saying a lot."

"Who says that?" he asked.

"People…very smart people." She grinned. "And I think they're right."

He couldn't help smiling back at her. His heart started to pound heavily in his chest, and he could feel the burning heat from his flushed face. He wasn't used to attention from girls outside of his family. He wasn't sure what to say or how to act without looking like a moron.

"So, you want to play chess or not?" she asked, oblivious to the effect she had suddenly caused in him.

"Yeah," he choked out.

He suddenly noticed the way she moved, her mannerisms were dainty and graceful. Her smile, warm and generous. Her thick dark hair was pulled back into a neat bun but a few wisps fell down by her large, luminous eyes. She was very pretty, and he wondered why he hadn't noticed her around school before. How could he have over-looked someone so cute? He turned his thoughts back to the game and tried to put full concentration on the task in front of him.

After an hour he said to his weary opponent. "Checkmate."

"You beat me! You told me you've hardly ever played before!" she exclaimed, tossing the board to the side.

"I haven't, I honestly haven't!" he proclaimed, realizing that others were beginning to stare at them.

"I don't believe you. I've played this game all my life and I've never been beaten that badly," Rachel pouted, staring at the many pieces of his that were still on the board. He could see the tears in her eyes, threatening to spill over from the humiliation of losing to an amateur. Daniel knew if he wanted to keep her friendship, he would have to tend to her pride.

"You're right, I'm sorry. I wasn't telling the truth before, my sisters and I played chess all the time at home. I don't know why I lied," he fibbed.

"I knew it." Her tears cleared and her eyes lit up. "You should play Justin at the next tournament. He hasn't been beat yet!"

Daniel looked at his watch. "I should go." He stood up and heard his knees snap from sitting so long.

"So you'll come back next week?" she pressed and he considered it. He had been initially angry at Miss Temple for blackmailing him into joining the chess team, but now was glad that she did. It was a lot of fun.

"Yeah, I'll be here," he replied with a goofy grin.

"Good! I'm glad," she smiled back warmly.

"Thanks for the game, I'll see you later." He left and headed for the washroom to wash up for supper. He noticed that halfway up the stairs that he had a dynamic spring in his step. Usually girls made him nervous, but since Rachel did most of the talking, he hadn't felt any pressure. Chess is a game that requires a great deal of silent concentration but even when they weren't talking, he hadn't felt uncomfortable. She was like no other girl he had ever met, and he hoped that he could play chess with her again.

After he went to the washroom, he walked in his bedroom to find his thirteen-year-old roommate, Harold, slumped over his desk. As usual, he was poring over a textbook vigorously. Harold turned around to acknowledge him, his brow creased with frustration. His blond hair was a tangled mess, and he was dressed only in boxer shorts and socks. He was so skinny that his ribs were clearly visible when he took in a deep breath. Harold Benning was literally the living definition of a ninety-pound weakling; with scrawny limbs, sharp features and thick glasses. He was a fairly nice guy, and Daniel didn't mind him much but he was usually stressed out. Nothing came easy to poor Harold, he worked hard for every single mark he had ever received. All-nighters were nothing new to him, he spent every second of the day studying just to maintain the required eighty percent average.

"You okay?" Daniel asked.

"I hate history! I have so much homework, I'll have to pull another fucking all-nighter." Harold put his hands to his temples and rubbed them gently.

Daniel found his lack of vocabulary amusing, Harold swore constantly and was always angry.

"There's my usual homework, and then I have to re-write another test next week. I have to study like mad for that because I'm still on academic probation." He took off his glasses and rubbed the lenses against his shirt. "I had an algebra test this morning and I have a feeling I failed it too. I just didn't have enough time to study for it."

Daniel was glad he didn't have to study quite so hard. He averaged a ninety-seven percent in all his tests, mid-terms and what assignments he did complete. He got an eighty-eight percent in a calculus mid-term that he hadn't studied for and was mildly surprised that the mark was so low.

"How do you do it, Bradley? How do you get by? I never see your nose in a text book, all you do is read that fantasy crap!" His tone was accusatory as he pointed at Daniel's 'Lord of the Rings' battered paperback on the dresser table.

ISOLATION

"I don't know," he mumbled.

"It's not fair. I have to bust my ass off and you seem to have all the time in the world and still get nineties!" he spat out.

Daniel couldn't think of an appropriate response, and was surprised at the intensity of Harold's animosity. Harold immediately threw his hands up. "Geez, I'm sorry. I didn't mean anything by it. I just need some sleep. I can't even think straight any more."

Daniel watched him rub his blood-shot eyes and felt immense pity for him.

"It's okay, want to come down for supper with me?" he asked while grabbing his sweater out of the closet. The dining area was always cool.

"No, I'm not hungry. I don't have time to be hungry. I'll see you later." Harold turned back to his textbook, indicating that the discussion was over.

Daniel walked out, thinking to himself that it just didn't seem right for a thirteen-year-old to be that stressed out.

* * * * *

Daniel was studying at his desk after dinner that night, when a knock at the door startled him. Gerry Krane, a thin freckle-faced senior stuck his head in and informed him that he had a phone call. He stepped out of his room and went to the hall pay phone, with a strong feeling as to who it was on the line.

"Hi, Mom," he said into the receiver.

"It's not Mom, it's me," a friendly voice giggled.

"Hey, Katie, what's going on?" he asked cheerfully.

"Nothin', just wanted to hear your voice. We miss you."

He could hear his little sisters' voices in the background and the mere sound made tears spring to his eyes.

"I miss you guys, too. How are things at home?" he asked, feeling stupid for feeling so sentimental all of a sudden.

"Okay, I guess. We'll be done school soon because of the garden, which is nice in a way. Dad is busy out in the fields and Mom is helping him and volunteering for the church. She's doing bake sales and running the reading program at the library, basically the same as every other year. They're fighting a lot more though. *A lot* more."

There was a pause and than she laughed stiffly. "I'm sorry, that was stupid. You don't need to hear about stuff like that!"

"Yes, I do, Katie. Tell me, what's going on." Daniel leaned against the wall and clutched the phone tight. Her voice sounded funny, and a queer numbness spread throughout his body.

"It's nothing. Really. Well, you know how Mom and Dad bicker and carry on. They're just getting older and crankier is all."

"Really, is that all?" he questioned, not feeling relieved in the least.

"Yes, that's all. Don't worry, you silly old goose, I swear all you ever do is stew about things. How are you? How is boarding school life?"

He didn't want to talk about himself but answered her questions and tried to sound enthusiastic. He was worried though; there was an edge to her voice that he had never heard before. He knew her well enough to know that she was holding something back. After speaking briefly to Maddy and Evie, he said good-bye to Katie and hung up the phone with a heavy heart. He couldn't put his finger on it, but something about that conversation just wasn't right.

* * * * *

'So, how have you been, Daniel?" Miss Temple asked at their session the next week.

He grimaced at the question. "I'm so exhausted. My roommate, Harold, snores when he actually *does* sleep and wakes up most days at five thirty to study. Sometimes he stays up all night cramming and his desk lamp keeps me awake. He talks to himself and swears when he studies and gets himself all worked up. Because finals are in a few weeks, he's getting worse. I haven't had a decent nights sleep in over a week!"

"Have you talked to him about it?" she asked and he shook his head.

"He's stressed out enough. I'm not going to cause him any more problems."

"Well, you have a right to have a decent nights sleep," she stated crisply.

"It's no big deal. I have other things to worry about." He tried not get angry, but instantly felt hot under the collar. "My teachers think I should stay on for summer school because I don't have certain courses. My Mom didn't do a good enough job educating me, that's what Mr. Barker said."

"Did Mr. Barker *really* say that?"

"Not in so many words, but yeah," he replied bitterly.

His biology teacher, Mr. Barker, had boisterously and publicly expressed his indignation at Daniels lack of education in sciences and foreign languages. He felt a student with such meager schooling should not have made it through the admission process. He thought this school was for the elite, who had already demonstrated their academic excellence and merely needed guidance. It wasn't for those who hadn't even grasped the basic fundamentals.

Barker embarrassed him in front of the whole class within his first week of school. When he didn't answer a tricky question properly, Barker used that as an example to prove the less than mediocre education one can expect to receive from home schooling and public schools. Daniel decided that the man was an arrogant asshole, and that the only fitting revenge for such humiliation would be to ace his course. He went on to earn a solid A's in his class, but Barker was not easily impressed. Instead, he turned around and protested that Daniel needed to take summer courses to catch up with his other classmates. His theory was that while Daniel could understand the material they were currently studying, he did not have a solid base for the subject, and would need a more thorough grasp of it before he took more advanced courses.

"There's no way I'm staying here for the summer, my father needs me at home. He needs help during those months."

Miss Temple knew this would be a problem, and decided to confront it when she was better equipped with information. "I'll talk to your instructors and the school administrator and we'll get to the bottom of this."

"There is nothing to get to the bottom to. I'm not staying here!" Daniel folded his arms defiantly.

"Daniel, it's going to be okay. We'll work this out," she said quietly.

"No one cares what I think or feel and you all make decisions for me like I'm an idiot. I hate it! I'm so sick of this crap! I just want to go home!" He was practically shouting now.

"We only want what's best for you, Daniel, settle down. I do care what you think…we're all just trying to do what is best for your future." She tried to placate him, hoping those worlds would bring him some comfort but he turned on her with startling fierceness.

"That's just it, Miss Temple. You all look ahead too much, why don't you think about what's best for me *right* now. My dad needs me, and I need the summer off. Period. There is nothing more to discuss. I'll make up those courses some other way, some other time."

"It's not that easy, Daniel, and you know it."

"All I know is that I don't need teachers and guidance counselors telling me what to do all the time. If you really want what is best for me, you'll talk to my teachers and the dean and explain to them that my father needs my help during the summer months. Will you at least do that?"

He watched her purse her lips until they were a thin, straight line. She narrowed her eyes on him and said in firm, cold voice. "I know you're feeling frustrated but that is no reason to be rude. I demand an apology."

"Look, Mr. Barker..."

"An apology!" she snapped and slammed her palm on the top of her desk. "I have never been anything less than civil towards you Daniel, and I expect the same consideration back from all of my students. Since you are clearly upset, I will forgive your lack of manners. But in the future, please have the decency not to raise your voice or curse in the presence of a lady."

His eyes widened at her sudden flash of temper, for she was usually so reserved and controlled. She was obviously not one to cross and he mentally stored that little tidbit of information away in his brain.

"I repeat, I will look into this for you and we will go from there. If you carry on like a spoiled brat, I will leave it in the hands of Mr. Barker." Her eyes did not waver from his. "Is that what you want?"

"No," he muttered. "I'm sorry Miss. Temple."

"Fine. Now before you leave, I want to discuss something else with you." She cleared her throat and continued. "About the chess team, after I gave it some thought, I decided that you can have the choice whether you want to stick with it or not. I'm not going to force it on you, you can quit if you like. You took the test, passed it and fulfilled your end of the bargain."

Daniel stood up. "Well, I...uh...I think I will stick with it for a while. I played the other day, and it was okay."

She smiled and he watched her eyes light up. "I thought you didn't know how to play."

"I didn't really." He smiled back. "But like you said...I'm a fast learner."

* * * * *

Daniel woke that night to the muffled sounds of sobbing and sniffling. He opened his eyes and called out to the darkness.

"Harold? Are you okay?"

When there was no response he sat up and turned on the desk lamp beside his bed. "Harold?"

His roommate was lying on his side, his back turned towards him. His body was visibly shaking.

"Hey, what's wrong?" he asked, peering at him in confusion.

"Turn off the fucking light!" Harold cried.

"Not until you tell me what's wrong." Daniel tossed his covers off and slid his legs over the edge of his bed.

"Can't a guy get any privacy around here?"

"No. Tell me what's going on," Daniel repeated. "Did something happen today?"

Harold sighed, rolled over and asked for a Kleenex. Daniel threw him the box on his desk. He watched him clumsily wipe his runny nose and rub his squinted, bloodshot eyes.

"If I fail, I'm out. One more failed exam and I'm finished here. The dean called me in his office today to tell me. It's not even a matter of if I fail, it's a matter of when." He paused to wipe his nose again.

"I have a history exam in a week and there is no way in hell I can pass it. I just can't do it...my father's going to fuckin' kill me!" His voice broke and he started to sob. Tears streamed down his cheeks. Snot ran from his nose freely and puddled above his upper lip.

"You can pass Harold, you just have to study hard and..."

"That's just it!" Harold interrupted him with bulging eyes. "I study as hard as humanly possible and I still barely pass. I'm not like you Daniel... nobody's like you." He looked up at the ceiling and shook his head.

"Maybe your attitude is the problem,"

"Fuck you, what the hell do you know about anything?" Harold pointed at him. "You barely make it to your classes and never do your assignments. You hardly do anything but walk around with a huge chip on your shoulder. You're lucky you do so well on your tests or you'd be on your way out too."

"You don't even know what you're talking about." Daniel scowled.

"The biggest difference between you and me is that I *want* to be here and you don't. But you're the one that belongs here and they just keep me around because my family practically funds the place." He put his fingertips to his temples. "But I've been failing now for so long, that I'm pulling the school average down and making them look bad. They finally have to put their foot down and get rid of the dead weight."

"You wouldn't be here if you didn't meet their standards, Harold, why are you beating yourself up like this?"

"They have to pay the bills, too, buddy. Look at this place, look how nice it is. Who do you think pays for it all? It comes from friendly donations from the students families, so that their children can have the very best education possible. So what if three percent of their students are average dim bulbs, it doesn't really matter in the grand scheme of things. Everybody gets what they want; the school gets more funding, the parents have the satisfaction of telling everyone where their son went to school and the child gets the best education possible. However, if the child is an idiot like me, it all turns into a nightmare from hell."

Tears filled his eyes again and he added softly. "You don't tell someone like my father that you failed. You just don't. He doesn't know what the word means." A single tear fell slowly from his right eye and Daniel turned away. He couldn't bear to look at his misery. He knew Harold's father was a prominent corporate lawyer and came from a wealthy, distinguished family. Larry Benning had high expectations for his only son, and had hopes that he and Harold would open their own law firm after he passed the bar exam.

"You're not going to fail Harold." Daniel stood up and walked over to Harold's desk.

"I'm not in the mood for a pep talk. Just turn off the light and leave me alone," Harold groaned, putting his hands over his face.

"I'm not going to let you fail." Daniel pushed papers and books around on his cluttered desk until he found what he was looking for. "So…you're studying the history of the French Revolution. Your notes here are on the events that happened during the mid-eighteenth century through the Napoleonic era. That's what the exam is on right?"

"Yeah, so what?" Harold shrugged.

"I've studied all this before, it's not so bad and a week should be long enough to get a good handle on it. Look, I'll tutor you if you want." He sat down at his desk, text book in hand. "Do you want me to help you or do you want to sit there and cry all night?"

"Fuck you," Harold snapped.

"I'm only going to ask one more time, Harold. I'd like to help you out here. This stuff isn't all that tough if you just take the time and go over it properly. It's just memory work; fitting all the dates and people in the right order in your brain so that it makes sense to you. You can do this, I know you can." Daniel looked him straight in the eye and they stared each other down for a few seconds.

"It's a waste of time!" Harold exclaimed dramatically.

"Fine. Go tell your father that. That you failed because you wouldn't even bother to study. That you thought this was all one big waste of time. I'm sure he'd love to hear that while he's kicking your sorry ass back to Vancouver."

"Or for…" Harold exhaled loudly and sat up. "Okay, you're right. I need help."

"I'd be honored to help since you asked *ever* so nicely," he smirked and tossed the text book at him. Harold flipped through a few pages a looked up at Daniel with an odd expression on his face. "You're an unusual fellow, Bradley. Just when you think you have someone figured out…"

"The only thing unusual around here is the God-awful stench coming from your side of the room!" Daniel joked and they both howled with laughter.

Chapter Four

"Phone for you, Bradley!" someone shouted from the hall the next night while he and Harold were studying.

"Mommy must miss you an awful lot," Harold teased.

Daniel punched him lightly on the shoulder. "Don't slack off while I'm gone." He stood up and headed for the door.

"Yeah, yeah," Harold griped.

Daniel went down the hall to the pay phone and noticed the Steward twins walking towards him.

"Hello," he said into the phone.

"Hi, honey, it's me," his mother sang sweetly. A small smile reached his lips. It was always nice to hear her voice. It was comforting to know that she was somewhere out there thinking about him. "How are you?"

"I'm fine, just studying for finals. How is everyone down there?" He looked up to see the twins walking slowly past, staring boldly at him with cold, menacing eyes. He wondered what they were up to, and why they were looking at him so strangely. He had never even spoken to either one of them before, so there would be no reason for them to have any animosity towards him.

"Oh, everyone is fine," she laughed nervously, and Daniel looked away from the twins and focused on her voice again. She didn't sound right. He felt the same uneasiness come over him that he had had when Katie called.

"Mom? Everything okay?" he asked and she laughed thinly again.

"Of course it is, silly. The girls are in bed now, they're tired from working out in the garden all day. It's been raining so much that it has been hard to get anything done outside. This is the first nice day in over a week. Your father...he's been a bit frustrated with the weather."

"It's been that bad?" He was surprised. The weather in Rowland had been cool but sunny since the first of April.

"We got just over four inches last week and the fields almost flooded."

"Oh." He looked up to see that the twins were gone and a rush of relief flooded over him. There was something about those two that made him wary.

"I got a call from Miss Temple today. I was outside but Katie said she wanted to talk to us about summer school? I have to call her back tomorrow, but…are you planning on staying on through the summer, Danny?"

He could hear the strain in her voice and felt a tightness in his chest. If Miss Temple had called his parents, that meant she hadn't been able to help him after all.

That creep, Mr. Barker, had gotten what he wanted and now he'd be stuck in a stupid classroom all summer while his dad struggled without him.

"I don't know, Mom, they were talking about it but I told them I couldn't. I told them that I had to help dad out around the farm, but they say I don't have all the required classes. That if I want to take more advanced courses next year, I'll have to catch up during the summer."

"Is that what you want, Danny?"

"No! No, it's not what I want, but it's not up to me, Mom. *You* talk to them, you tell them that I can't! They don't listen to me!" he exclaimed.

"I will, because…your father got a bit upset when he found out about it. It will cost more money for you to stay on there through the summer months."

"I know, Mom, I know. Look, call Miss Temple and talk to her. Talk to the dean too, maybe I can make up the classes some other way." He felt sweat break out on his brow and wiped it away with his palm.

"I gotta go, sweetie, your father just came in from the barn."

"Can I talk to him?" he asked eagerly.

"Right now isn't a good time, and this is long distance and all. Look, I'll talk to that woman and call you back when I find out what's going on. Okay?"

Her words came out in quick jumbles that he could barely understand.

"Okay, Mom."

"Alright, I have to go now. I love you, darling, bye," She hung up the phone abruptly and after he hung up, he walked wearily back to his room.

"You okay?" Harold looked up from his textbook.

"I'm fine. Lets take a break, I want to go for a walk." He grabbed his jacket off the back of his chair.

"A walk? Where?" Harold stood up.

"Anywhere. I just need to get out of this room," he said grimly, knowing that he wouldn't be able to concentrate on anything concrete for a while.

"It's seven-thirty, you don't want to go outside, do you?" Harold pulled on his jacket as well. Harold was deathly afraid of the dark, and kept a nightlight or lamp on all through the night. The thought of walking outside in the dark would probably send him into a mini panic attack.

"No, I just want to walk the halls for a bit."

"Alright."

As they walked out of the room, Harold touched his arm gently. "Did you get bad news or something? You look upset."

"My parents are pissed that I have to go to summer school. My dad needs my help around the farm and I think I'll be stuck here thanks to, dickhead Barker," he snapped, hating the scrawny bastard more each second that he thought about him.

"Well, look at the bright side. If I don't fail my finals, you'll be hanging out with me this summer."

"*That's* the bright side?" Daniel exaggerated a loud groan.

Harold gave him a friendly shove in return.

They walked down the stairs to the main floor, and as expected, the place was quiet and lifeless. They walked down the wide corridor, left the boys dormitory and turned a corner that led into the main hall. Trophy cases and portraits of past prime ministers, religious and scholarly figures lined the walls. The halls were dimly lit, one lightbulb hanging from the ceiling flickered on and off erratically.

"This place gives the creeps at night." Harold shivered. "Let's go back."

"Do you hear something?" Daniel stopped. "Listen!"

"It's a piano, someone is playing in the auditorium." Harold shrugged. "The music students practice there every night."

"Let's go see." He grabbed Harold's arm and pulled him along.

"Do we have to? Can't we just go back to our room?" Harold pleaded but Daniel ignored him.

They went halfway down the hall, stood in front of the auditorium double-door and listened silently.

"That's Mozart, Elvira Madigan," Harold whispered.

"How do you know that?" Daniel asked skeptically.

"My mother plays the piano and only listens to classical music. If you grew up in my house, you pick up on that kind of stuff."

"I want to see whose playing." Daniel opened the door and peered inside.

Twenty-feet in front of them sat Rachel Sheldon in front of a baby grand piano. She played softly, but the room reverberated with the soul-wrenching strains of music originating from her nimble, tiny fingertips. Her long hair flowed down her back in a tumble of exquisite curls. A large spotlight from the back focused solely on her, it gave off the only light in the darkened theater. Another music student sat beside her, turning the pages of her sheet music.

They stepped inside, let the door close behind them and watched Rachel play for almost two minutes. "She's good," Daniel whispered and Harold snickered.

"Good-looking you mean."

"No, I mean that she's a good piano player. Listen to her, she's amazing."

"You got a thing for her, Bradley?" Harold sneered.

"No, *do* you?"

"Sure. I got a thing for all the girls, it don't get me nowhere though. For some reason they don't find my coke-bottle glasses very attractive." He took off his thick glasses and cleaned them on his shirt.

"Gee, I wonder why not." Daniel turned back to Rachel. "We better get back. We have a lot more studying to do tonight."

"Don't remind me." Harold rolled his eyes.

Daniel cast one more lingering gaze on Rachel, and reluctantly left the auditorium.

* * * * *

Daniel walked briskly down the hall the next morning. He had been pulled out of his algebra class by the school secretary, and told to go to the dean's office immediately. He knew he hadn't done anything wrong but he couldn't help feeling the unpleasant churning of butterflies at the concept of seeing the dean alone. Dean Wilkens was a huge bear of a man, with a potent presence. Daniel was terribly intimidated by him, even though he had never been anything other than polite and courteous toward him when they passed in the halls. When he was let into his office, Daniel was surprised to see Miss Temple inside waiting for him as well.

"Come on in, Daniel. Have a seat," Wilkens said gruffly and waved him in. Miss Temple wasn't smiling and Daniel knew then what the meeting was about. He sat on a wooden chair beside her.

Dean Wilkens leaned back in his own leather chair across from them and sighed. "I'm afraid you're not going to like what we're about to tell you."

"It's about summer school, isn't it?" He looked down at his hands miserably.

"Mr. Barker was right Daniel. You're well versed in English, history, and geography, but lack in math and the more scientific subjects like chemistry and biology. At the end of your education here, you also should be fluent in two other languages. You don't even have a foreign language course this semester. You're behind your fellow classmates, do you know what this means?" Miss Temple asked.

"No, what?" Daniel replied dully.

"If you plan to graduate with your peers when you're eighteen years old, you're going to have to spend every summer until then in summer school to make up your missed courses."

"That's insane!"

"Watch your tone, young man," Dean Wilkens said sharply.

"I'm sorry, sir, but come on. I can't be in school full-time for four straight years. That's crazy!"

"We'll arrange some sort of short break for you during the summer, but you are behind the others your age and that's the plain and simple fact. You need to take some pre-requisite courses to even take some of the more advanced courses. Summer school is the only way for you to get the credits you need to graduate when you're eighteen. Unless, of course, you want to remain here at the school for a longer period of time." Dean Wilkens let his voice trail off.

"But my father..."

"I spoke to your family this morning. They are aware of the situation and your mother discussed hiring a young man down the road to help your father when he needs it. You shouldn't worry about that, Daniel, your parents will work something out. You need to focus on what is most important, your studies. Your parents are working hard to afford for you to be here, so you need to do all that you can to maintain your high marks," Miss Temple said firmly.

Daniel lowered his head and rolled his eyes. They didn't understand, none of them did. Of course his mother would tell Miss Temple exactly what she wanted to hear, she wouldn't cause a scene. They couldn't afford to get a hired hand, it was simply out of the question. He was a burden on his family, in every sense of the word, but still they allowed him to remain here. There was nothing he could do though. It was out of his hands.

"Alright," he sighed. "I'll go to summer school."

* * * * *

While miserably walking back to his algebra class, Daniel turned a corner in the hall and saw Rachel a few feet ahead taking a drink from a water fountain. She stood up straight, wiped her mouth and looked his way.

"Hi Daniel!" Her eyes lit up and she started toward him. His heart began to thud powerfully in his chest.

"Hi."

"Where are you going?" she asked. Her hair was pulled into a tight braid that fell down to her shoulder blades. He was so busy noticing how pretty she was that he barely heard what she said.

"Um...uh...back to my algebra class, room eleven."

"Ew, yuck. I hate math and science, I just don't understand that kind of stuff," she grimaced. "Mr. Barker or Mr. Neville?"

"Barker," Daniel spat and she nodded.

"He's a jerk, I've had him twice and I swear he marks harder than any other teacher here. He's on some sort of power trip or something." She shook her head. "So, have you signed up for the tournament this weekend?"

"Chess tournament?"

"Yeah, it's Saturday from nine o'clock in the morning until whenever. You really should come out, it's a lot of fun." She started to back away from him.

"I *really* have to go, I'm late for my piano lesson but sign-up with Mr. Neville. He organizes the tournaments, just let him know before Thursday."

"I don't know." He wasn't sure he was up for a tournament just yet.

"Oh, come on. It's not competitive; it's just for fun. Everyone has a good time, you really should come." she pleaded, putting her hands into a prayer position. "Pretty please?"

He couldn't possibly turn her down when she looked like that. "Alright, I will."

"Good. I have Mr. Neville this afternoon so I'll sign you up then. Okay?" She was practically yelling, she was so far down the hall at this point.

"Okay!" he called back. She turned a corner and was gone.

He wondered how in such a short time period, he had been talked into going to summer school, participating in chess tournaments, and being a tutor to another student. Things were changing rapidly in his life, and it seemed like everything was out of his control. Part of him liked the changes, but another part was terribly frightened by them.

* * * * *

"Read over the next five pages and I'll ask you some questions on it," he ordered. "Then we'll go over your study notes again."

It was the night before the big exam and Harold was anxious and stressed. Daniel looked over at the clock hanging in their room. It was ten o'clock and his mother hadn't called yet. He was certain that she would have called either last night or this evening to talk about him staying on for summer school. The fact that she hadn't made him nervous, and he recalled the last few conversations he had had with her and with Katie. They had seemed tense and on edge. As if something was on the tip of their tongues but they were afraid to say it. But what? What were they so scared of? What was going on at home?

"Are you okay?" Harold hit him on the shoulder and Daniel snapped back to reality. "You've been staring off into space for almost five minutes. Are you feeling alright?"

"I'm fine, just a little tired." He rubbed his eyes. "Give me your book and I'll ask you some questions."

"Look, if you're not up to it you can call it a night. You've helped me out a lot, I can probably take it from here. Why don't you just go to bed?" Harold offered but Daniel grabbed the book from his hands.

"I want you to pass Benning, so I'm going to push you until this information is ingrained in your brain. We're quitting at midnight, not a minute more or less. You need your sleep so you're not pulling one of your senseless all-nighters. Now, on page thirty-five..."

"You know, I never would have thought you'd make a great tutor but in the last few days I've seen a different side of you," Harold interrupted, and looked at Daniel in what could be perceived as a gaze of admiration. "You're a completely different person than I thought you were, I don't even know how to explain it."

"Are you trying to distract me from quizzing you?" Daniel asked shortly, not knowing where the conversation was going.

"No...I'm just saying that I appreciate all that you've done for me the last few days. I know you have your own exams and work to do, so...thanks."

"You're welcome," Daniel replied quietly. The strange thing was, that he *really* liked tutoring him. He initially offered to help him just to get a buddy out of a jam but after a few days he began to actually enjoy testing Harold on information. Even more strange was that all along he had truly wanted to drop out of school, go back home and work with his father. But now his feelings were mixed. He was starting to like it here; he had a friend now and he would die before he admitted this to anyone else, but he had a small crush on Rachel. He liked most of his courses too; they were challenging, and interesting and

ISOLATION

the teachers kept him on his toes. In the last few weeks, he started to feel as if he fit in here, like he actually belonged. But then he felt guilty about that, because he knew this was not what his father wanted.

Him even being here was all his mother's doing. It was clear that his parents had very different aspirations for him, and were still feuding over it as well.

He was so confused, what was he supposed to do when he graduated? Who should he disappoint? His mother or his father, and would any decision he made satisfy either of them? Did it even matter what *he* wanted?

He felt imprisoned by the hopes and fears of the two people that mattered most to him, to the point where he knew it would eventually immobilize him from making either one happy. Himself included.

"Daniel?"

"Uh? Oh, okay." He looked down at his textbook and forced himself to focus. "Alright, what page were we on?"

* * * * *

"Daniel. Daniel Bradley," Mr. Neville checked over his papers, and looked for his name. He pointed to the left side of the room.

"You're playing against Todd Steward first, over there at table five."

Todd Steward? He groaned inwardly, of all people to play with! There were twenty-five other chess players in the tournament and they just *had* to pair him with the biggest, ugliest, meanest kid in the school. He was shuffling unhappily over to his table when someone grabbed his arm from behind. He turned around to Rachel's beautiful face.

"Uh…hi," he sputtered out, feeling the familiar race in his pulse rate.

"I'm glad you could make it. Who are you playing first?"

"Todd Steward," he grumbled and she laughed.

"He's not as good as player as he thinks he is. Just don't let him intimidate you."

"He doesn't intimidate me," Daniel replied, a little too quickly.

"You know, we break for lunch at noon. Do you want to meet up then and eat together?"

He could barely respond to her question, he couldn't believe that this unbelievably pretty girl wanted anything to do with him. "Sure!"

"Okay, well they want us to go to our tables now. I'll see you later." She skipped away and he felt very lucky and honored in that moment. There was something about her, something that made him feel better whenever she was around. She was so sweet and nice, but he secretly hoped that she wasn't like that to everyone. He hoped that there was a tiny part of her that thought of him as highly as he thought of her. It was unlikely, but he could hope.

"So you're my first victim." Todd was already at their table, with a welcoming condescending smirk. Daniel wanted desperately to physically wipe that expression off his ugly mug, but instead sat across from him calmly with a forced, tight smile.

"Hello, Todd."

"So you're the new geek around here. The one that thinks he's hot shit," Todd said in an irritating voice that made Daniel seethe.

"I don't know what you've heard about me, but I'm sure most of it is probably untrue. I'm new to this game, I'm just learning, so give me a break today." Daniel attempted to be civil but the look on Todd's face told him that civility was not his style.

"Oh cut the shit, you arrogant prick," he cursed quietly. "Rachel told us that when you two played, you whipped her ass. She's almost a good a player as my brother you know. She's the third best chess player here, ranked under me, of course. So you're obviously not new to the game. I don't know what kind of crap you're trying to pull here, but it's not going to fly with me. Understand?"

"I'm not trying to pull anything," Daniel responded defensively and felt his blood start to boil in his veins. Who did this guy think he was, talking to him like he was a child that he could just push around. They had just met and Todd had already ripped right into him. Daniel tried to restrain himself, but he was just about to push the table into his chest and tell him where to go when Mr. Neville called their attention to the front of the room. The over-zealous man flashed his absurdly white teeth, made a little speech and indicated that the games were on.

"You know, I'm really going to enjoy this." Todd sat back in his chair with a filthy, malevolent grin.

Daniel leaned forward and spoke so softly that only his opponent could hear. "I think the rankings are going to change today."

Todd's face froze in surprise. "What did you just say?"

"I said there isn't a doubt in my mind that I won't kick your fat half-witted ass," he replied, surprising even himself with the confidence in his voice.

Todd sat up straight in his chair, but before he could say a word, Daniel swiftly moved his wooden pawn.

"Your move."

ISOLATION

* * * * *

Daniel didn't have a competitive bone in his body, or so he thought. He never had the opportunity to find out if he did, growing up on the farm. He didn't have the chance to play with other kids, other than his sisters, who weren't interested in sports or competitive games. They were usually too busy to do that sort of thing anyway. When he had played chess against Rachel, he had been so immersed in making the right moves that he hadn't been concerned about winning so much as in just playing the game properly.

But this time he wanted to win. Not just win, he wanted to brutally humiliate and annihilate his opponent. He was excited, adrenaline pumped through him viciously, giving him energy and motivation. Time seemed to literally stand still for them. Todd seemed just as intent as he to win; and it was quickly obvious that he was, indeed, a better player than Rachel. Todd's gruff exterior completely belied his aptness; he looked like a bully but had the sharp mind of a nerd. It was an exhausting mental challenge for both of them; their nasty banter muted as their mutual respect for the others game grew and their concentration intensified.

Mr. Neville called out, startling them both from the reverie, that it was time for a lunch break and everyone began to file into the dining hall.

"You're good, Bradley, but not that good," Todd said shortly as he walked away. Daniel was about to issue out an equally clever response when he noticed Rachel bustling towards him.

"How are you doing?" She grinned.

"Good, still playing Todd," he said as they fell in the lunch line with the others.

"Really? Whose winning so far?"

"We're about even," he replied, though he planned to change that very soon.

"He's pretty good, but his brother Justin is phenomenal."

"So I hear," Daniel muttered, unimpressed.

"I saw you, the other night when I was playing the piano. You were with Harold," she said.

"Oh, yeah. We were just out walking around, heard some music and decided to see where it was coming from."

He wondered if they could have gotten in trouble for that, he knew that they were not allowed to wander around after eight o'clock at night and boys were absolutely forbidden to enter the girls dormitory at any time. Maybe they weren't allowed in the auditorium either.

"You're a very good piano player, amazing really."

"Oh, I'm not that good. But you should have came up to the stage and talked to me. You were out the door before I realized it was you." She looked up at him coyly. It was in that instant that he knew that she felt the same for him as he did for her. That she had a crush on him too. A pleasant tingling sensation raced up his spine but he tried hard to conceal his excitement.

"Next time I will," he returned shyly, and they stood in awkward silence until they got to the front of the lunch line. He wondered if others noticed the flush on his face or the trembling of his hands. Once they received their food, they sat at a table together, and shot demure smiles at one another between bites of lasagna, salad and french bread. Normally girls and boys were not allowed to eat together and had different lunch periods, but the school made exceptions for special events.

He noticed Todd sitting with Justin across the room behind Rachel. They were both glaring blatantly at him. He knew that he shouldn't care, that he shouldn't sink to their juvenile level but shot an equivalently malignant look back at them. Todd followed suit by sticking out his tongue at him, and Justin opened his mouth showing Daniel a grotesque sight, his mouth full of half-chewed food.

He responded by giving them both the finger, and they laughed with childlike astonishment. The three boys played their game of immaturity throughout the whole lunch period, unbeknownst to Rachel, who was busy batting her pretty eyelashes and eating as daintily as possible.

* * * * *

Two hours later, Daniel proclaimed in a loud, smug voice. "Checkmate."

Todd stared down at the board in surprise and then disgust. It was a close match, either one of them could have won. Instead of feeling victorious, though, Daniel suddenly felt fearful of how Todd would react. True to his personality, he pushed the table away from him and glowered down at Daniel.

"You were just lucky that time, twerp, next time will be different. I can guarantee you that."

While Todd barreled away to find his brother, Daniel called out cheerfully. "Thanks for the game, Steward!"

They had accumulated a bit of a crowd around their table an hour earlier, when word spread of the evenly matched game going on. Everyone cheered at Daniel's victory, but most were surprised that a newcomer had beaten out one of the best chess players in their school. Everyone milled about, talking eagerly amidst themselves of the game that had just transpired; of the new player that no one knew a thing about, and of how furious Todd had been. Rachel stood amongst the crowd, laughing and clapping with delight.

"That was great!" she gushed when she approached his table. He stood up alongside her. "So tell me the truth, where did you learn to play so well?"

"I don't really know. I think, like he said, I just got lucky," Daniel replied modestly.

"Well, I got beat out by Kenneth Lackey, so I'm done," she said. The crowd had started to lose interest and were drifting away from his table to another. One of Rachel's friends called her name and waved for her to join them.

"I have to go," she said reluctantly. "I guess I'll see you later. Congratulations again on your big win." She stood up on her tip-toes and kissed him full on the cheek. Daniel was so surprised, he almost lost his bearings and had to grip the table for support. She looked up at him with nervous wide eyes and scurried off to her friends. Daniel swallowed hard and blinked a few times. It had happened so quick, he almost wondered if he had imagined it. A couple of other students witnessed the display of affection and whispered excitedly about it to one another.

"Bradley!" Mr. Neville called out over the crowd and waved at him. "Over here, you have another match!"

Daniel wandered over towards the teacher, knowing that after that kiss, there'd be no way that he'd be able to concentrate on chess anymore.

Chapter Five

"That coffee is going right through me, I'm going to have to stop at the coffee shop up a few miles." Daniel broke from the story, and handed her the thermos cup. "It tastes good though, is there any more?"

"It's empty, I finished it off a while ago," she said, disappointed that they had to take a break. She wanted to hear more, for it had been so long since she had been able to get more than one word responses from him.

Thunder rumbled furiously in the distance and rain continued to pour relentlessly, soaking the earth. It was just after five o'clock and the roads were still dark and quiet, enabling them to make good time.

"It's funny to me that you quit at the good part. Before Justin kicked your butt in that chess tournament. I seem to remember him beating you in no time flat and taking first place," she teased.

"Yeah, yeah. I was getting to that," Daniel mumbled.

"That chess tournament started that whole silly feud between you and the Steward boys. It's hard to believe you were once so immature." She turned to him. "I remember all that, I remember it because I was there. Which means that you're avoiding the real issue yet again. These events that you're describing are not the things I want to hear about. I want to know what happened to you at the end of that summer, when you went home for that two week break. When..." She couldn't bring herself to say what happened, partly because she didn't know what did.

"I was getting to that. Why do you have to push me! I told you to let me tell it my way but you just can't do that can you! You always have to pressure and nag. Just this once, can't you let me do it my way?" he raged, saw the coffee shop ahead and turned on his blinker to signal his turn.

The truth was, he couldn't just out and talk about that summer. It was too hard. He had to do it gradually, like pulling off a band-aid. He was opting to do it slow to put off the inevitable pain and discomfort. Why couldn't she understand that? Didn't she see how hard this was for him, to recall memories that he worked so hard to repress for almost twenty years? He was stuck in a strange transitional period, where his future was too uncertain and barren to contemplate, and his past too intensely painful to face. It was a stressful night for him, and here Rachel was, coaxing him to expose a lifetime of hurt in just a matter of minutes. It wasn't that easy.

He pulled into the parking lot and found a space. "Do you want anything other than coffee?"

"No," she replied curtly. He opened the car door and raced into the coffee shop. Run away like you always do Bradley, she thought irritably.

She ejected the Madame Butterfly tape and put on the radio. She turned the dial to a popular soft rock station and froze. The song playing raised goose-bumps on her flesh. That was the beauty of music; it brought a memory or moment to life and enhanced the very essence of it. The haunting, beautiful voice of Patsy Cline brought her back to the innocence of her thirteenth year. When she had rebelliously snuck Daniel into her dorm room on a humid July afternoon. Her roommate, Sally Darren, had went home for the summer and had left a radio hidden away in a closet.

Rachel dug it out and turned it on to off-set their nervous, awkward silence. She found a clear station and turned around to look at Daniel. He was sitting stiffly on her bed, his face a deathly pale, with sweat gleaming on his worried brow. She sat beside him, took his hand and squeezed it gently. He lowered his head and looked at her. Really looked at her, and it felt as if his eyes were boring down into her very soul. His eyes shone with a vivid fire and passion but unfortunately he turned away with polite shyness. She impulsively reached up, put a hand to his cheek and turned his face back towards her. She kissed him then, her first real open-mouth kiss and it was as magical and wonderful as any adolescent girl can envision. She could have kissed him forever, with Patsy singing softly in the background. Every sensation about that moment was delicious; the sweaty but pleasant touch of his hand on hers, the afternoon sun basking on her face from the open window and the slight breeze that washed over them from it. It would be years before she realized how life-altering that moment was. She had felt alive and happy then, in the most complete sense of those two words. Her mild crush on Daniel blossomed to full-blown love and devotion the moment their lips had touched.

Rachel stared at the radio as if in a trance until the song ended. Icy shivers raced through her nerve endings. She had never felt so many varying emotions at once. It started with a quivering chin; a twitchy nose and then the tears ultimately announced themselves. She didn't bother to wipe them away. The effect that he had on her originating from that kiss, had clearly yet to dissipate.

She truly thought that she was over him. She thought that twenty tumultuous years, and a final bitter break-up would severe all romantic feelings that she had for him. But bizarrely enough, she was just as much in love with him now, possibly even more so, than she was then.

There were so many questions to this sad obsession she had for him, like why she wanted so badly for him to fall back in love with her, when she knew at this point, that he was incapable of giving her what she needed? Why did she want to save him from himself. Why did she *even* care when he had caused her so much pain over the years.

It didn't seem fair that she had wasted the best years of her life on a man who reached the peak of his emotional maturity at the age of fourteen.

It was fate's cruel joke for her to have a soul-mate, with an untouchable soul.

* * * * *

Daniel rapidly sloshed through the flooding parking lot, hands full of take-out and was just about to get in the car when a deafening crack of thunder shook the sky. He jumped, and almost dropped the two coffees in his hand.

The sound of thunder, to him, sounded disturbingly like a gun shot.

It had been almost twenty years since he had heard a real gun fired, and if he never heard that sound again, he'd be a lucky, lucky man.

He climbed in the car; dripping wet and handed Rachel a Styrofoam cup of coffee. "I can't believe this rain, it's insane out there."

After he settled himself in, he finally looked over at her. His face dropped and his eyes widened with concern. "Rachel? What's wrong? Why are you crying?"

"I'm just...worried about your mother." She wiped her cheeks and sniffed.

He eyed her for a few seconds and then started the car up. "I am too." He pulled back unto the highway and took a sip of coffee.

"Are you going to continue, with your story I mean?" she asked and noticed his body stiffen. "I'm not trying to pressure you, I just..." She couldn't finish, her lips started to tremble.

"You weren't crying about my mother, were you. You were thinking about us," he stated and a single tear slipped down her cheek.

This was a mistake. Going to Aldon to with him was a judgement error of epic proportions. What made her think that she could handle this?

"So what if I was!" she sputtered and instantly regretted her admission.

"Damnit, Rachel! I have enough on my mind as it is with my mother, I can't deal with you, too. Why do you have to act like this now!" he swore.

She shifted her weight so that she was completely turned towards the passenger window. She didn't want him to see her face. She had never felt so helpless and angry in her life, and cursed herself for feeling that way. She was usually strong and controlled, but not around Daniel. He brought out the best and worst in her, and his power over her was both frightening and infuriating.

She hated him for making her feel an inch high. Like she were a mere schoolgirl who couldn't control her emotions, but that was precisely how she acted around him. It didn't give him justification to casually disregard her feelings though.

How she longed for the simple days before that fateful kiss, when her one and only love was music. She didn't want to love Daniel Bradley any more.

She didn't believe in fairy tales or miracles, she was past believing she could change him. She simply didn't *want* to have feelings for him, but her stubborn heart wouldn't listen to the rationality of her brain.

* * * * *

They were silent for nearly twenty minutes, and the dense tension between them seemed to grow into its own tangible being. The intensity of the storm eventually calmed to a steady rainfall, its consistent patter on the car roof was rather harmonious and peaceful. It was Daniel who broke the silence, only when he had finished his large coffee and tossed the empty cup in the plastic bag he kept for garbage in the back seat.

"I don't want to argue with you Rachel, I'm not up for it right now. I'm trying to tell you something. I *want* to be honest with you but you just have to let me do it my way." He didn't look at her when he spoke, and she wouldn't look at him either. He continued with his story regardless of the bitterness she still exuded.

"Yes, Justin beat me in that tournament and the whole thing proved to be a rather humbling experience. The Steward boys took notice me from then on, and went out of their way to prove that I was no match for the likes of them."

He sneezed and continued with his story.

"Harold came racing into our room the following Monday and was in such a frantic state that I was sure that he had failed that test. It took him a minute to spit the words out but he had passed, getting a record high for him at eighty-five percent. He said he nearly fainted from shock when the teacher handed him his test back. The final was worth twenty-five percent so he passed the course even though he had failed the mid-term. He would still have to make up other subjects up in summer school but he would be allowed to stay on for the next term. I don't think I've ever seen Harold that happy, he was grinning from ear to ear for hours on end. He was laughing and joking, it was like he had a completely new personality."

Daniel smiled slightly at that fond memory. He had never once even considered the fact that Harold *could* fail. He knew all along that if they tried hard enough that he would do fine, but Harold wasn't quite so optimistic. He had started packing his bags the day after the test, and had prepared his speech mentally of how he was going to tell his father that he had failed out of private school.

Daniel had been more excited about Harold narrowly passing that test than he was of his own academic success. He had received near perfect scores on all his tests but barely gave it a seconds thought. When something came easily to you, you tend to take it for granted, and that's exactly what he did.

"Harold's parents came up for a visit that weekend and I got to meet his father, who he spoke often about. I was very intimidated by Larry. He was a tall, beefy well-dressed man that made his presence known when he entered a room. I remember everything about him. He wore a perfectly-tailored three-piece black suit, a flashy college ring and the shiniest shoes that I've ever seen. He was a man of expensive tastes, and high standards, you could sense that about him immediately. Harold's mother, Ruth, was a pretty little thing that looked like a trophy wife to me. She was beautiful but placid, like a doll with no personality or real characteristics. Larry certainly made up for her dullness though. He was boisterous and crude; and it was hard to believe that little old Harold was spawned from such an unlikely couple."

"They picked Harold up and took him out to dinner in Rowland. They stayed in our room for fifteen minutes at the most, but in that small amount of time, Larry made a huge impression on me. I don't know how to explain it, but his whole demeanor was very impressive and exciting. He had it all. Money, education, a great career that everyone respected, a beautiful wife, and a son who wanted nothing more than to please him. He had the world by the tail and you knew it. He was happy, self assured and walked with a confident stride that I had never seen before." Daniel swallowed hard. "He was so unlike my father. He was a miserable old fart that never wore a suit in his entire life and worked his ass off from morning til night every day. And it got him nowhere."

Rachel heard the change in Daniels voice and turned to look at him.

"I didn't want to be like that. I didn't want to be old and poor and still working like a dog. I didn't want to be my father. I decided then and there that I wouldn't return home to farm, that I would graduate and go on to university. I would become a professional of some sort…I would be someone important like Larry Benning."

Rachel felt her insides turn, she had never in her life heard Daniel speak so candidly. She had never even heard him speak of his father, it was one of many subjects that she was forbidden to question him about all throughout their relationship.

"I saw a lot of other families visit or pick-up their children and they were all like the Bennings. Wealthy and nicely dressed, mannerly and polished with a slick, rich elegance. I looked at my family differently and was ashamed of where I grew up. Of how poor we were, and of both my parents. Mostly of my father, though. He, who had never read a book in his life; who wore ripped blue jeans and manure stained work boots every day and always smelled like cow shit. I wanted him to be like Larry. Articulate and charming with worldly knowledge and a taste for the finer things."

Meeting Larry Benning had made him acutely aware of the differences between him and all the other students around him. The extremity of those differences made him embarrassed. He knew his father sensed that change in him the next time they met, could tell that his feelings had changed towards him. Perhaps that had been his fear all along.

"It's ironic. Harold envied me for my book-smarts, and I envied him back for the kind of wealth his family had. The easy life they led that someone like me could only dream about. But I guess you always want what you can't have."

He stopped speaking, could no longer form concrete thoughts in his mind and suddenly remembered where he was headed. All this talk had made him forget what this trip was really for. He was going home. To the place where it all began…and ended.

"Daniel?" Rachel called out and startled him. "Are you okay?"

He honestly didn't know any more. He gripped the steering wheel, and drove with a gnawing fear of what lie ahead.

Chapter Six

Daniel stood with his arms folded, looking at Miss Temple's large book collection in her office, on a quiet Friday afternoon. She was late for their appointment, their last one before she left for summer vacation, and he glanced down at his watch for the tenth time in two minutes. It was unlike her to be late, she appeared to be the most organized and efficient person on the planet.

"Good afternoon, Daniel." She breezed in the door swiftly and settled herself behind her desk. She indicated with the flick of her wrist that he should sit down as well. He did. She offered no apology or explanation for her tardiness, and simply asked how he was doing while pulling papers out of the notebook she had brought in with her.

"Fine. I passed all my exams and start summer school next week. I was real thrilled to find out that Mr. Barker is teaching two of my courses. I'm sure he'll make sure I have plenty of homework," he said dryly.

"Mr. Barker has high standards for *all* of his students, so to keep him off your back you just have to do the work he assigns and do well in his courses. Just remember that he *is* a great teacher, one of the best here, you can learn a lot from him." Her tone was condescending.

"I'll try to remember that," he replied shortly.

She opened up her notebook and placed her small reading glasses on the end of her nose. "I was just in a meeting with Dean Wilkens. He's not pleased with your current antics and recent association with the Steward twins."

"I don't know what you're talking about," he lied, feeling a tinge of uneasiness but forced an innocent smile on his face. It was a beguiling smile that always went over well with his mother but it was apparent that Miss Temple was no fool.

"Oh, I think you do. Let's see…" She peered down at her notes. "From stealing each other's clothes in the change rooms, taping 'kick me or I'm an idiot' to one another's back to starting food fights. You three have made utter nuisances of yourselves the last three weeks."

Daniel knew that there was no way to deny it so he replied sincerely. "But they started it."

"Original defense," she scoffed and shook her head. "Really. What's gotten into you, Daniel? While I'm certainly glad that you're interested in expanding your social circle, I hardly think pulling pranks on other students is the best way to make friends or to spend your time."

"Yes, I was in on the food fight but they started it and all the rest. They stole my clothes first and I did it back to them. They put signs on my back so I did it right back," he sighed. "I beat Todd in a chess tournament and they've been after me ever since. I'm not just going to let them get away with stuff like that. The first few times they did something it seemed like all in good fun but now they just won't leave me alone."

"You ignore them. Period. If they don't get a reaction from you, they'll leave you alone. They know they can get to you, get a rise from you and get you to play their game. But you seem to be the one getting caught, not them." She took her glasses off. "They're staying on through the summer, did you know that?"

"No, why...did they both fail a course?" he asked hopefully but was actually surprised. He thought they both did well academically.

"They're upgrading. Several students do that," she explained. "To get into the university or college of their choice and to be eligible for a full scholarship, students have to have marks in the mid to high nineties. Most can pass their courses here but few can keep up with the rigorous workload *and* do extracurricular activities while maintaining such a high average. We offer the opportunity to upgrade during the summer. There are certain requirements needed but I hardly think you'll have to resort to that. Your marks this semester were impressively high so as long as you keep up with what you're doing, you'll be fine."

She continued in a serious monotone. "Back to what I was saying though, Dean Wilkens is rather concerned that you three will distract one another this summer. He takes his holidays in July and August, I'm off for the entire summer, and there are only a handful of teachers staying on. It's imperative that each student behave in a responsible and mature manner during a time when there is less supervision. Anything less will reflect poorly on their record. We have high expectations of our students here, and feel that they should expect a lot from themselves."

"Miss Temple, you don't have to worry about me acting up or anything. I just wish the Stewards would leave me alone and bug somebody else," he whined.

"You're only responsible for your own actions, Daniel, so if they do something to you again, just report it to a teacher and go about your way. Justin and Todd will soon find some other way to spend their time. Be aware that the school doesn't think highly of such antics, so it's best if you detach yourself from this kind of mischief if you want to be in good favor with the teachers. They can make your life a living hell if they so choose," she warned and he knew she was right. There was nothing to be gained from retaliating to their pranks; other than trouble.

"If I have your word that you'll be on your best behavior this summer, I'll inform the dean that you have been warned and have promised to act accordingly. I hope that this subject is closed." She closed her notebook and pushed it away. She then looked back up at him with a softened facial expression. "So, have you spoken to your family recently? You haven't spoken of them in quite some time."

He looked away. "My mother calls once a month. She said my dad was upset at their phone bill and now she's only allowed to call every three weeks. Our conversations are always short and to the point. She doesn't say much, just wants to know if I'm alright. I don't know…" he trailed off.

"What's wrong?" Miss Temple pushed, noticing his discomfort on the subject.

"It seems like she's holding something back from me. That something happened or is going on at home that she won't tell me. I don't how to explain it, but her voice doesn't sound right. When Katie called, she sounded the same way. Maybe not, maybe I'm imagining things," he muttered but she knew instantly that someone like Daniel does not imagine such things.

"Have you asked one of them if something is wrong?" she asked and he nodded.

"They both told me things are fine and that I should focus on my studies and not worry so much."

"Then you should listen to them. I'm sure everything is fine. If it was anything important, one of them would tell you," She paused for a few seconds. "I wanted to tell you before I left for the summer that I am very proud of the way you have stepped up and pushed yourself this semester. I know how hard it is to start a new school, and especially in your case when you were educated at home for so long. But you did it, Daniel. You did brilliantly in all your courses and you've fit in quite nicely. I think you'll do just fine here at the academy."

He blushed at her kind words.

She stood up. "Well, then, I guess that will be it until September."

ISOLATION

He stood up as well and she led him to her office door. "Have a good summer, Daniel."

"You, too. Are you doing anything special on your holiday?"

"I'm going to travel further west to visit my sister who I haven't seen in a year, and relax around her pool. I'm also going to try to catch up on my reading." She gave him a warm smile and winked. "Stay out of trouble, young man."

"I'll try. Good bye, Miss Temple," he said with a wave and as he walked away, it suddenly occurred to him that he wouldn't be seeing her for several months. It was like a blow to the stomach; how was he supposed to get by around here without her advice, witty jabs and inspiring words. It dawned on him that he actually looked forward to their regular Friday appointments. She was the first person who had befriended him here, and spoke to him like he were a fellow intellectual, not just a kid. She had consistently been there for him, was genuinely interested in his well-being and truly believed in him. It was going to feel strangely quiet and empty at the school during the oncoming summer days. An unsettling feeling of isolation overwhelmed him then, and stayed with him for several hours.

* * * * *

The summer months of 1962 in Rowland were oppressively dry and humid. The remaining students and faculty at the academy ambled about like the walking dazed in the stifling hot weather. Everyone had a sweaty wet sheen to them, and energy levels were low, if not non-existent. The days went by slowly, as if the heat were weighing down not only them but time as well.

Daniel had four classes; two in the morning and two during the hottest part of the day. Fortunately, Rachel was in his last class, which was geometry, so he had at least something to keep him alert and focused. He fought hard to not daydream about her, knowing it was silly to be so smitten by someone, but he couldn't seem to stop staring at her. He had to conceal his feelings though, for if Harold or the Steward twins knew the extent of his crush, they'd tease him mercilessly.

Todd and Justin must have received a good reprimand from either the dean or Miss Temple because they hadn't pulled any stunts on him in weeks.

They completely ignored him actually, giving Daniel the idea that Miss Temple had taken matters into her own hands. That gave him a funny feeling, though, knowing that a forty-five year old woman had become his protector here, but he was grateful for the reprieve.

He found his summer courses fairly easy, even though a lot of it was new material. Mr. Barker's attempts to prove him inferior to his fellow classmates failed miserably. Since there was more free time to do homework, he studied hard to keep Mr. Barker's superiority complex in check. There was no way that he was going to fail the mans class, and the teachers belligerence towards him gave him the extra motivation to study like mad, even during a suffocating heat wave.

He also continued to tutor Harold, who found his studying tips and advice more beneficial than any that he had received from his top-notch teachers.

He started to pull marks in the upper eighties and his confidence slowly increased. He loosened up a bit, and relaxed with the sound knowledge that he wasn't the dunce he once thought he was.

Harold and he even found time to goof off and have a little fun. Both loved to read comic books, and any discussion related to the subject resulted in a lengthy argument about who the best superhero was, and which power would be the best to possess. They told each other late-night ghost stories in attempts to spook the other out, and talked of subjects only adolescent boys found interesting. They found themselves in fits of giggles often, particularly during these midnight chats when they were beyond exhaustion, sending them into wildly delirious states. One night in particular, when it was almost three in the morning, Harold suddenly stood up, bent over and let out an explosively loud fart. Daniel thought that he would literally die laughing. They were told a minute later to 'keep it down' from the hall supervisor; a stone-faced senior wearing purple pajama bottoms with matching slippers. After he closed the door with an authoritative frown, they pushed their faces to their pillows and howled with laughter at his feminine attire. Daniel laughed 'til tears streamed down his flushed cheeks and his gut ached.

He had never had so much fun and woke each morning with a smile on his face and a bounce in his step. Despite the heat, Mr. Barker's constant reproach, and the nagging thoughts of his family at the back of his mind, he was having the best time of his life.

* * * * *

"I have great news! You can come traveling with my family on your summer break!" Harold burst into the room on a quiet Saturday afternoon. He had just spoken to his father on the phone and sat down on his bed excitedly.

"My dad has this new client in Calgary that he's going to meet with. My mom decided that she and I are going with him and we're going to stay there in a hotel for a *whole* week. We're going to see Banff and see the mountains and after we're just going back to our house, but dad said if you wanted, you could come with us to Calgary and he would fly you back so that you could spend your last week off with your family. He'd cover the flight cost and everything. Isn't that great? What do you think? Do you wanna come?" he prattled all this information off in a hurried, eager voice and ultimately had to stop and catch his breath.

Daniel put his book down. He had never traveled or flown before, and as tempting as the offer was, he really wanted to go home on his two-week break at the end of August. He missed his family, all of them. Not as much as when he first arrived here, but they were still always near his thoughts. He wanted to go home for many reasons, but mostly to see, for himself, if all his concerns these past months were groundless.

"Thanks, Harold, but I really have to go home on my break. My dad needs help around the farm and I don't even think they'd let me anyway. They wouldn't want your dad paying for everything, and my parents wouldn't be able to afford it," he declined.

"No! It's fine! Really! He doesn't mind at all. *Please* come…for me. I'll be so bored in Calgary with just my mom to hang around with. She's as fun as an old shoe, you'll be doing me a huge favor if you come."

"Sorry, bud." He shrugged and turned back to his book. "Thanks anyway though."

"Aww, shucks." Harold slumped. "So I'm stuck with the old bat again. If she forces me to go shopping every day, I'll never forgive you, Bradley."

Daniel was reminded again how different their families were. The Bennings' traveled at will, stayed in hotels for great lengths of time and had money to spare to do as they pleased. The Bradleys' never left the small town of Aldon, and saved every penny to make their payments and to afford groceries each week. Money was always an issue, and the stress from the lack of it was evident on his parents' faces most days. He doubted either of them would ever be on a plane, and that thought disturbed him. He wanted them to have an easier life, to not have to worry and work their lives away.

"You'll live," he muttered irritably to Harold, who snapped his head up at the odd tone of his friends voice.

"You okay?" he asked and Daniel nodded without looking up from his book. Some things just couldn't be explained.

* * * * *

"He awoke one night to the sound of foot-steps and something leathery rustling around. It was a quiet and muffled noise, just loud enough to wake him up. It was coming from inside his closet. The boy sat up straight, and though his room was dark, he could see the door handle of the closet turn slowly. Something was trying to get out. He wanted to scream, to hide or run into his parents' room but his legs wouldn't move. He sat there frozen solid as his closet door opened with a sickening creak." Daniel spoke in a hushed monotone while ominously holding a flashlight to his chin in their darkened room. He was telling Harold a scary story, after much pleading. Harold thought he told the best stories and begged him often for one but Daniel saved his stories for Saturday nights. It gave him a full week to think up a good one.

"When the door was completely opened, he heard the sound of someone or something breathing inside. He found the courage then and got up and ran in a panic. He raced to his parents' room and on his way out, something caught his eye. A pair of gleaming red eyes flashed at him from inside the gloomy darkness of the closet and a raspy voice whispered, 'Next time, next time.' The boy refused to go back into his room. His parents eventually had to move out of their new house because he begged to leave and had become an insomiac. The day that his family moved, they loaded up their vehicle and climbed into it to leave. As they were pulling away from the curb, the boy looked out the back window up to his old bedroom window. He saw a wide set of smiling jagged teeth and bulging eyes leering from behind the sheer curtains. A clawed hand waved good-bye to him maliciously. He screamed for a full hour and would never fully recover from that sight. Twenty years later, he would still be sleeping with the lights on without ever getting a full nights sleep. Whenever he heard about people having heart attacks in their beds or dying suddenly in their sleep, he knew that the thing he saw had gotten to someone else. That it had scared them to death, that they had died of shock. So he refused to spend the night in a room with a closet, and warded off sleep as long as he could, for fear that the thing...would finally fulfill its promise to him."

Daniel let out a long, morbid cackle and flashed the flashlight on and off.

"Wow, that was truly awesome," Harold gasped with awe. "You're a great storyteller, Bradley, that was just as good as any story I've read in a book. Have you ever thought about becoming a writer?"

"No," he scoffed at the compliment but laid down in bed with a satisfied smile. Later, after Harold was snoring noisily, his words resonated in his mind. He did like making stories up, it came easy and his mother always told him he had a vivid imagination. Maybe Harold had something there.

That night, the seeds of dreams were planted.

* * * * *

The summer school term finally wound down and they were once again in the midst of final exams. Neither Harold nor Daniel were stressed out about it this time around though. They had plenty of time in a day to study and were well prepared. They breezed through their tests and at the end of exam week, they started packing their suitcases for their two week vacation.

"It's always strange going home. When you walk in your bedroom after being away for months on end, it doesn't even feel like yours at first. Your stuff doesn't feel like yours, it feels different but nothing's changed. Just you. Then, just when you're getting used to it, and it starts to feel like home again, you're holiday is over and you're right back here again," Harold complained as he folded a white shirt and placed it neatly into his suitcase.

"This place starts to feel more like home then your real home," Daniel summarized and Harold nodded.

A sharp knock on the door made them turn and Larry Benning burst in. "Good morning gentlemen!" He went straight to his son and used his thick arms to swallow him in a fierce bear hug. "It's good to see you again, m'boy."

"Dad!" Harold cried out in annoyance as he tried in vain to push him away. When Larry finally pulled back with a hoarse laugh; Harold's glasses were left awry on his nose and his hair was a tousled mess.

"I'm not a kid any more! You shouldn't do that every time you see me, it's embarrassing."

"Nonsense. I can do what I want to show my pleasure in seeing my own son. The day you can fight me off is the day I stop trying to hug you," He stated with a smirk and winked at Daniel. They both knew full well that gangly old Harold would never be strong enough to fend him off. He probably couldn't even stop his own mother from hugging him if she really wanted to.

"So, Bradley, Harold tells me you're quite the little genius. Said you're helping him a bit with his homework, which is quite commendable. Lord knows the boy needs all the help he can get!" he joked but added soberly, "But seriously, that's real nice of you to take time away from your own studies to tutor him. Don't think that it's not appreciated." His eyes never wavered and Daniel liked that about Larry. He was a man who looked right at you when he spoke, and told you exactly what he thought. That was integrity.

"Oh, it's nothing, sir." He blushed modestly and gave Harold a sharp look.

Harold didn't notice; he was still trying to fix his glasses.

"Such modesty. That's what I like about you boys, you still know your place. Give you a few years and you'll be arrogant jack-asses like half the men I work with who think the world owes them something. Don't get me started though," he laughed again and whacked Harold hard on the back. "You packed yet?"

"Oww!" Harold exclaimed and glared at his father. "That hurt!"

"You're getting soft, m'boy. A few weeks with me is exactly what you need." He winked at Daniel again, who chuckled politely. "Too bad you couldn't come, Bradley. Maybe next time."

"Yeah, hopefully next time. Thanks for the offer, though."

Larry snapped Harold's suitcase shut and picked it up off the bed. "What all do you have in here boy? Geez, I swear you're a worse packer than a woman... everything but the kitchen sink!"

He walked out of the room and Daniel was once again astounded by his positive energy and good nature. You couldn't help but get in a good mood when he was around.

"See what I have to put up with?" Harold rolled his eyes and his shoulders sagged with exasperation.

"Oh, he's not so bad." Daniel grinned but Harold coughed in disagreement.

"You try living with him! It's enough to drive you crazy." He shook his head. 'Have a nice break though, see you in a couple weeks."

"You, too. Have fun in Calgary."

They shook hands briefly, uncomfortably. They both had a sinking feeling that they'd miss one another but didn't want to show it.

"It'd be more fun with you," he added and with that, he left. Daniel watched him go, realizing that he had spent more time with Harold in the past eight months than he had with anyone else. It felt funny to be apart from him, even if it was only for a few weeks. He was his first real friend, and he knew things would have been a lot different without Harold as a roommate.

"Bradley!" a classmate from down the hall called out to him. "There's a guy downstairs that says he's your father. He said he'd meet you out in the parking lot. He didn't want to come up."

"Okay, thanks," he said and quickly grabbed his suitcase. He raced down the hall and through the main floor, waving farewell to the classmates he passed. He went out the main entrance and into the glaring sunshine where he spotted his father having a cigarette in the shade of a tall willow tree.

"Dad!" he called out and hustled over to him. Joe Bradley turned around and looked at the son he hadn't seen or talked to in eight months. Daniel almost stopped in his tracks, the man before him looked nothing like his father. He was gaunt and weedy, very unlike the burly, muscular physique that Joe worked hard to maintain. His face had an unhealthy yellow hue to it, but his full-grown beard covered most of his skin. His eyes were puffy, bloodshot and watery, as if he had been crying for days on end. He was wearing his usual clothes but they looked excessively filthy and stained, and reeked powerfully of manure. He looked slovenly sick but apparently didn't have the presence of mind to be aware of his ghastly appearance.

"Dad?" Daniel asked tentatively when he got closer. It was clearly his father though, as humiliating as that was. His father flicked his cigarette unto the grass.

"Come on." He walked towards the truck that was parked a few feet away.

Daniel followed behind him, and tried to ignore the hard stares from a well-dressed couple walking past them.

He opened the truck passenger door, and the potent smell of stale cigarettes wafted over him and nearly brought him to his knees. Once he caught his breath, he was surprised to see that Sam wasn't inside. His father never went far without the old mutt.

"Where's Sam?" he asked as he climbed inside, trying to ignore the odor.

"He's dead," his father answered dully, without an ounce of emotion.

Daniel, half in and half out of the truck stared at his father in stunned silence.

"Get in the damned truck already so we can get the hell out of here!" Joe snapped and spittle flew from his dry lips.

Daniel obediently got inside as quick as he could, shut the door and Joe immediately roared out of the parking lot with squealing tires. With a violent jolt, he shifted gears and pushed the accelerator to the floor. He completely floored it down the long, one-lane drive-way and barely slowed down to turn unto the main road. He cut off another car doing so, narrowly avoiding an accident, and its horn honked angrily at them for miles. The old truck made loud unhealthy clunky sounds, indicating it would not hold up to such treatment for long. Daniel gripped his seatbelt with both white-knuckled hands while they sped down the highway at top speed. He could smell liquor on his father's breath, and as he watched him light up another cigarette, he realized his father was not even close to being in a sane frame of mind. There was a blank deadness in his eyes, and a cold fear that he had never experienced before washed over his entire body.

Daniel wasn't just afraid for his safety, he was afraid of the stranger beside him.

Part Two

Chapter Seven

When they pulled into their driveway in Aldon, over six hours later, Daniel almost cried out in relief. He had never been so uncomfortable and restless in another person's company for such a long stretch at a time. They had spoken only a handful of words to one another throughout the entire trip.

Daniel had asked about the crops, the weather and the livestock and Joe had merely clipped off one word responses. Joe did ask if he had passed all of his courses, but when Daniel boasted of his high marks, he seemed unimpressed. Hurt by his coolness, Daniel turned to look out the window and they traveled the rest of the way in complete silence.

The sun eventually disappeared under gray, heavy clouds but the sky appeared undecided as to whether it wanted to spout rain or not. Such weather was a dismal sight and Daniel succumbed to its depressing influence. It started to rain just when they entered Aldon, but it was merely gentle sprinkles that caressed the windshield lightly.

Maria and the children were waiting on the porch steps when they pulled up and he gave them a friendly wave. He noticed immediately that their smiles looked tight and frozen. His mother shot an uneasy glance at Joe, and she looked almost as haggard as he. Daniel looked over at his father and his gut-reactions over the past several months were confirmed. Kate and his mother had kept something from him, it was obvious that his father had changed and that he was the source of all the problems here, but why? *Why* had he changed? What had happened to make him act so strangely? Why was he so angry? What was going on around here and why wouldn't they tell him about it?

He opened the truck door and jumped out, not knowing what awaited him in his home away from home. He recalled what Harold had said just before he left. *It's always strange going home. When you walk in after being away for months on end, it doesn't even feel like yours at first. Your stuff doesn't feel like yours, it feels different but nothings changed. Only you.*

But that wasn't the case here. He hadn't changed, but everything else had. The air here felt different too. It felt eerily cold for August and a harsh wind breezed over, spattering him with fresh rain. Whatever it was that was going on here obviously wasn't good; and as Katie walked stiffly towards him with dull eyes, he felt a new wave of fear.

* * * * *

While unpacking his suitcase late that night in his room, his tired mind branched off in various unpleasant directions. He had endured a nightmarish trip home with his father, experienced a bizarre homecoming from his family and now was completely exhausted. He had eaten a meal of beef stew and homemade fresh bread quickly, without tasting it, and simply longed for the comfort of his bed. It was too late to look into family secrets tonight, that could wait until tomorrow.

Those plans perished with the sound of a soft knock at the door. Katie opened it and let herself in. She looked tired herself; her eyes were slightly puffy and her lips were tightly drawn. Even her hair didn't have its usual shine.

"Hi." She went to his bed, sat down on it and crossed her legs. "You were quiet at supper, you really haven't said much at all since you got home. Tell me what things are like at this school, tell me what your friends are like and how your courses were."

It was obvious that she was trying hard to sound natural and light, but there was a definite strain in her tone. He felt pity for her, knowing that his mother had probably warned her not to tell him anything. Had reasoned that his ignorance would be in his best interests. Did they think he was stupid? That he wouldn't notice that something was seriously wrong here? That he wouldn't try to figure it out?

"Katie, don't act dumb with me." He perched himself up on top of his desk. "I know something is going on with Dad. He's gone slightly mad or something, but I don't understand why. What happened? When did he start acting like that?"

She lowered her head and sighed. "I can't talk about that, don't ask me to."

"Why not?" he exclaimed. "Did Mom tell you not to tell me? Dammit, Katie, I'm part of this family and I deserve to know what's going on!"

"You're part of this family are you?" She snapped her head up. "You don't even live here any more! You live hundreds of miles away and only come home for a few weeks out of a year. Mom only talks to you for a few minutes a month, so tell me what good does it do to have you stew about this and fail your courses and throw away Mom and Dad's hard earned money. How does that help us? What good does that do anyone?" Her lips trembled uncontrollably. "You can't help us."

"Let me try." He stood up. "Is he hurting any of you? Has he hit you?" He was almost afraid to hear the answer.

"No. He hasn't touched me," she whispered and he could have screamed with relief. She hadn't lied, but she wasn't completely honest either. He *had* been abusive, but not with her.

"How much is he drinking?"

"Every day, more and more." She looked up. "He spends most of his time in the shed. We don't really know what he does out there. He doesn't talk to anyone unless he's hollering and he doesn't even come in for meals any more. He…he got worse after Sam died."

"How *did* he die?"

"He got run over by the truck two months ago. He was following Dad too closely when he was backing up and Sam couldn't get out of the way in time. He was getting old and slow, and you could tell that he was having pain in his hips and back legs. He didn't die immediately though; Dad had to get the shotgun out to finish him off." She closed her eyes and took a long time before continuing.

"When dad saw that he had run him over, he started screaming like a madman. He even started crying when he lifted up the shotgun, I almost thought that he wouldn't do it but he did. The sound of the blast was deafening…I've never heard anything so loud. When Sam was dead, Dad knelt down beside him for a long time. It was horrible. We all cried for days, but thankfully Evie and Maddy didn't see it happen."

Daniel had to fight off his own tears. He couldn't remember a time when Sam wasn't around, and though it was clear it was Joe's dog, they had all loved him dearly.

"Not long after you left, Dad just started acting funny. He would get real mad real easy and he and Mom fought more often. Mostly about money, but it was pretty obvious that he didn't like you being off at school. They fought about that a lot."

He felt a hard stab of guilt in his chest, knowing that his education had caused so many problems. But he had made it clear from the beginning that he didn't want to go, did that still make it his fault?

"What does…"

"No, I don't want to talk about it any more." She put up her hands as if to ward him off. "I can't, not tonight. We can talk some other time, I promise.

You just don't know what it's like to live with him, it's so tiring." Her shoulders sagged and her eyes looked old and worn out. "Tell me about your school now, tell me happy things."

He wished so badly in that moment that it was her that had to go away to school, not him, so that she wouldn't have to endure whatever she endured here. It was obvious that it was wearing her down, more so than the younger girls, who Katie and his mom had obviously sheltered from the brunt of it.

He decided to tell her what he knew would bring a smile to her face.

"I have a girlfriend." He forced a smile. "Her name is Rachel."

"Really?" Her eyes sparkled. "What is she like? Did you two meet in class? Have you held hands? Is she pretty?"

He laughed at her string of questions. "She's very pretty and smart. She's an amazing piano player and wants to be a musician."

"Wow, she must be good then," Katie gasped.

"She is. I met her playing chess, we're both on the chess team."

"Really? I didn't think you liked chess that much. You've hardly ever played it."

"I like it more *now*." He grinned and she giggled.

"You didn't answer my question. Have you held hands?" she teased and he leaned forward and whispered. "Better than that. We kissed once."

"Oh, I don't believe you!" She hit the bed with the palm of her hand. "Now I know you're lying. You're so darned shy, you'd never kiss a girl."

"Well I didn't really kiss her. She kissed me. One Saturday, a bunch of us were playing chess but it was just too hot to sit in that stuffy auditorium. I was playing against her and she asked me if I cared whether we finished the game or not. I said 'no', and she said we should find something cooler to do. She led me up to her room, which is against the rules, but we got away with it. We were in her room, and she just kissed me out of the blue."

Katie looked skeptical but he didn't know how to prove what he was saying was true. "It was strange but nice at the same time, I was so nervous I didn't even know what I was doing. After we kissed, I ran out of her room in a panic and have barely spoken to her since. She probably thinks I'm an idiot now."

Katie laughed. "Well, I believe that!"

Daniel folded his arms, realizing that he hadn't given much thought to Rachel lately. He really should have said good-bye to her before he left for the summer break. That would have been the nice thing to do since they were practically going steady. After their kiss he had felt like avoiding her, though he still liked her just as much, if not more.

"Well, I should probably go to bed. Tomorrow is another long day." She stood up. "It's nice to have you back, Danny."

He hadn't heard anyone call him that in a long time and it sounded funny to him now. "I'm going to find out what's causing Dad to act like that, and when I do I'll make sure things go back to normal around here. I'm not going back to school until I know you're all going to be alright," he said with conviction and her face drooped sadly.

"That's exactly what Mom said you'd say."

* * * * *

His mother woke him just after nine o'clock the next morning. She sat on the edge of his bed and gently rubbed his arm until his eyes flicked open.

The blazing sun streamed in through the window, blinding him with its warm rays. He put his hand up to shield his eyes. He had forgotten his routine, to pull the shade down before bed.

"Time to get up, sleepyhead," she sang softly. He sat up and she smiled tenderly at him. "It's so nice to have you back, Danny. It's wonderful to have all my kids under one roof again. You don't have any idea how much I've missed you." She squeezed his arm affectionately.

"I've missed you all, too." His voice was dry and hoarse, he coughed into his hand.

"I know that Katie talked to you last night, even when I told her not to," she said. "Let me make this clear right now, I will not allow problems in this house to interfere with your education. Whatever happens here, stays here, and we will deal with it in our own way. It's nothing for you to worry yourself over, your father is just a little stressed out is all." She stood up, and walked towards his desk with restless fingers that tugged anxiously at her plain house-dress.

"Money has been a bit tight this year, the weather hasn't been co-operating and with you away, Joe's had a lot more on his plate. And it was hard for him when Sam died, especially the *way* he died….and…he's never been one to handle stress well." She turned around and looked hard at her son. "But it has nothing to do with you, so don't get yourself all worked up about it."

"But it's more than just that isn't it, Mom." Daniel ripped off his bedcovers and sat up on the edge of his bed. "There is something seriously wrong with Dad. I saw it as soon as he picked me up at school, he isn't right…"

"Stop it!" she snapped and pointed at him. "I will not have you speak that way of your father. You will speak of him with the respect that he deserves. There is nothing wrong with him."

"Mom, he's…" he started but she cut him off.

"I repeat, there is *nothing* wrong with him. Quit filling your head and Katie's head with utter nonsense, I will have no more of it. Everything is fine. Now wash up for breakfast, you have a big day ahead of you." With that, she left his room.

She was right about one thing, he did have a big day ahead of him.

* * * * *

Putting on his old work shirt, and blue jean overalls was an odd experience, not just because they were a tad too small. They didn't feel like his clothes any more, just like his musty-smelling room didn't feel like his either. When he looked at himself in the mirror, he had to admit that he now preferred the look of the school uniform over his work clothes. The uniform was clean and polished, giving one a smart, refined look. He once despised it but it grew on him, as did many other aspects of the confining school. It was funny how people adapted to change. It was rather frightening, actually, how one could shed their skin so easily.

After brushing his hair, he went downstairs and was relieved to hear the friendly banter of his younger siblings. At least some things hadn't changed.

The distinct, mouth-watering aroma of fried bacon filled his nostrils making his stomach grumble expectantly. Oh how he had missed his mother's cooking. He walked into the kitchen, and all the girls stopped what they were doing to look at him. He wondered if they had forgotten that he was in the house. The two youngest girls were coloring and writing at the table, Katie was washing dishes at the sink. His mother was about to start canning peaches; the counters and floor were cluttered with cardboard boxes of the fruit and mason jars.

"Good morning."

They all said good morning back and went back to what they were doing. His mother stood up from the table where she was having a coffee. "There is bacon already fried and I'll scramble some eggs for you too."

"Bacon and toast is fine," he declined.

"Nonsense. No son is mine is going to do without a decent breakfast when he's only home for a short time. He'll eat like a king if I have any say about it." She winked at him while she walked over to the stove. He got a tall glass out of the cupboard and poured himself some orange juice. He sat down beside Evie and asked her what she was drawing.

"A cow, can't you tell?" She sounded offended.

"Sure I can, it looks great." He sipped his juice and smiled at Maddy. She stared at him blankly, as if she had never seen him before.

"Your father told me he wants you to stack bales today. He wanted you up earlier to help milk the cows, but I thought you should have a day to sleep in after such a long trip. I helped him today, but you'll have to get up extra early tomorrow morning to finish chores before church," she stated while cracking eggs into the sizzling frying pan.

He stifled a groan of disgust at the chore before him. It was morning and he could feel the smothering humidity already. It would be hell in the dusty shed by mid-afternoon, when the sun was at its strongest.

"Where is Dad?" he asked.

"In the shed, I think," his mother replied as she whipped the eggs around with a whisk.

"I want to talk to him." He stood up but his mother was on him like a whip.

"You will sit and eat your breakfast first," she ordered and pointed at his chair, indicating that he should return to his seat. The girls stared at him with wide eyes, their crayons stationary in their little hands. He reluctantly gave in and slumped back down into the chair.

Katie shot him a dark look and continued washing dishes lethargically.

He knew they feared that he would start trouble and make things worse. But they had to get worse before they got better. His father had to know he couldn't continue on like this, disturbing everyone else's lives. It wasn't right that they had to walk on egg shells in their own home, terrified of doing or saying the wrong thing to set him off. The tension in this house was palpable, and as the eldest son, he felt he had the responsibility to set things right. He had to set aside his own fears of his father, which he wasn't entirely sure he could do.

He ate his breakfast in rapid speed and scurried out to the shed. His mother watched him through the screen door with worried eyes and wrung her hands on her apron. She exchanged a knowing look with Katie, who noticed her own hands trembling in the soapy water.

* * * * *

When he walked into the shed, he wasn't exactly sure what would transpire between him and his father, but was decidedly relieved with what he found. His mother had been misinformed. Joe was already out in the fields with the three mulboard plough, ploughing the ground for next years crop.

So he went to work. Going through the motions, his mind on everything but what he was doing. Stacking bales was usually irritatingly monotonous, but today it was suffocatingly hot out, and thick blisters formed quickly on his softened hands making it that much worse. Another body to pass him the bales from the wagon would have made the job easier, but today he was alone with his thoughts.

He went in the house for lunch at noon. His mother fed him two cold meat sandwiches, potato salad, chilled apple juice, and a pear. She sent him a thermos full of ice water and another pear and he was back to the hayloft. By suppertime, he was worn out. He ate a meal of leftover stew by himself, and went straight to bed. He wasn't used to such physical labor anymore.

It took him a few hours to fall asleep but was relieved that Katie didn't come in his room to talk. He stared at the ceiling, not able to shake off the foreboding feeling that had overcome him since returning home.

* * * * *

The next morning, Daniel awoke promptly at five o'clock and went to the barn for chores. His father was not in sight so he started without him. Joe, in fact, did not show up at all, so he spent the next hour and a half feeding and milking the cows alone. Later, fatigued and dirty he went inside to shower and dress for church.

With a towel wrapped around his waist, he dug out his best clothes from his closet, and was hardly surprised to find that they were far too small. He was obviously still going through a growth spurt; his pants barely covered his ankles, his dress shirt felt tight and confining and the cuffs didn't even reach his hands.

For as long as he could remember, he had been going to the St. Andrews Catholic Church in Aldon on Sundays with his mother and Katie. They went at seven thirty in the morning, and prayed for a half hour before the eight o'clock mass.

There were two masses because the small church could not hold more than forty people. The later one was at eleven o'clock but the earlier one was the busiest.

Today when they entered, the church was cool and gray. It was like a silent, eerie tomb lit dimly by a mass of flickering wax candles. The two rows of wooden pews were split by a wide central aisle, like many churches. Maria went to her usual spot, the back pew on the right. She knelt beside it and crossed herself. Once sat down, she stared blankly at the rosary in her hands. Daniel and Katie went around to the other end of the pew, crossed themselves and knelt to pray, their elbows perched on the pew in front of them.

Daniel watched his mother from the corner of his eye, not liking the forlorn look on her face or the way she twitched nervously. Despite her obvious agitation, she looked pretty, with the sides of her hair up in a barrette and the rest of her hair falling down over her shoulders in gentle curls. She wore a white blouse, a loose scarf around her neck and simple long black skirt and heels.

Father Reilly appeared at the front of the church and flashed them a warm smile. The Father was a short, stout man in his late-forties with a balding head and grey wisps of hair around his ears. His hairy hands clasped a thick black bible comfortably on his bulging belly as he strode around to light more candles.

His mother suddenly stood up and walked down the aisle towards the priest.

Daniel shot his sister a bewildered expression and turned back to see what his mother was doing.

"Good morning Mrs. Bradley." Father nodded politely when she approached him at the front.

"Father, I know you have mass soon but I need to talk to you...alone." She cast an uneasy glance at her children.

"Would you like to go to the confessional booth?"

"No, just...just somewhere private."

"Of course. Come with me." He led her out of the sanctuary and left the two children staring at them in confusion.

"What's going on?" Daniel whispered.

"I don't know." Katie sat down on the seat.

"Mom looked upset this morning."

"She always looks that way."

"Does she usually go in to talk to him?" Daniel asked and sat down on the pew as well.

"No." She looked down at her hands.

"You're holding something back from me. What's going on? Tell me." He was trying to keep his voice down but it felt like every word he said echoed in the empty room.

"They got into another fight last night. I heard them." She frowned. "Didn't you?"

"When I finally fell asleep, I slept hard." He bit his lip. "Do you think that's why she wanted to talk to the Father?"

"I don't know, I said."

"It doesn't seem right, her going off to talk to him alone. Something's wrong." He knew it, every part of him screamed that something was terribly wrong but he didn't know what to do about it. Katie didn't want to talk about it any more, so they spent the next fifteen minutes in strained silence.

When his mother finally appeared, rushing towards them from the choir room he thought she looked as if she were about to cry.

"Are you alright, Mom?" Daniel asked in a fretful voice. She grabbed them both by the crook of their elbows and led them out of the dark, dismal church.

"I will be," she replied firmly.

"Aren't we staying for Mass?" Katie asked.

"Not today, hon. I don't feel well and just want to lay down for a while."

The sun blinded them when they walked through the double doors together. Several parishioners were already coming up the walkway for mass.

They stared at them in puzzlement while the three breezed by without a word. Maria stood tall, head held high. No one would ever guess that this poised, attractive woman was in tremendous agony, but Daniel knew that she was. And though he would never know what happened between her and the priest that morning, it would be decades before he stepped foot in a church again.

* * * * *

"Daniel?" Rachel called out, he had blanked out on her yet again. He was re-living that week prior to his father's death in his mind, and could vividly recall each second of it as if it were yesterday. The whole week played out in his mind like a movie. A horror movie.

Something in the sky caught his eye. It was an understatement to say he was grateful for the distraction. There was a brilliantly colored rainbow off to their left, amidst the gloomy clouds and it was a glorious sight. He remembered what a colleague of his, an English literature professor, had told him about rainbows. He had said, *despite what many think, a rainbow isn't really shaped like an arch. It actually forms a circle. The center of the circle is on an imaginary line between the sun and your head. Most people don't know where a rainbow comes from or why it looks the way it does. Not enough take the time to appreciate what a natural miracle it really is.'*

Daniel always remembered that, and found it interesting because it proved his theory that most people didn't fully see, comprehend or appreciate half of what was in front of their very own eyes. He certainly didn't. He stared at the rainbow absently, wishing he could be anywhere but in this car heading toward Tarlington with Rachel. He didn't want to talk about his father any more; or think about his mother and the horrible things that happened in their home. He didn't want to feel anything about anything or anyone. But Rachel wouldn't allow him to hide from reality for long.

"Daniel what happened next?" She pushed.

He couldn't tell her, he couldn't explain what happened that week in any rational manner. He tried to summarize. "Every day, Dad got a little worse. He yelled over every little thing, started throwing things and just totally freaked out. When I finally found out...or saw rather that he was hitting my mother, that was the final straw. I took her aside and told her to take the girls to my Uncle Steve's and stay there. He wasn't safe for them to be around anymore, and the girls were terrified. They didn't understand what was going on. None of us did." He clenched his teeth, remembering their raw fear and confusion. Their panicked faces drove him to do what he did next.

"I watched them drive away through the living room window and went out to the shed to talk to my father." His heart started to race as he remembered each torturous step to that building, and recalled the alarming amounts of adrenaline that coursed through his veins that night.

"Daniel, what did you do?" Rachel whispered, fearfully thinking of his irrationally short temper. Wondering what he was capable of, if pushed to the brink.

He gripped the steering so hard, it felt as if his knuckles would burst through his own skin. "I killed him."

Chapter Eight

Daniel laid in his bed most of the next day, listening to the sounds of mourning family and friends tread carefully throughout his house with muted, curious voices. He held a well worn book in his hands, reading the same line over and over, without registering the simple text. Nothing would distract him, nothing calmed him and nothing felt right. The last twenty-four hours felt like an unsettling bad dream that he just couldn't wake up from.

His father couldn't be dead.

It just wasn't possible.

None of it seemed possible yet he couldn't dispute what he had seen with his very own eyes. The blood-soaked reality sat in his stomach like a large, undigested meal, reminding and sickening him at the same time.

Near ten o'clock, his mother's elderly, rather eccentric aunt Myrtle, brought him up a mug of scalding hot, honey sweetened tea. Beside the mug, on a pretty doily was large blueberry muffin that his neighbor, Mrs. Carlyle, had freshly baked and brought over in an overflowing basket.

"You must eat, darling. You must keep your strength up." Myrtle placed the tray on his nightstand and interlaced her wrinkled, brittle-nailed fingers over her protruding belly.

"I'm not hungry." He turned his attention back to Dickens, *A Tale of Two Cities*. A good book, for him, was usually like chicken soup for the sick; comforting and healing. But not today. There was nothing on earth that would give him a bit of consolation today.

"Perhaps you should come downstairs then. It would do your mother good to see you up and around," she nodded encouragingly.

"I think I'll stay in here for a while longer," he muttered, refusing to make eye-contact.

"Darling." She lowered her significant bulk on the side of his bed and leaned forward until they were almost face-to-face. She smelled strongly of peppermint candies, coffee, hair-spray and cigarettes. The combination made his already tense stomach roll in disgust.

"I know what happened yesterday was awful. Horrible really, death is always a tragedy but sometimes it's good to talk about it. You know, get it out of your system." She batted her lashes persuasively. "Sweetie, no one around here seems to know what happened. Doctor Jones and Sheriff Brody won't disclose the specifics and your mother, of course, is much too distressed to even speak of it. She's barely said two words all day. But you were here last night when it happened weren't you dear?" she inquired with the subtlety of a begging dog.

His body stiffened under his white bed sheet. A flush of annoyance overwhelmed him, but his face remained emotionless and unobliging.

"All your family and friends are here and they want to help you get through this terrible time. But no one has any clue what happened, and I think that we have a right to know how Joe died." Her voice lost its false politeness as unadulterated curiosity overcame her. She, a woman who had blatantly disapproved of his father, was practically drooling in anticipation at hearing the details of his demise and to have first-hand knowledge about it. He wanted to smack her with his hard-covered book, and his fingers even tightened the edges of Dickens unconsciously. But memories of the night before unfolded before him, and they had a sedating effect.

"Tell me what happened, Danny. Tell me what you saw," young Sheriff Brody had asked, while sipping a cold cup of coffee in Daniel's room around nine o'clock the previous evening.

Warren Brody was thirty-seven, tall and thick with chiseled features and a bristly mustache. He was well-liked in the community for his honesty, easy manner, and fair sense of justice, like his father who had held the position before him. Brody dealt little in such matters as these though. Most of his days were spent arresting traffic offenders, and handling domestic disputes and reckless youths.

"Nothing." Daniel sat on his desk chair, arms folded tightly around him. His right leg had started shaking spasmodically an hour earlier, and no matter how much he willed it to stop, it simply wouldn't.

"Come on Danny. You must have heard something. You must have heard the gunshot." Brody sat down on his unmade bed.

"I did." Daniel had nodded, and continued to stare at his leg which clearly seemed to have a mind of its own.

"What time was that around?" he questioned mildly, pulling his notepad out of his jacket.

"I don't know. I didn't look at the clock." Both legs were at it now. He watched them with morbid fascination.

"Did you go out to see your dad, Danny?"

Daniel swallowed hard, his throat was raw from screaming. "No."

"You told your mom that you were going to. That you wanted to talk to your dad and..."

"But I didn't," Daniel cut him off. "I was too scared to."

"Did your parents have a fight tonight?" Brody rested the notepad on top of his thigh. Daniel knew that his mother had told him everything that she knew, had told him all about their quarrel, and he wasn't about to recite the same thing. He didn't think he could, even if he wanted to.

"Danny. Was there a fight between your parents?" Brody repeated.

"Yes, there was a fight but I didn't go in the shed tonight," Daniel snapped. "After my mom and sisters left, I just came up to my room. I didn't know what to do, I was scared and confused. I just sat up here and thought about what to do next...and then I heard the gunshot," he lied. The fabricated words flowed effortlessly and convincingly from his mouth. He was good at storytelling. His legs quit moving.

"Danny, is there anything else that we should know about? Anything you saw or heard that might explain what happened tonight?" Brody stood up.

Daniel turned away. "No."

Brody stepped toward him, placed his large hand on Daniels shoulder. "I don't mean to badger you about all this, I know how hard it must be for you. I just want to get the facts straight." He squeezed firmly. "I'm sorry, Danny, I just can't imagine what you're feeling right now."

Daniel felt his breath catch in his throat and closed his eyes.

Dr. Jones and Sheriff Brody later reported that based on their findings, Joe Bradley had died by his own hand. Therefore, there would be no formal investigation into his death. Maria, slouched miserably on the floral couch in the living room immediately snapped to attention. She wiped her stringy hair from her face, stood up and voiced her concern with how the community would react to the word 'suicide'. It was a powerful word with dreadful connotations that would taint the entire family, she said with such powerful conviction, that it moved all who heard her. The authorities understood her anxiety, and because they had such enormous respect and sympathy for her, assured her (after much discussion), that if anyone asked, they'd inform them that Joe had died in a tragic farming accident. They earnestly promised not to divulge the details of her husbands death to anyone.

Relieved, she tearfully hugged and thanked them all for their empathy. That was the last time she had spoken.

"It was a farming accident," Daniel repeated what the officers had said, to

Myrtle, who still hovered over him anxiously.

"Oh!" She winced. "I know that! But what happened? What *killed* him?"

Daniel bit his lower lip, and when she fervently repeated the question, he tasted blood.

* * * * *

The night after the funeral, he pulled back his bed-covers, climbed out of bed and pulled a T-shirt over his freshly tanned, taut shoulders. Silently, in the dimness of his nightstand lamp, he packed his suitcases with pursed, angry lips. After he clamped the bulging luggage shut, he left his room to call his uncle to tell him to pick him up a day earlier then they had planned. On his way downstairs, he passed Katie's room and stopped. He stood before the closed door with heavy, doleful eyes. She, like her mother, had not absorbed the recent events well and had been on doctor prescribed sedatives for the last two days, while kind neighbors cared for Evie and Maddy. Maria and Katie were grieving the same way, privately and internally, and yet their feelings towards Joe couldn't have been more different.

Daniel placed his open palm on her door, wanting badly to go inside to tell his sister all that had happened in the shed that night. To relieve his aching burden, to share the pain that they were both experiencing. He stood there for almost two minutes, frozen in indecision and filled with a complexity of emotions that he didn't understand. He didn't want to be alone in this, but he couldn't unload on his sister, who had enough to deal with. She would have to live daily with the visible aftermath, while he would leave and have only memories to haunt him.

When he eventually walked away from the door and placed his hand on the banister on the top of the staircase, he did so with full knowledge that he would leave in the morning without saying a word to any of his family members. And as wrong as that was, he couldn't picture a scenario where anything would be right, ever again.

* * * * *

The next morning, he stood nervously at the entrance of his parents' driveway with suitcases in tow. He was waiting for his Uncle Steve, Maria's older brother, to pick him up to take him back to Rowland.

Brightly-colored feathered birds announced the arrival of a new day with hopeful music as the bleeding orange sun peeked over the flat landscape that enveloped him. As he breathed in the cool, morning air, he saw his uncle's red truck in the distance and his nerves began to settle slightly. But it wasn't until he was in the tidy cab and the truck was in gear, that he felt like he could breathe freely again. When they passed the cheerful sign on the outskirts of Aldon that informed them that they were now leaving town, and to come back soon, he almost chuckled with somber disbelief. He definitely would *not* be coming back soon.

It was a quiet, uncomfortable trip. They did not talk about the tearless funeral, or about the vast amounts of food that the community felt obliged to drop off at their door as if such a loss left them queerly ravenous. They didn't talk about his mother, who had barely spoken since seeing her husband's corpse and now walked about with a blended expression of numb disbelief and indescribable sorrow. They didn't talk about why he was leaving early, or about anything that mattered. His uncle gave him space and silence, two things that he desperately needed.

"Take care of yourself now," Steve said quietly when they finally reached the school and parked in the main parking area for visitors. Other families were arriving as well and he noticed many mothers were milling about, with tears in their eyes and tissues clamped in their formal white gloved hands.

He looked away. Not wanting to see their farewells, their wholesomeness.

"Thanks for the ride." He got out and grabbed his suitcases. He was truly grateful for Steve, a single, overweight bachelor who worked at a tire plant in Tarlington. He did well for himself and offered to rent out their land, care for their livestock and assist them financially. He would move in soon and take over things until his mother got a grip on herself. Daniel didn't know what they would have done without him. He certainly wouldn't have been able to go back to school and they probably would have had to sell everything and start over.

"Thanks for everything," Daniel said with as much conviction as he could muster.

"If you need anything, you call me," Steve said firmly, his bleary eyes glued on his nephew.

Daniel nodded and walked away with his own eyes planted on the ground. He knew no matter what, no matter what happened, he wouldn't call anyone for anything.

He was on his own now.

ISOLATION

* * * * *

"Hey! Good to see you, old buddy!" Harold exclaimed when Daniel walked in their room. He plunked his suitcases on his bed and sat down wearily beside them.

"Did you have a good break?" Harold asked and sat on his own bed across from him.

"Not really," Daniel muttered and put his hands through his tangled hair. He had never felt exhaustion like this before, he felt like he could sleep for at least ten years.

"Mine was great! We did a lot of neat things and went to see this movie with Marilyn Monroe. You would not believe how gorgeous she is; she's something else, I tell you. I haven't been able to stop thinking about her. Have you seen any of her movies before?"

"No," Daniel replied hollowly, and stared at the floor with his head in his hands.

"Well, you should. Too bad you couldn't have come, you would have had a great time."

"Yeah. It is too bad," he repeated, thinking to himself that things might have turned out differently if he *had* gone with Harold. Maybe his father would still be alive.

"You okay? You look a little sick," Harold inquired.

Daniel took a deep breath in but did not raise his head. "My dad died last week."

"Oh, God. I didn't know. I'm sorry." Harolds eyes bulged and his color blanched. "What happened?"

"It was a farm accident. Just a stupid fucking accident." Daniel shook his head. "I don't really want to talk about it though if you don't mind."

"Sure, I understand. I'm just real sorry, man, that's so awful." Harold stood up and placed his hand on Daniel's slouched shoulder. "Is there anything I can do?"

"No." Daniel stoop up abruptly, almost knocking Harold over. "I have to go to the washroom."

"Are you sure you're okay?" Harold called out after him but he did not bother to answer. He raced down the hall and ignored the other guys he knew, lingering around with curious eyes. He went into the washroom, to the long line of sinks and turned on the faucet. He let the cool water run on his hands for a minute and then slapped it on his face.

He didn't know if he could do this. He couldn't handle the stricken expressions on peoples faces, the sympathy that they offered or their gestures of affection that made him ill. He wanted things back to normal; where people acted natural around him and didn't treat him like a fragile piece of glass. He wouldn't break or shatter.

Not in front of them anyway.

He put his wet, dripping hands to his face and breathed deeply. The sight of his father's bloody face flashed before his eyes and gripped him. Daniel felt a sob slip up his throat and choked it down. He had never felt so angry, depressed and helpless all at the same time. He felt like crying and screaming and tearing something apart. He looked at his pathetic reflection in the mirror and slammed his palms against it.

"You okay?" A voice behind him asked and he turned to see Justin Steward leering at him. He hadn't heard him come in.

"I'm fine." He headed for the door and slammed his shoulder into Justin's on his way, knocking him off balance.

"Hey! Watch it, Bradley!" Justin exclaimed but Daniel kept on walking.

If Justin had of provoked him in the least, he would have loved to have a full-out bare-knuckle fight right then and there. But Justin obviously wasn't as stupid as he looked, and they both went their separate ways.

* * * * *

His encounter with Rachel the next day was just as awkward as it had been with Harold. Sometimes Daniel felt as if he had to comfort others; that it was his job to ease *their* pain when it was *his* father who had passed. Rachel had never even met the man but still succumbed to a mild bout of tears, carrying on as if the news truly pained her. He could not imagine being that empathic; it must be a horrible way to live.

He was glad to be back in class, distracted by the daily academic grind. He thrust himself into his studies and spent most of his time at the library so that he wouldn't have to deal with Harold. He no longer had it in him for small talk; Harold's consistent chatter and attempts at jokes to make him feel better got on his nerves. He avoided Rachel as much as he could too because she was the same way. The only person he couldn't avoid was Miss Temple. The first time he met with her for their usual Friday appointment, he noticed how thick and musty the air was in her office. It needed a good airing out after the summer humidity. Daniel looked out the window behind her and wished he could be outside, in the warmth of the fall sunshine instead of cooped up in her gloomy office. He would have preferred to be *anywhere* but here under her fierce scrutiny.

"You haven't answered my question."

"I told you, it was an accident," he replied.

"I want to know what happened specifically. I have family members that are cattle ranchers and own workable land. One of my uncles lost an arm when he was young so I know how easily accidents happen on the farm." She cocked her head to the side. "It would be good for you to talk about it, to relieve some pent-up emotion."

"I don't have pent-up emotion. I'm fine. I just don't want to talk about it is all."

She sighed. "I don't think you're fine, Daniel. Your father is dead and it must have affected you. You have to have *some* emotion over his death."

"You want me to cry?" he asked sarcastically. "Will that make everyone feel better if I just break down and cry? 'Cause you're gonna be waiting a long time if that's what you're waiting for."

"I don't want you to cry," she stated stonily. "But maybe you should. In order for someone to get over such a tragedy they must go through several stages. I think you're in the denial stage, still in shock over what happened and not able to accept that he's really gone. You're also angry. Angry that he's gone and angry that you couldn't have prevented his death. In order to move on with your life, you have to confront and accept the events that have happened. You have to reveal your true feelings to someone you trust, or more importantly, to yourself."

"There is nothing to reveal. I've accepted that he's dead. I saw his body."

"Do you trust me?" she asked and he shrugged with a slight nod.

"I'm going to tell you something personal about myself because I trust you, Daniel. It has to work both ways if we're going to be totally honest with one another. I realize it can't all be you throwing yourself out on the line to have your feelings and actions analyzed." She cleared her throat.

"The reason I spent the summer at my sisters is because she's very ill. She has a terminal illness and her husband is having a hard time working, taking care of her and the house and the kids. She was given six months to a year to live."

Daniel stared at her, not sure what to say or if he should say anything at all.

"I've known she's been quite ill for some time now, but I didn't know how bad it had gotten until this summer," She swallowed. "It's hard to believe that someone that close to you can be taken away. Can suffer so horribly. I feel so helpless and useless. An experience like that humbles you to your place in the world. Makes you see what's really important."

She reached for a tissue on her desk but her eyes were still dry. "Carol is simply wasting away in her bed for all to watch, completely aware of what's happening to her. As much as we pain to see her suffer, it must be that much worse for her."

Daniel folded his arms and looked at the floor, willing himself not to run out of the room in a panic. Why were women so anxious to spill their souls and torture themselves? Why couldn't they just grin and bear it like the rest of the population. Why did they have to over-think everything. Did they actually enjoy crying and dwelling on this crap?

"It'd be easy to be angry. Angry at God and the world, but that doesn't do anyone any good. Things happen that we can't explain and we just have to have hope that things will get better. Life goes on and there will be brighter days. I do believe that." She forced a weak smile. "Now…can you tell me what happened to your father, Daniel? Can you tell me how you feel about his death?"

He looked up, and said in monotone. "I told you already. He died in a farm accident. He's gone, I'm fine and that's all there is to say about it."

* * * * *

They just wouldn't give it up. Miss Temple, Rachel and Harold were annoyingly aggressive in their individual pursuits to reach and heal him in his time of personal anguish. But they failed in all their attempts. He became a fourteen-year-old recluse, who hid in corners of the library to avoid any sort of human interaction. He took his lunch back to his room so that he could eat alone because he knew if he sat in the cafeteria, Harold would be all over him. He didn't want anything to do with any of them and as a result, everything came crashing down around him.

It started with Rachel.

First she was angry that he had quit the chess club. She didn't understand why he would give it up and no answer he gave satisfied her. Then she was hurt that he hadn't gone to her piano recital when she had personally requested that he attend. He hadn't forgotten about it, which had been his excuse. He just hadn't wanted to go.

"I know you're going through a lot right now, but you don't have to be so selfish. Ever since you came back from summer break, you've been really distant towards me. Rude is probably the better word for it. Is there something else going on? Is there something I should know?"

They were standing in the hall and other students peered at them curiously as they passed.

"There is nothing going on, I'm just real busy right now."

"No busier then anyone else." She put her hands on her hips.

"I just don't have a lot of time, that's all. And it's not as if we're going steady or anything." He bit his lip, knowing that that was the worst things he could have said.

"Oh. I see. You're right, we're *not* going steady." Her nostrils flared. "Well, you should know then that Justin Steward asked me last week to be his date for the Fall Formal this Friday. I will assume that it's okay with you if I go with him. 'Cause like you said, we're not going steady or anything."

"If you want to go with him, that's fine with me," he challenged and noticed that others were now blatantly staring at them.

"Fine! I will!" She stormed off and left him standing there with his mouth agape. The Fall Formal was a dance for the senior students, and he was surprised at first that Justin was even going. But Justin and Todd did hang out with the older, popular crowd. It bothered Daniel that Justin had even asked Rachel, when everyone knew that they were pretty much going steady. Did he do it just to piss him off? If he did, it had worked.

He spent the rest of the week stewing about it and every time he saw Rachel in the halls or in class, she gave him the cold shoulder. He wasn't sure what to do about it or if he should do anything at all to smooth things over. Maybe it was just easier this way. It wasn't as if he wanted a girlfriend, anyway. But that didn't mean he wanted her to be with Justin either.

On Friday night, around eight o'clock he snapped the book closed that he was studying from and went down the quiet hall to the washroom. He entered one of the stalls and pulled his pants down. He sat on the cold seat and was just about to go when he heard the washroom door fling open. It sounded as if three guys walked in; they were all talking loudly about the dance. He recognized one of the voices.

It was Justin.

They talked about the girls they were taking as they washed their hands and checked their hair. Daniel gnawed on his lower lip and gripped the toilet seat. If they said one word about Rachel, he didn't know what he'd do.

"So, what's this girl like that you're taking Steward? I don't really know the younger girls all that well," One of his friends asked off-handedly.

"She's a hottie. Real early bloomer, hardly any of the other girls in our grade even have a chest yet. I'm hoping to get her outside during or after the dance…see how far she'll go," Justin bragged.

The other two laughed and Daniel could feel his face flame with anger. He bit his lower lip so hard that he could taste the metallic taste of blood, but barely noticed.

"You're so full of shit. She's what, thirteen, fourteen years old? How far do you think she'll possibly go?" the other asked, incredulously.

"I'll take her as far as she'll allow, and maybe a little bit further." Justin boasted. Daniel stood up quickly and started zipping up his pants.

"I thought she was with that Bradley kid, that weird guy that rooms with Benning."

"Bradley's a moron. She's not with him anymore, if she ever was. The guy doesn't have everything going on upstairs if you know what I mean. Book-smart maybe, but he's got a screw loose somewhere," Justin snided as he slicked back his hair.

"That so!" Daniel slammed the stall door open and stepped out. The two older students jumped in surprise and embarrassment but Justin merely blinked twice.

"You make a habit of eavesdropping, Bradley?" he asked, his eyes never moving from his hair.

"No. But you sure have a habit of making an ass of yourself ," he shot back, walking towards him with both fists clenched. The juniors nudged one another uneasily, half-hoping for a fight but not sure whether they'd want to interfere or not.

"You got something to say to me?" Justin lowered his comb slowly and turned around. If he was nervous or uncomfortable, he didn't show it.

"Yeah. I think you're an arrogant prick and it's about time I told you so." He looked around the room. "I see that your dip-shit brother isn't around to protect you this time, so I'm doubting that you have anything to say back to me."

Justin pointed his comb at Daniels face. "You're not even in my league, you stupid fuck. I wouldn't waste the breath to tell you what a sorry, pathetic loser you are…"

Before he could finish his sentence, Daniel snapped and lunged forward with lightening speed. He cocked his arm back and punched Justin full in the mouth as hard as he could. Blood sprayed from his lips as he fell backwards to the floor and his eyes rolled back into his head. The two juniors charged at Daniel to hold him back but before they could, Daniel jumped on his chest and started pummeling his face. His jabs were quick but efficient. Justin didn't even try to ward off the blows. The first punch had nearly knocked him unconscious.

"Christ, Bradley! Get off of him!" one of the students yelled as he pulled on Daniels shoulder. Their efforts were useless, he wasn't getting off until he was good and ready.

"You're going to kill him!" the other screamed and that's when he stopped, his fist in mid-air. They pulled him up to a standing position and looked down at Justin. His face was a swollen bloody mess. He was still conscious though, and his groans sounded like a mewling cat.

"Go get a teacher or the school nurse. Get somebody!" one yelled at the other and the blond one promptly raced out of the washroom.

"Are you nuts? This kind of shit could get you suspended!" the frazzled junior exclaimed to Daniel and leaned over Justin to ask if he was alright.

Daniel put his hands to his face and tried to catch his breath. He didn't know what had come over him but one thing was for sure, he definitely felt a lot better.

* * * * *

"I don't even know what to say to you," Miss Temple sighed the next morning. She put her fingers to her temples and massaged herself in small circular motions. She had just spoken to the dean and they were still working on a suitable punishment for Daniel. They had already dismissed suspension, as it was his first offense and Justin merely had swollen eyes and lips. He wasn't even seriously hurt, only his pride had been wounded.

"First of all, how did it start?"

"He started talking trash about me with his friends in the bathroom and didn't know I was in the stall," Daniel explained. "I came out and confronted him and he lipped me off in that cocky, stuck-up way of his and I just decided I wasn't going to take it. I don't really know what came over me. I just wanted to shut him up…and started hitting him and couldn't stop."

"So you instigated it. You punched him first."

"Yeah, but he was the one who provoked me. You should have heard what he said!"

"It doesn't matter what he said. You should be able to control and handle yourself in a mature and responsible fashion. Rational people don't go around hitting people when they get angry," she fumed.

"You didn't hear what he said," he repeated. "You just don't let that kind of stuff go. You have to stick up for yourself. That's what men do."

"No, men don't. Real men don't allow themselves to sink to that level. Mature men control themselves. It shouldn't matter to you what Justin or anybody thinks."

"I don't care *what* they think but I'm not going to let them put me down right in front of my face." He waved a dismissive hand. "You don't understand, you're a girl."

"I understand more than you think, Daniel," she retorted wryly. "I think you have a lot of anger inside you that you need to express. This fight was merely an outlet, a way for you to unleash some repressed emotions. I don't think Justin would have had to say very much for you to provoke a fight with him."

"I think you're wrong." He stood up. "When you and the dean decide on my punishment, come and get me. I'll be in the library."

"Don't interrupt me when I'm talking young man, I'm not through with you!" she chastised and he sat back down.

"Your little confrontation last night wasn't the only reason that I wanted to talk to you this morning." She took a long drink of her coffee. "I told you a while back that my sister Carol is quite ill. Well, she's gotten worse. Her family is not handling her change in condition well and I have offered to go and help them through this horrible time."

"So you're taking a leave of absence?" Daniel asked but she shook her head.

"Not exactly. I've decided to retire."

"What? You're too young to retire!" he gasped.

"Yes, I am too young but I've inherited a nice sum of money from my deceased husband and parents so I am very comfortable financially. I don't need to work; but I've always found it challenging and fulfilling so I didn't really feel the need to quit. I certainly didn't see the point in staying home, doing nothing all day just because I could afford to." She set her coffee cup down. "But now someone needs me. I only have one sister, and I could not in good conscience ignore her pleas to be with her now. I want to be with her in her final days. So I have decided to move out west permanently."

Daniel was speechless, literally speechless.

"I have informed the school faculty that I will be leaving in three weeks."

ISOLATION

"Three weeks? No! You can't." He shook his head and whispered. "I don't *want* you to go." His face was grief-stricken and she smiled sadly at the sight of it. A part of her was relieved that she had finally reached him, had finally gotten him to express some real emotion.

"I'm sorry, Daniel. I don't want to go, but it's something I have to do. I will miss you terribly though."

He jumped up and ran out of the room, startling her with his abruptness, and slammed the door behind him. She was flattered that he cared so much about her leaving but hated to abandon him like this. It was clear that for all his macho attitude and display of bravado, he was still just a lost and lonely little boy.

* * * * *

He charged into his bedroom and hurled the door closed behind him. Harold was at his desk studying and jumped at the noise.

"Something wrong?" he asked, spinning around in his chair.

"No," Daniel muttered and flopped himself on his bed. He laid down on his side, his back facing his friend. He knew he was about to cry, and was desperate not to do it in front of Harold.

"Did you get suspended?"

"No. They haven't done anything yet, they can't decide what to do with me," Daniel replied, teeth clenched.

"I saw Justin a little while ago in the hall. He looks as if you went at him with a baseball bat. Man, you really did a number on his face." Harold gripped the back of his chair excitedly. "What the hell did he do to get you so pissed?"

"He just said the wrong thing at the *wrong* time," Daniel replied irritably.

"Shit, man. Everyone is talking about it, no one can believe you just went berserk like that. Ted and Craig won't stop talking about it, they said you just flew off the handle and..."

"Look. I really don't give a shit what Ted and Craig have to say about it," Daniel cut him off. "I don't want to talk about it."

Harold slammed his hand against the chair. "You know, Bradley, you've had a real shitty attitude ever since you got back from your summer break. I know your father just died and all, and you're going through that but you don't have to be such a jerk to me. I'm just trying to be your friend."

Daniel sat up and swung around. "If you were a real friend, you'd know when to shut up and leave a person alone. But no, you just keep talking and asking questions. Are you that stupid that you can't take the hint?"

"You know, for a while there I actually felt sorry for you." Harold stood up, his face a crimson red.

"I don't want your damned pity!" Daniel spat. "I just want you and everyone else to leave me the hell alone!"

"Don't worry. You won't get pity or *anything* else from me ever again!" Harold exclaimed and raced out of the room.

Daniel stared after him, feeling as if he should follow him and apologize but laid back down instead. He hadn't cried since his father's death, and had promised that he wouldn't do it here, but he broke his promise that day. His chest heaved painfully, as if something massive was constricting his lungs. Thick tears streamed down his cheeks, but he hurriedly wiped them away.

How could things get so bad so fast? Why did he feel so alone when there were so many people around him, he wondered as he wrapped his arms around himself. He fell asleep that way, in a tight fetal position, but even his dreams were filled with pain and loneliness.

* * * * *

They threw a surprise going-away party for Miss Temple in the auditorium on the Friday that she left. Everyone was invited and several teachers and senior students made moving, dramatic speeches. After she made an emotional speech of her own and thanked everyone for coming, the school band struck up. They played in the background while everyone ate cake and ice cream and personally bid her farewell. She was touched by it all, and broke down crying twice.

Daniel didn't attend. He stayed in his room at his desk and studied for a biology exam. His mind however, wasn't on science. He stared absently in his notebook for a while and eventually decided that it was useless to study. He was too distracted. He got up to look out the window.

It was almost four-thirty, and he had heard that Miss Temple wanted to leave around that time to catch a bus in Rowland at five-thirty, that would take her to the nearest train.

He suddenly saw her walking towards her car in the faculty parking lot, which was directly within his view-point. She was carrying a large cardboard box, and a fellow teacher beside her was carrying another box as well as her leather suitcase. She abruptly stopped walking and turned his way. He felt his chest tighten when she raised her head and looked directly up at his window.

ISOLATION

He couldn't see her facial expression but she nodded her head slowly, still gazing up at him and he waved back. He knew that she could see him. He stepped forward and pressed his palm flat against the windowpane. She stood there for a few more seconds and then continued on towards her car. His gaze shifted to the surrounding snow-capped mountains that shrouded over the school, and the sight merely reinforced the sense of entrapment, isolation and helplessness he already felt.

He was trembling all over. He turned his attention back to Miss Temple, and closed his eyes when her car started to pull away. He closed the curtain, sat on his bed and put his head in his hands. He cursed himself for not taking the opportunity when it was open to him. He could have spoken to her once more before she left, but had stubbornly refused to. Now he regretted it. He wanted to tell her the truth about his father, to get it off his chest and to relieve this crushing weight inside. She was the only one he had considered being honest with, but now she was gone.

His secret would remain buried.

Chapter Nine

Three Years Later

The bell rang at three thirty on a rainy Tuesday afternoon and woke the students out of their bored reveries. They grabbed their books and scrambled out of their seats even though their teacher continued lecturing. Daniel was in English literature class; learning about authors that were beyond his time and the classics that they had birthed. After he got his books and notes together he too stood up to leave but noticed the teacher pointing at him.

"I need to speak to you before you leave, Mister Bradley." Professor Masterson called out over the clatter. Daniel cursed mentally. He considered William Masterson to be the oldest and grumpiest teacher of the lot. He was in his early fifties, completely grey with a full mustache and beard and a penchant for clip-on ties and mix-matched socks. He was amusingly eccentric; he didn't interact with the other faculty and disregarded their courses as fluff. He wore the same-colored tweed suits with suede elbow patches over his stocky, ill-proportioned frame every day like clockwork. He talked to himself quietly when he walked down the halls and used the word 'damn' often when he was lecturing. He was a strange man, a self described 'recluse by nature' who preferred his own company to others.

He wasn't even a good teacher; his public speaking skills were nil and he had a tough time relating to his young students. He didn't attempt to get to know any of them either, and had obvious contempt for those who did poorly in his classes. But his love and respect for literature was evident, and his knowledge of books and authors was astonishing. To Daniel, he was an educated fool. He stuttered and stumbled over his words in a muffled, cantankerous way but if you took the time to listen, you could learn a great deal. It was a pity really, he was probably the brightest out of all the teachers here but the students viewed him merely as a source for jokes.

"Yes sir." Daniel approached his desk, wondering what on earth he could have done to earn the old bugger's attention. Professor Masterson rarely spoke to his students one-on-one, and it usually meant that you were in trouble if he wanted to talk to you alone after class.

"I read the short story you wrote for my creative writing assignment," he said and rustled through his disorganized desk until he found the copy.

"Here we are. *Myth of Madness* it's called, yes?" He looked up at Daniel who was momentarily distracted by his bushy gray eyebrows. He had never seen eyebrows that thick or wild before; they looked like two angry caterpillars squiggling around his beady little eyes.

"Yes sir, that's my story."

"Do you have a fondness for the supernatural?" he asked loudly, as if the very concept was absurd. Daniel shrugged. "I guess. You said we could write about whatever we wanted."

"That I did." He nodded. "I was very impressed with your writing. I'm not thrilled about the genre you selected, horror is not my cup of tea but there's a place for everything I suppose. Your writing style is unique, and you have an incredible grasp of the English language for one so young. How long have you been writing?"

"I've never really written anything before. I've made-up stories before but I've never written any of my stories down until this assignment. My Mom always made me do English assignments at home that focused on correct grammar and spelling, and she made sure I improved my vocabulary by learning a new word every day."

"Admirable." Professor Masterson muttered and Daniel detected sarcasm in his tone. "Why don't you take a seat young man. I don't like having conversations with people who hover over me. One has to respect others personal space if they want others to respect their own."

"Yes sir." Daniel grabbed a desk at the front of the class, dragged it loudly until it was directly in front of his teacher's desk and sat down.

"Yes, well, as I said I was thoroughly impressed by your writing. I have to admit, I've been disappointed with most of the work I mark here. I started my career teaching English in public high schools and though there was a diamond in the rough every few years, I never came across one true potential writer. I thought I had it made when I transferred here. I thought the talent would be boundless, that there was the possibility of teaching the next Hemingway. This is supposed to be the cream of the crop but it seems the more intelligent you are in science and math, the stupider you are in the arts. In writing in particular. Most of my students here can't write worth a damn, though they try to impress me with their bloated vocabulary. They prattle off all the books they've read and studied but most of them don't read anything other than what their assigned, and wouldn't recognize good writing if it jumped on their ass and bit them," he scoffed.

Daniel nodded politely but wondered where in the world this speech was going and what it had to do with him.

"I've always said, you either have it or you don't, and you do, Mister Bradley. You do." His eyes gleamed. "By just reading just one of your stories, I can tell that you have the makings of a fairly decent writer. Don't get a swelled head on me, you're no Jules Verne or anything but I definitely see some potential here. There is nothing I can teach you that will make you a better writer. If you have a vast imagination and the ability to read, spell and form a sentence you have the basic tools. Writing is an art, and like everything else, if you want to improve it you have to practice. All anyone else can do for you is provide encouragement and inspiration." He coughed abruptly into his hand and audibly cleared phlegm from his throat. "So, that said, I should probably ask you if you're even interested in becoming a real writer. It takes time and preserverance and I'll hound you every step of the way, but if you're willing, I think you'll be pleasantly surprised by the talent that lies within you."

When Daniel didn't immediately reply, he threw out his hands in exasperation. "So?"

"Sure, I guess," Daniel replied, he was bewildered by the man's rambling. "But I don't understand, sir, what exactly do you want me to do?"

"I want you to write, Daniel. I want you to write until you're sick to death of it, and then I want you to write some more," he smiled grimly.

* * * * *

Daniel stared at the empty page in front of him. Masterson had told him to write a twenty page story in one night on whatever subject he chose. It seemed like a time-consuming but simple task, but it was harder than it sounded. The more he stared at the blank page before him, the foggier his brain became. He didn't know why he bothered; it wasn't worth anything on his final mark anyway because the other students didn't have to do it. He was tempted to crumple the paper and tell the man to find some other pet project, but he knew he wouldn't. He was surprised and flattered by Masterson's words on his writing skills and a bit curious to see if he really did have something. His sisters and Harold always raved about his stories, but they were not avid readers so they didn't have anything substantial to compare him to. But

Masterson was a literate man, a professor of English and therefore knew what good writing looked like.

Daniel sighed and pressed the tip of the lead pencil to the paper. He recalled that in class one day, Masterson told the class that his favorite book was the *Count of Monte Cristo* by Alexandre Dumas. It was a tale of action and adventure and redemption. He was stumped for an original storyline so he decided to use certain aspects of Masterson's favorite yarn. He obviously liked that sort of theme so Daniel formed a similar plot in his mind but set in a different time period. The entire twenty pages focused on the main character, who was wrongly convicted of murder trying to escape out of prison with the assistance of another inmate. When he read the finished product two hours later, he was too tired to see the plot holes or the distinct similarities in the book he was copying from. He decided that it was good enough anyway.

"This is crap." Professor Masterson crumpled it up and threw it in the garbage the next day after class.

"What's wrong with it?" Daniel proclaimed, resisting the urge to retrieve the papers and flatten them out. He was well aware of Masterson's temper, and could see the blaze in his eyes today. He wasn't about to add fuel to the fire.

"Do you think that little of me that you would scrounge together bits and pieces of a classic piece of literature and pass it off as your own, butchering it in the process and expect me of all people not to notice? Do you think I'm an idiot, Mister Bradley?" he demanded.

"No sir, I just..." he stuttered.

"I asked you to do a creative writing assignment, do you know what that means?"

"Yes, sir."

"It means you have to be creative and write your *own* story!" Masterson exclaimed. "Do you know what plagiarism means?"

"Yes, sir, I do." Daniel lowered his head in resignation.

"Good. I'm going to assume you had a temporary bout of insanity last night and will let it go this time, but next time I will not be so forgiving. So let me guess, you had a case of writer's block, right?" He stroked his beard thoughtfully. "You couldn't whip up a story out of thin air and panicked. Tell me if I'm warm."

"You're right, sir, I couldn't think of anything. I just thought if I could borrow an idea from somewhere else, I could get started and go from there."

I don't know what I was thinking but I didn't mean to flat-out copy anything." he declared sincerely.

"Ideas don't come from nowhere, Daniel, they come from within. They come from here." Masterson pounded his chest with his closed fist. "When you write about what you're interested in, about what you know and love, it pours unto the pages. When you let the reader in on a piece of something that is a part of you, it's like opening a brand new world to them, and a connection is made. If you don't know or care about what you're writing about, why should anyone else?"

"I don't have anything to say though, I can't think up an original story," Daniel admitted.

"Everyone has something to say, everyone has a story. The story itself isn't the most important element anyway, the real key is to tell the tale in a way that reaches and connects with people. A bum on the street corner can tell a story about a burning house. But a good storyteller can tell the same story and make you care about the fate of the people that reside inside the house, and let you feel and smell the intensity of the flames. If the reader doesn't care about the characters, or get involved, the story doesn't work."

"I don't think I could ever be that good, not like Dumas or Tolkien. They're geniuses," Daniel sighed and Masterson leaned back in his chair and folded his arms.

"You're right, Daniel, you probably won't ever be that good. If in your mind you truly believe that, you never will be."

Daniel stared at Masterson, speechless at the blunt truth of his words.

"If you are willing to try though; to put the time and effort in, and risk putting your heart and soul out on the line every time someone reads your work, you *will* find out how good you really are." He leaned forward, eyes glued on the student before him. "Do you want to find out?"

Daniel didn't hesitate, "Yes."

* * * * *

So he wrote, and he wrote and he wrote. Before, during, between and after classes he wrote. And when he wasn't writing he was thinking about what he was going to write next. He ate, breathed and slept with his stories; they became who he was and defined his existence in his final year at Steinem Academy. The semesters slipped by like a dream. Classes passed by without him hardly noticing but he was fortunate enough that he didn't have to study hard to maintain his high average. He scarcely saw Harold any more. Though he still roomed with him, they were literally two passing ships in the night. They never spoke, and neither he nor Rachel gave him more then a passing glance in the halls. He didn't blame them. He had written them off with complete disregard to their feelings and though he missed them, it was easier this way. He was too busy to interact with others. Too immersed in his work and his time with Masterson. He pushed himself harder and harder, trying to impress and captivate the old guy with his work.

But it was more than just that. Masterson had given him a reason to get up in the morning, had given him a challenge and something to strive for. He found most of his courses to be tiresome and easy, and because he was bored, his thoughts often turned to his father, and the night he died. Writing was a distraction, it gave him the escape from reality that he desperately needed. Masterson had given him a way out of the dark trenches of his own mind.

Masterson himself was profoundly pleased with Daniels progress, what he submitted to him was beyond any of his expectations. The boy had a true gift of the written word. There was only one problem. Their preferences in genres differed drastically. Daniel wanted to write about ghosts, vampires, men rising from the dead, destructive aliens, and the apocalypse. This was all much to Masterson's dismay.

"What the hell is this?" he demanded after reading his latest work on a pack of hungry vampires that terrorize a young family camping in the woods. "Who the hell wants to read this supernatural crap!"

"Lots of people. Look at Edgar Allan Poe, Alfred Hitchcock, Bram Stoker and H.G. Wells. Their legends in the literary world and their work totally revolves around fictional monsters, the undead and the supernatural. You have to admit, there is a market for this stuff," Daniel reasoned.

"No respectable publishing company would ever publish this. It's too gory, too scary for the average reader. If you want to be highly regarded within certain circles, you *can't* write horror."

"I don't care about being 'highly regarded'," Daniel mimicked. "I just want to tell a good story."

Masterson sighed, and hoped that he was merely going through an adolescent phase. His talent was too good to waste on such mindless dime-store crap.

But Daniel didn't grow out of it. He kept writing his ghost stories, and got better and better at telling them. To the point where Masterson finally sat back in his chair one day with a bemused smile. He had just finished reading

Daniel's latest tale. The story was about the ghost of a young boy trying desperately to warn his motherless siblings that their love-struck young nanny was poisoning them. That she was trying to kill them all off to get their father all to herself. When the children finally listen to the ghost; instead of running off in fear at the sight of it, they frantically go to their father to tell him what's going on before it's too late. But he doesn't believe them and will not even consider the possibility that he has a ghost in his home or that his beautiful care giver is a murderer. It was a terrifying story, without Daniels usual lust for gore and blood, and was solidly told. Much is left up to the imagination of the reader which creates a tremendous amount of suspense. The characters were realistic and fully dimensional, like Masterson had taught him, Daniel made the reader care about the children being poisoned. You truly wanted them to find out what the nanny was doing and have the father believe and protect them.

"This is good," Masterson admitted begrudgingly. "Very good. Good enough to send away, I'm going to mail it to a magazine that publishes short stories. *Chills and Thrills,* I think the thing's called. I only know about it because a colleague of mine edits for it. I haven't talked to him in years but this is just the sort of stuff they thrive on," he told Daniel as he held up the sheets of paper. "If you type it up double-spaced, and number the pages I'll mail it in."

"Thanks," Daniel said excitedly.

A month later they received word that it was accepted. Not only did they print the story and pay him thirty dollars for it, but he had won their annual 'Best Short Story Contest' and was awarded fifty dollars more for first prize.

When Masterson handed him the magazine his story was published in, Daniel felt almost faint. The enormity of having hundreds of people, mostly guys his age, reading what he wrote made him queasy. But when he opened the pages to his story, and saw his name under the title, an enormous rush of adrenaline coursed through his body. He almost lost his sense of balance; the powerful effect it had over him was astounding.

"It's beyond words to see your own name, your own words in print. When you give that much to something, it's gratifying to see it all come together." Masterson said quietly behind him. "You were meant for this Daniel."

Daniel turned around, eyes wide.

"You're a writer," he said firmly. "It is truly your calling. You can graduate from here and do anything you want with your life, but you have the potential to be more than just an average literary lover like me. One that teaches and admires others works. You have the ability to write at a level that most can only dream about. Don't let *anyone* change or crush that creative spirit. Just set it free and take you where you're meant to go."

Daniel was so moved by his words that if Masterson would have allowed him, he probably would have hugged him.

* * * * *

Daniel graduated from Steinem Academy on a bright Saturday afternoon in June of 1966. They held the graduation service outdoors on the back campus. Because there were no trees near the stage, shade was scarce, but a slight breeze temporarily cooled off the large, self-fanning crowd. His mother showed up with Kate, and they sat proudly in the second row. His mother's face beamed radiantly when he went up for his diploma, and tears poured freely down her cheeks like a waterfall. As he shook the dean's hand and looked over the crowd with a stiff smile, he noticed Miss Temple sitting alone near the back. She too was smiling brilliantly and he gave her a small nod as he walked off the stage. He hadn't seen her in over three years and was instantly surprised how time had flown. He was writing so much any more, that time no longer bore meaning. He could pore over a single story for weeks and months and barely notice the world around him.

Immediately after the service, he pushed through the crowd to find his old counselor. He knew he probably wouldn't see her again after today and wanted to say the good-bye he should have said years ago. On his way over, he saw Larry Benning proudly hugging his son while his wife looked on blissfully. His heart skipped a beat. Harold was quite visibly mortified by his father's outlandish affection but in that moment, Daniel would have done anything to be him. Anything at all.

When he approached Miss Temple a few seconds later, she was speaking to one of the teachers. She glanced his way and excused herself from that conversation.

"Congratulations, Daniel," She put out her hand and he shook it briefly.

"Are you here to see me?" he asked and she smiled.

"I came to see *all* the students. I worked with every one of these graduates when they first arrived here at Steinem. It's always exciting to see my kids graduate and prepare for post-secondary school. It's like setting a bird free, and hoping it'll do well on its own."

"Your sister, is she..."

"She died. Over two years ago, it was inevitable but she went peacefully. I'm glad I took the time to spend her final days with her."

A silent second passed. He knew he should say something, but he didn't know what.

"And how are you?" she asked.

He noticed that she had aged a bit in the last few years. Her grey hair was much more prominent, as were the fine wrinkles around her eyes and mouth. As finely groomed as she was, the make-up and clothes couldn't hide the stress that she had endured the last few years. It looked as if the many losses in her life were starting to take its toll.

"I'm fine," he replied shyly and noticed his mother and Kate headed their way.

"I hear you're going to Western. Good choice, it's a great school. I also hear you got a full scholarship, that's wonderful!"

"Yeah." He nodded, knowing he wouldn't even be able to go to university if he hadn't gotten a full scholarship. His mother would never be able to afford to send him. But he had earned top marks through most of his courses and was even on the honor roll. "I'm going to major in English and minor in history."

"With the ultimate goal being…" she trailed off, waiting for him to fill in the blanks.

"An English professor." He wanted to tell her about his writing and about Masterson tutoring him but he didn't want his mother to hear. He wasn't ready to let everyone know about his writing aspirations just yet. It was still too personal.

"Excellent," she beamed. "I just can't believe you've graduated already. It just feels like yesterday that you walked in my office all homesick and sullen with straw still behind your ears."

"Hi, honey." His mother tapped him on the shoulder from behind and he turned around.

Maria was smiling but she had a pained look in her moist eyes. This was her baby, her one and only son who had gone and grown up on her. He was almost six foot three now, broad and muscular with a mysterious glint in his big brown eyes. He was so handsome, a true vision in his black grad hat and gown. But he looked like a stranger to her. She didn't know him anymore. The last time she saw him was the night before he snuck back to school with his uncle Steve. He hadn't said good-bye to her that morning, had simply left without a word or a note. That killed her. It was bad enough that Joe was gone, but to have Daniel rush off to deal with it on his own was heartbreaking.

She had called him as frequently as she could afford but it wasn't the same. She was no longer an important part in his life. She didn't know what he thought about, what he did in a day, what stresses he had, what foods he ate or what he did for fun. She had lost the two most important men in her life the day Joe died.

She never should have left Daniel alone that night, but everything had happened so quickly that she hadn't had time to think things through. And it was too late now to agonize over it. What's done is done. Dwelling on it was a waste of time, and she believed in expending energy wisely. She only hoped that her boy was strong enough to get through all this on his own, and more importantly, that it wouldn't hold him back.

"Mom, this is Miss Temple. She used to work here at the school as the guidance counselor."

"We met," Maria said and stuck out her hand. "Nice to see you again."

"It's a pleasure to see you, too, Mrs. Bradley."

They shook hands politely.

"You must be awfully proud of your son today."

"I am." Maria looked adoringly up at him. "He's done very well for himself. But I always knew he would."

Daniel stood there awkwardly, knowing that he should be basking in the limelight and enjoying the fruits of his accomplishments but he couldn't. He felt as empty as he always did.

* * * * *

When Daniel walked back in the school to hand in his gown and hat, he met Rachel in the hall. The thought of ignoring her and pretending he didn't see her crossed his mind briefly. But she walked straight towards him so boldly that he was forced to acknowledge her.

"Hey, Daniel." She smiled and stopped right in front of him, blocking his path.

"Hey." He swallowed hard and looked everywhere but at her face.

"I heard you're going to Western. Full scholarship and all, that's pretty neat."

"Yeah, it's okay. Where are you going?" He looked down at his feet and shifted his weight from side to side.

"University of Toronto. They have a pretty good music program. I didn't get a scholarship, though. I'm just going to live with my parents."

"Oh." A dark thought occurred to him. "Is that where Justin is going too?"

"I wouldn't know. We broke up years ago." Her eyes narrowed. "Didn't you know that?"

"No." An unexpected rush of relief washed over him. "Look, I gotta get going. My mom and sister are out there waiting for me."

"Yeah, I met them. They were sitting beside my parents and they introduced themselves to me. They're real nice, I got talking to Katie and she's such a sweetheart. Anyway, I just thought that…my grandmother lives near London and we visit her often. Maybe we could get together some time. Get some coffee or dinner or something some weekend. It might be nice to see a familiar face."

"Okay." He shrugged.

"Here is my parent's phone number. Feel free to call me some time." She handed him a small piece of folded paper.

"Okay. Well I better go." He started to walk away but she grabbed his arm.

"I've wanted to talk to you for a long time. We haven't really talked since that stupid argument we had so long ago." She blushed. "I feel bad about that. I don't like the way we ended things. I thought…"

"There you are!" A loud voice interrupted them and they both turned to see one of her girlfriends rushing towards them. "Rachel, I've been looking all over for you!"

"You better go." He slipped out from her grasp.

"I'll call you," he promised and practically ran, heart pounding all the way down the long hall. He finally turned the corner and stopped short in his tracks, gasping for air. He leaned against a locker and held his head down in shame. What was wrong with him? Here was a perfectly gorgeous girl that he truly liked throwing her phone number at him and he was running away like a scared rabbit! What an idiot he was! But the mere thought of taking her on a date put him into cold sweats. As much as he liked her, he didn't need the complications or stress in his life. He wiped the sweat from his brow and continued down the hall with her phone number clutched tightly in his hand. He turned another corner swiftly and almost smacked head-on into Miss Temple.

"Oh goodness!" She jumped back and clutched her chest. "You scared me."

"Sorry." He stepped away from her.

"I'm glad I ran into you though. I wanted to see you before I left." She stuck out her hand to shake. "I just wanted to congratulate you again and wish you good luck at Western. I know you'll do just fine there."

He shook her tiny, soft hand and when she turned to walk away, he said quietly. "I'm truly sorry about your sister, Miss Temple. I know how hard it must have been for you. I'm just…I'm sorry you had to go through that." He knew about loss, he knew about losing someone close. A part of him needed to acknowledge that to someone who understood. Someone who had helped him once.

Her feet froze in place, her back straightened to a perfectly erect posture and he heard her sniff softly. She turned toward him.

"I'm sorry about a lot of things that have happened in my life, Daniel, but one thing that I am very proud of, is the time that I've spent with talented, capable children like yourself." Her wet eyes riveted on his. "No matter where you go or what you do, I want you to remember that there is someone out there who believes in you." A single, mascara coated tear trickled slowly down her cheek.

"And when you believe in yourself, too, there won't be a thing in this world that you won't be able to do." She smiled gently, turned around and with a sinking heart, he watched her walk down the hall and out of his life.

Chapter Ten

His university years slipped by like a blur, so quick that his life there had a dream-like, hazy quality to it. He spent most of his time in front of his old Remington 32 typewriter in his cramped dorm room or in the library. Western, one of the oldest, most respected Canadian universities, is a city in itself; sprawled across four hundred and sixty-six hectares in London, Ontario with over sixty main campus buildings. He could easily blend into the crowd here, he was just another student number and loved the feeling of anonymity. The one big difference between this school and the one he had left behind was the girls. They were far more aggressive in this one. On a daily basis he was pursued and fawned over by attractive classmates vying for his attention. A tiny part of him was flattered, but he wasn't much interested. He had too many other things on his mind.

He was knee deep in his first full-length novel. After winning several writing contests, and publishing numerous short stories in various magazines, he felt he had what it took to write an actual novel. He wasn't prepared, however, for the amount of time it took to do so. It became an intricate balance of time-management skills to put equal amount of effort into his schoolwork and his book. He titled it *Isolation*.

It is about a middle-aged, successful horror writer, Jerry Quinn, who rents an isolated log cabin up north to pen his latest novel in. He is a loner, a womanizer, an alcoholic and avid drug-user. He has many ailments that he blames his many problems on, and he also uses his ample problems to justify his chronic use of alcohol and prescription drugs. He suffers from writer's block, and had desperately hoped that the tranquillity of such an isolated location would alleviate the problem. Not realizing that his substances would counter-affect whatever effects the seclusion would have had. While cooped up in the cabin during the long winter nights, he ruthlessly indulges in the many painkillers he brought along and immerses his mind into the warped plot-lines of his bloody yarns. One night in late December, while pounding on his typewriter and guzzling a full glass of whiskey, he hears a strange noise outside the cabin. He's curious as to what made the noise, but is too drunk to get up and see what it is. The next night he hears it again, and a sharp movement at the window catches his eye. The next night the noises outside grow louder, closer, and something flashes by the window again. In the daytime, he can think of rational explanations for what he has seen and heard, and blames it primarily on the large consumption of booze and drugs he had taken the day before. But when the night rolls in, all his explanations go to the wayside. Something was out there. Something wanted to scare him. It wasn't human and it wasn't an animal. He wished it were. His circumstance was far more terrifying than anything he had ever written and at first he tries to embrace the intense emotions he was feeling to relay it into his work. But at night, he is too scared to type or write. He is too scared to move. Whatever out there was getting more bold, and one night the thing in the window stopped moving and stared right back at him. He passed out at the sight of it and the next morning packed his stuff to leave. He races hysterically outside of the cabin, into the bone-chilling cold where the dreary white landscape and frigid bare trees disillusion him with its eerie vastness. He is devastated to discover that his car won't start. He doesn't have a phone either because the cabin doesn't have phone jacks. There are no neighbors within walking distance and the nearest town is over fifty miles away. Much too far to walk in this weather, he'd freeze to death before he ever got to his destination.

He was totally isolated out here. He couldn't leave and he couldn't get help.

He was stuck until spring.

Once he realizes the stark reality of his situation, he decides he simply won't stay another night. He goes immediately inside and polishes off his many bottles of pills with a flask of vodka. Before he falls into endless sleep, he writes a letter to his estranged daughter explaining why he did what he did and apologizes for his neglectful treatment towards her.

He recalls the memories of a past he has worked hard to forget; of the terrible abuse he had endured at his father's hand as a child, of the shameful poverty he had lived in until his first taste of literary success and the pain that he had caused in many fine women and loyal friends. He cries until the tears won't come, and finally accepts and welcomes the fate that he has tempted for years.

It is then, when he is lying in bed, wearily drifting off to eternal slumber that he remembers what he had seen in the window the night before. He remembers the monster, the dull eyed hairy beast that had scared him unconscious. He had been looking at a face he hadn't even recognized.

It had been his own reflection in the window. The monster was none other than himself.

When Daniel was twenty-two, he finished writing this novel and sent it out for Masterson to review. He was estatic, although he still wasn't a fan of horror novels, he thought Daniel had written a 'haunting piece of art'.

He called him immediately after reading it. "I liked it. It's nightmarish but complexly engineered, unlike most horror novels. It's emotionally engaging because the main character is no hero. He's flawed and gritty, an impulsive train wreck but you want him to survive. I like the way that you explore the depths of his fear. Fear of the unknown is much more powerful and interesting than what you can see and understand. And the fear of what you're becoming is even more frightening."

Daniel couldn't have been more relieved. He knew his harshest critic but most ardent fan was Masterson. He sent his five hundred page novel off to ten publishing companies, ones that Masterson helped him select, and waited anxiously for a response. It was two months before he heard anything, but when they came, they came in twos. He received two rejection letters in the mail on the same day, both from large publishing houses in Toronto. He nailed those letters on the wall in his dorm room and stared at them for hours. They were motivation if nothing else. Motivation to succeed and to overcome. He would be good enough for them some day, one day they would regret rejecting him. He received two more rejection letters and nailed them up as well. Three weeks later he received two more and pounded them into the wall with a mighty force. He read them over so many times that he could recite every line on each letter. He tried not to let them get to him, but he was starting to doubt that *Isolation* would ever see the light of day. He became so dejected that he couldn't bring himself to start writing again, or to even think about the plot outline for another book.

He called Masterson and told him this, and was surprised when the old man became irate. "You've barely even begun your writing career and you've already given up on it. What kind of horse shit is that!"

"But I..."

"But nothing! Who cares if nobody picks this one up now, maybe it's just bad timing. The worst thing you could do right now is quit writing," he growled. "Did you know that the truest testament of a person's character is revealed when they are confronted with failure? When faced with a larger than anticipated challenge, most fold under the pressure, but it is the select few that rise to the occasion and push themselves to the limits with that much more determination. Those are the ones that succeed, not just in their goal, but in life. It is only when we overcome our fear of failure that we see what we're truly capable of."

"Did you hear what I just said?" Masterson demanded.

"Yes, I did, but it's just so hard." He didn't know if he could stand receiving another rejection letter. The very thought made him ill. What little confidence he had in his writing was withering away with each letter.

"Don't give up Daniel. You have too much to give to just let it go like this. Give it time," Masterson advised softly.

Late that night, Daniel sat at his typewriter and closed his eyes. Masterson was right. He couldn't let this disappointment discourage him. He wasn't ready to give up. Not when he knew he still had something to say. A story that had to be told. He began to type; slowly and tentatively at first but within minutes his fingers were moving at such a swift and natural pace that they appeared independent from his body. It felt good to be writing again, it felt right. And at three in the morning, he looked tiredly down at the fifteen sheets that he had written and smiled. He had to do this. Not for anyone else but himself. It didn't matter if anybody ever read his work.

And with that new resolve, came a fierce tenacity like nothing he had ever experienced.

* * * * *

Two months later, when he was completely submerged in his second novel, he received a letter from a small company in Toronto that specialized in undiscovered fictional authors. He opened the envelope despondently, knowing exactly what the first lines would be, '*We thank you for submitting your manuscript, but regret to inform you...*'. But as he read the letter over, his heart began to pound. They had accepted it! They had actually accepted his novel and a contract was enclosed. He laughed out loud and re-read the letter several times. He was standing in the middle of a hall and other students stared at him balefully as they walked around him.

He was a real writer. A published author!

He walked down the hall dreamily and went to the pay phone to call Masterson. Tears filled his eyes as the phone rang, and when Masterson finally answered, the good news trickled incoherently off his tongue.

"You sound so surprised," he chuckled. "Didn't you believe me when I told you that you were a good writer?"

"I just can't believe this is really happening," he breathed, feeling very near to hyperventilation. All this time he had wanted to get published so bad, but now that it was happening, it didn't even feel real.

"It's happening. And it's only the beginning," Masterson stated.

* * * * *

Daniel finished his second novel immediately after the first was published.

Both were printed by Canon publishing but only one received rave reviews from the critics. *Isolation's* cover page was full of praise including;

> *Engrossing and suspenseful...grabs you by the throat*
> *Compelling and terrifying...in the realm of Edgar Allan Poe*
> *A natural storyteller...a promising young talent that hooks the reader on the very first page*

His second novel, *The Other Side* was considered too dark and controversial for the mainstream, but critics still could not deny his gift for the written word. They considered him to be the 'next big thing' in the literary world.

That story revolved a young man recovering from a near-fatal accident who has a disturbing afterlife experience that leaves him delusional and paranoid.

Half of the novel centers on the main characters drugged, harrowing hallucinated perspective on life and death, as he tries to figure out what happened to him and what's real and what is an illusion. The other half focuses on the medical professionals trying to determine what caused his mental breakdown and their theories on what he claims to have seen when he was considered dead.

Daniel did extensive research on theology, philosophy and mythology and interviewed a prominent psychologist, physician, and priest to make the dialogue and plotline realistic. The *Other Side* earned more critical acclaim than royalties, but his work was getting noticed, and for a young writer, that was an accomplishment in itself.

He kept pushing himself harder, and while working on his masters, he was already busy doing research for his third novel. He was hungry for success, hungry for something he couldn't define. The money he received wasn't very much but it came in handy. He didn't do it for the money, though. Cash was just an added bonus.

Masterson envied yet was baffled by his relentless, compulsive drive. Daniel didn't understand it either, but still he wrote, late into the nights and first thing in the morning before class. He couldn't stop writing, even if he wanted to do. He was obsessed with it, and it wasn't until he met up with a very special woman, that he thought about anything other than the next line on his typewriter.

* * * * *

He was walking on campus one May afternoon with his head held low, munching an apple, completely preoccupied as usual. He was headed to his Modern British Literature class, but his thoughts were on the tricky chapter that he planned to write that evening.

"Daniel? Daniel Bradley?" a familiar voice called out. He looked up.

It was Rachel, of all people, ten feet from him standing amongst a small crowd on the lawn. While he blinked in surprise, she left her group and jogged over to him with her right arm raised in greeting. He had thought when he left Steinem, that he would never see her face again. He was glad that he was wrong.

She hadn't changed much; gotten slightly taller, had filled out a bit and had longer hair but she was still very much the same. She was beautiful. He felt the usual rush when she was near, but walked over to her as nonchalantly as he could.

"Fancy meeting you!" She laughed and tossed her long hair to the side.

"What are you doing here?" was all he could say.

"My brother's studying business here, first year. My parents and I are just visiting."

"Oh." He looked at his watch. He was going to be late for class.

"Am I holding you up from something?" she asked, her smile faded.

"No, no. I just have to get to class in a few minutes that's all."

"It's been a while, hasn't it. What's it been, six, seven years?"

"Yeah. Time flies, eh?" he replied quietly.

"Yes, it does. I graduated last year. I'm helping my mom teach piano. Still living with my folks, how pathetic is that?" She giggled good-naturedly. Part of him wanted to ask her if she was seeing anyone but if she was, he didn't want to hear it. "I've heard through the grapevine that you're working on your masters. That's great, Daniel. And your novels, wow, I've read them both and they're fabulous. *The Other Side* was a bit dark and philosophical for me, I don't think I fully understood it, but *Isolation* was great. You're doing so well, Daniel, really you are. Though I'm not surprised, you were clearly the brightest and most motivated of us all at Steinem," she smiled.

He stared at her and wondered why he didn't take the chance so many years ago. She was the perfect girl, so nice and sweet and beautiful. But here she was, and he still didn't have the courage to pursue her.

"Thanks," he mumbled.

"Well, I better get going." She pointed to her parents, who were watching them cautiously. "It was nice seeing you, though." She started to walk away.

"Wait!" he choked out, surprising himself. She turned around, eyes wide.

He couldn't believe how striking she looked, with the sun shining on her hair. Her trim, luscious frame hidden under her silk white blouse and pleated skirt.

"I was just wondering how long you were in town. Maybe we could get that cup of coffee you mentioned on grad day. I don't know, you don't have to or anything but it would be nice to catch up I guess," he rambled.

"That would be nice, Daniel. Are you free later today?"

"Yeah. I have classes til four. How about…I don't know…dinner tonight?"

"I can't. We're having dinner at my grandmother's tonight, it's kind of a formal affair and I know I wouldn't be able to get out of it. Maybe it won't work out after all," she said dispiritedly.

"Are you free now?" he blurted, his classes already forgotten.

* * * * *

They went to busy coffee shop nearby and ordered coffee and pecan pie.

'Their specialty,' he said. They folded their arms awkwardly on top of the table and pondered upon what to talk about. They had been friends so long ago, and so much had changed, it was hard to fall into natural rhythum of dialogue.

"Are you working on another book?" she asked, as a bored waitress leaned across the table and poured them coffee.

"Yeah. I'm right in the middle of one."

"How do you find the time with all your school work?" She shook her head in amazement.

"My time is all scheduled in precise detail from the moment I get up to the moment I go to bed. It's all about time management, but I have to get seven hours of sleep, or I'm useless."

"You're so organized," she sighed. "I'm envious."

"If I wasn't organized then nothing would ever get done." He sipped the coffee. It was so hot that it burnt his tongue.

"Are you seeing anyone?" she asked bluntly and he shook his head.

"Have you *ever* had a girlfriend?"

"No." He knew then that he would be required to ask her the same question, even though he didn't want to. "Are you seeing anyone?"

"No." She tapped her fingers on the coffee cup. "I was seeing a guy in university but it ended when we graduated."

He almost said 'that's good' but caught himself. He found it very hard to believe that someone like Rachel was still single. He would think guys would be climbing out of the woodwork to be with her.

"My grandmother will probably give me the third degree about this subject tonight. She thinks there is something wrong with me; twenty-four and still single and living with my parents. Her and her cronies like to talk about how strange I am, putting so much time and effort into my career. I've been taking business courses at night and they think it's just a waste. That I'm throwing away my youth and my chance to get married. Their terrified of me becoming an old spinster like my Aunt Edna," she laughed hollowly but he could tell that she didn't find it at all funny.

"Do you *want* to get married?" he asked.

"Do you?" she shot back. The waitress arrived and delivered their large pieces of pie on shiny white plates.

"No," he replied when the waitress left.

"I don't either. Not now at least. I have too many plans, too many things I want to do before I settle down." She took a bite of the pie. "It's good."

"What are your plans?" he asked.

"I don't know, something with music obviously, but I'm not sure what I want to do. I don't want to work for anyone else, but I'm not sure if I can start something myself."

"Sure you can, if you want to start your own business. What's holding you back?"

"Some things are hard to do and when you're a girl, it's even harder." Her eyes narrowed.

"That's just an excuse. If you wanted it bad enough, you'd do it," he stated curtly and she stared hard at him.

"That's easy for you to say. Everything comes easy to you," she snapped. "Some of us have barriers in our way, things to overcome."

"I've worked hard for *everything* I've ever had." He set down his fork. "Nothing has ever been dropped on my lap."

"I know. I'm sorry, I didn't mean anything by it." She put up her hands. "I just get defensive when I talk about my career. I haven't gotten a lot of support from my family and sometimes I wonder why I even bother. Maybe I should just give up and get married and start a family like the rest of the girls my age."

Daniel shook his head. "I think that's the last thing you should do."

"Most of the guys I know think that the one and only place for a woman is in the home. Barefoot and pregnant."

"If that's what they want to do, then that's fine. But if girls like you have something they want to accomplish and want to work, then who is anyone else to say that they shouldn't." He picked up his fork and started back into his pie.

A moment of silence passed between them. Daniel scraped his plate clean and she sipped her drink and watched him thoughtfully.

"I'd like to see you again, Daniel," she whispered and his eyes lifted to meet hers. For a few seconds they merely stared at one another, their eyes speaking volumes. She reached across the table and touched his hand.

"Tell me you don't feel the same way."

He didn't say a word.

* * * * *

This was the beginning of their on again, off again romance. They saw one another sporadically after that, whenever she could fool her parents into thinking she was visiting her brother, and took the train up to spend the weekend with him. They would go to dinner at various restaurants and sample exotic foods, talk into the late hours in coffee shops and walk leisurely hand in hand around the aesthetic campus. Most of the time he was too busy studying or writing to see her anyway, so it was only one weekend per month on average that they were together.

The first time they made love was a tender but clumsy affair several months later. Fortunately his roommate went home every weekend so Daniel had the room to himself for two whole days. While they drank cheap red wine in his rumpled bed late that Friday night, they talked of students that they had known and events that had happened back at Steinem. It was mostly Rachel filling him in on things that occurred that he hadn't noticed, or cared about at the time.

"So what was with you and Miss Temple? I would see you talking to her in the halls. Did you actually like her?" Rachel asked, her index finger fingering the rim of her glass playfully.

"She was all right." Daniel shrugged. "When I first came to the school, she was the only one who really tried to get to know me. I was homesick and miserable for the first few months, and she helped me through that tough time. She encouraged me to work hard and get involved in things. She was real nice, tough, but nice."

"Tough is right. She was a hard-ass as far as I'm concerned," Rachel scoffed. "She might have been nice to you, but she was a bitch to the rest of us."

Daniel found that hard to believe. "What do you mean?"

"She just had this air about her, so snooty and full of herself. Like she owned the place."

"I didn't notice that. She was real assertive and always wanted the last word but I never once thought of her as bitchy."

"Her husband died the year before you came. He was older than her by ten years, and had a massive stroke when they were in the middle of eating dinner one night. He was hospitalized for months on end after that, and couldn't speak, walk or feed himself. I heard that he didn't know who he was or where he was, and the doctors didn't seem to think his condition would improve either. She renovated her home with medical equipment so he could live there and hired twenty-four medical care for him but continued working. She came to the Academy every day like clockwork like it never even happened, She didn't take time off to be with him or act like it bothered her in the least. About a year later he died, and she was at the school at the time." She burrowed her brow distastefully.

"I don't even know why she works at all, I hear she got a huge inheritance from him. He was just as well-off as her parents, so she didn't need to work."

Daniel turned away and took a long drink. He knew that Miss Temple had probably worked hard and acted aloof in a desperate attempt to distract herself from reality. From the grief that bubbled beneath the surface. That it was her way of coping with her loss, and he thought there were worse things a person could do then keep themselves busy. Rachel had never experienced a loss as great as that, and therefore, couldn't fully relate or understand.

"I heard, too, that she wasn't able to have children, and they say that's why she was so hard on her students. I guess she had five miscarriages when she was in her twenties and gave up trying after that. I don't know, I just can't picture her as the motherly type anyway." Rachel winced at the thought.

Daniel simply didn't want to hear any more about it. He respected Miss Temple and felt a strange sense of loyal towards her. He didn't want to hear any more derogatory comments about her or hear gossip about her private life.

"Enough about that. Tell me about you and Justin. How did that ever start up?"

Her smile diminished and she answered shortly. "I don't really remember. It was so long ago." She took a long gulp of wine.

"Bull. You remember everything else that happened in that school," he said dryly. "What in the world did you see in him anyway? I always thought he was an arrogant bastard."

"He *was* a bastard, but so were you!" she exclaimed and stood up. "You're practically a genius, right, so did it ever occur to you, Mister smarty-pants that the only reason I was ever with Justin was so that I could make you jealous?"

Daniels face reddened.

"It was all simply to get your attention. But it didn't work. You and Justin had that one fight in the boys bathroom the night of that dance when we were like thirteen, and I fooled myself into thinking that you were fighting over me. I was flattered, but afterwards you still didn't talk to me. Didn't even look my way. So I thought the way to motivate you to do so was to date the one and only guy you despised in that school. I thought that would catch your interest and make you jealous."

She put her hands through her hair. "I was a stupid adolescent twit. I wasted two years on that idiot for nothing."

Daniel stared into space. "I had no idea."

"What was I thinking, dating and playing mind-games at that age, anyway!"

She plopped down beside him. "If I could do it all over again, I would do it a lot differently but it doesn't matter in the long run. We're together now, aren't we?"

He put his arm around her waist affectionately and they smiled at one another. She leaned towards him and their lips met and parted.

They kissed passionately for a few moments, until Rachel pulled away and stood directly in front of him. She slowly unbuttoned her cotton blouse, took it and her white bra off to expose her small, round breasts. His face didn't leave hers as he pulled off his own shirt to reveal his thick, broad upper body. They idly stared at one another, half-bared and totally exposed. She made the first move, as always, and bent over to blow out the candles on his dresser. She crawled into bed with him, pulled the covers over them and felt at home in his strong, needing arms.

* * * * *

Later, Rachel drifted off to sleep with a contented smile across her lips.

Daniel remained awake, hands clasped behind his head, staring fixedly at the ceiling with a frown. This was a mistake. This whole affair was a mistake and he should have known better. His theory all along had been that the less involved he was with others the better. Relationships were complicated, and required time and energy. Being alone carried less responsibility, less expectations and less chance of being disappointed. Or more importantly, of being a disappointment.

He didn't want to hurt her, so he needed to do something now before it got more serious. He decided that in the morning, he would break it off.

* * * * *

She awoke the next morning and immediately knew something was wrong.

There was a tension in the air, the wonderful vibes from the night before had clearly dissipated. Daniel was back to his old self, but she wasn't about to let his usual grumpiness ruin her morning.

He was already showered and dressed, scribbling away on a notepad at his desk with his back turned towards her. She got up and dressed without a word and he didn't acknowledge her. She pulled back the window curtains to let the sunlight in and smiled at the faded blue sky. London was already alive and bustling.

"Do you want to go for breakfast now?" she asked while fastening her hair into a high pony-tail.

"I'm not hungry," he replied without looking up.

She slumped at the edge of the bed and frowned. "Is something wrong?"

He dropped his pencil on the paper he was writing on and stared at it. "We can't let this go any further."

"What. What can't go further?"

"Us. This." He waved his hand around. "I shouldn't have let it get this far."

"Oh." Her voice hardened. "You're having second thoughts. Well, you sure didn't have any last night!"

"It was a judgement error and I'm sorry." He inhaled deeply. "I can't give you what you want, Rachel. I have to finish my masters and this novel… I'm busy. I don't have anything to give to you or anyone right now."

"You're breaking up with me? We finally break through to the next level of our relationship and you're ending it! You can't be serious."

"I don't want to hurt you by leading you on."

"I think it's a bit late for that! I thought we had something here."

"You were wrong."

Those three words were like a punch in the stomach. They took her breath away. "Why are you doing this?" Tears sprang to her eyes. "You have feelings for me, I *know* you do."

"I've just realized that things between us have gone too far. I'm not comfortable with it anymore, I'm trying to be honest with you."

"But you're not being honest, with me or with yourself. I know you don't want to end this." She stood up and and went to his side. "Look at me."

When he didn't, she hollered, "Look at me!"

He did but it was a true test of endurance to look up at her tormented face.

"Look me in the eye and tell me you don't love me. I won't leave until you do," she demanded in a quivering voice.

He answered firmly, his eyes fixed on hers. "I care for you, Rachel. I do. But not in the way you want me to."

She stared at him for a few more seconds and then swung around. "Fine."

She clamored around to find her things and once she had everything she had brought with her, she stormed towards the door without a backward glance.

"I was wrong to think you had grown up. You're still the selfish bastard you always were."

The door slammed behind her.

* * * * *

Rachel listened to him recall those tumultuous times and was astonished at how little things had changed between them over the years. They were still struggling with the same issues, and she was stupid enough to take him back, allowing him to hurt her time and time again.

They got together three months after that, when he dug out her crumpled faded phone number and called her on a dark, lonely night. They stayed together almost six months before he got cold feet and withdrew again. A few months later she called him, and they were together almost seven months before the same thing happened. It became a sick pattern, and Rachel fell for it every time.

Her mother, Joyce, watched her only daughter fraught with agonizing despair over each break-up and asked her one day when she was weeping on her bed. "Why do you always go back to him honey, when you know that he's eventually going to break your heart again?" She placed her hand on her daughter's back to comfort. Rachel didn't raise her head from the pillow and simply uttered in a muffled voice. "I don't know."

"There are other boys out there. Boys who would treat you better." Joyce simply did not understand what kind of hold this fellow had over her.

"I don't want anyone else. I wish I did," Rachel sighed bitterly.

Her grandmother, Barbara Sheldon was most concerned about the situation and requested to see her alone at their next visit. They sat in the expansive library over tea and Rachel was awed as always at her grandparents' marvelous home. Her grandfather, Henry, was a respected doctor from an accomplished, wealthy family and though she was proud of her ancestry, it was only the men that had made the grand achievements. The women took care of the homes, the children and volunteered for hospital fund-raising and charitable events. And though these were noble things to do, it wasn't what she wanted to do with her life. Her grandmother couldn't understand that.

"No self-respecting young woman chases a man. My goodness, didn't your mother teach you the basic art of attracting and keeping a mans interest?"

"I guess not, Nanna," Rachel said wearily and sipped her tea.

"In my day, women did not behave in such a loose fashion. I'm appalled. Really I am. To hear of you going back to this fellow time and time again when he keeps breaking it off." She fluttered her eyes in frustration. She was an attractive woman in her seventies with long grey hair bundled into a tidy french twist. Her make-up was always immaculately applied in bold colors, her nails were regularly manicured and coated with gleaming red polish and her colorful, flowery dresses were from the finest stores in Toronto. Barbara was so feminine and proper, so unlike herself, that she sometimes wondered if they were truly related.

"Really, Rachel," she scoffed. "I'm surprised at you. I thought you would have done much better for yourself. You're a pretty girl but you're not a young woman anymore, you're options dwindle each day."

That was it, she had had it. It was hard enough to live with the rejection but to justify herself over and over again to her relatives and friends was getting to be too much. She slammed the tea cup down on the saucer and stood up.

"You know, Nanna, I'm just as appalled at you. When I was a little girl, you always told me that I could do anything I wanted. That if I wanted to live big, I had to dream big, like Papa did. But now I know that those were just words. You were full of shit."

Barbara wrenched back as if she had been slapped.

"Because I'm a girl, I'm really only *allowed* to dream of a wealthy, successful husband, a big house and nice things. To dream or pursue anything else wouldn't be proper. And forget about waiting for love, that's a minor issue because time is wasting and youth is fleeting. I got to hurry up and find someone before I'm old and ugly right? Well, I don't think that way, Nanna, I'm sorry to disappoint you but I have different aspirations than you, not better just different. And if you can't find it within yourself to accept me for who I am and what I do, than maybe I shouldn't come and visit you anymore."

Barbara took a moment to think before speaking and then said coldly. "Sit down."

"If you're going to give me a lecture, I'm leaving."

"*Sit* down," Barbara seethed, not used to being talked back to. Rachel reluctantly sat back down and folded her arms defiantly.

"It's obvious that you have the Sheldon spirit. If your grandfather were alive, he'd be very impressed. You may be partly right on some issues but there's one thing I have to say in defense of what I said earlier. If this fellow, Daniel, can't see you for who you are and how wonderful you are, than he doesn't deserve you." She reached across the coffee table and grabbed her granddaughter's hand.

"It hurts me to see you treated so poorly time and time again. You could do so much better. Why in the world do you keep going back for more abuse?"

"Because he's everything I want in a partner. He's talented and artistic, and much more intelligent and articulate than anyone else my age. He's driven and successful but not arrogant in the least. He's very modest about his accomplishments. He's different from any man I know, the way he thinks and analyzes the world around him. And, Nanna, he's so gorgeous. Movie star gorgeous, you know. You'd have to see him to know what I mean. He's perfect except for one thing."

"What would that be?"

"His repression, his complete indifference to the world around him. Since his father died, he has this sad, lost look on his face most of the time. As if he has a huge hole not just in his heart, but in his soul. It's obvious that he hasn't healed certain wounds but I know that if I could just reach him and get him to open up then…"

"You can't change him, Rachel," Barbara interrupted.

Rachel dropped her grandmother's hand and reached for her cup of tea.

Barbara put her fingertip to her chin thoughtfully. "Even if he is this intriguingly flawed but wonderful catch, it doesn't justify you dropping everything at a moment's notice every time he fancies your company. You have your pride, my dear."

"I don't want a lecture, Nanna."

"I'm just giving it to you straight. The fact of the matter is, I don't like where this is going and I don't think this man is the right one for you. Although I don't approve, my advice to you is this. If you're going to spend half of your life waiting around for a man to take notice of you, then at least make the *most* of that time. Don't make it even more of a waste."

"I'm not *waiting* for him to take notice of me," she replied indignantly and gulped her tea with a flushed face.

"Of course you are."

"No, I'm not!" Rachel repeated.

Barbara stood up, sick of her granddaughter's stubbornness and walked out of the room haughtily with her dress billowing dramatically behind her. While leaving the room, her hand on the golden door handle, she declared, "Rachel, if there is one thing I learned in the three years of nursing I did in the ICU where I met your grandfather, it's that you can't save someone that doesn't want to be saved. If he's as wounded and conflicted as you say he is, then he'll never be able to give you what you want. He'll be too absorbed in his own issues, his own pain. Perhaps you should think long and hard about how long you're willing to wait for a man…and about what that says about you." With that, she left the room, closing the door sharply behind her.

Rachel did think long and hard about her words, and they became the motivation she needed for what she did next.

* * * * *

In 1974, Daniel finished his masters program at the same time that he completed his third novel, *The Devils Moon*. The following fall he was starting the Doctoral Program in English Literature when *The Devils Moon* was published. It surprised everyone, he more than anyone else, by racing up the bestseller lists from coast to coast and topping them for a solid three months. He became a worldwide name and sales for his other two novels doubled. Talks were in the works of adapting *The Devils Moon*, a story of a young security guard working on death row who bonds with a spiritually reformed convicted murderer whose life story changes his opinion on capital punishment and life itself, into a screenplay.

Soon, he was the talk on campus, and was asked to make speeches at not only his own school but at colleges and universities across the country and at various social functions, academic clubs and book stores. His publishing company encouraged him to go on book signings and readings to promote his work while several reporters from mainstream newspapers across North America begged him for exclusive interviews. He found the attention invasive, shied from it and refused to promote his own work. He told his exasperated agent 'that his words would sell themselves'.

Masterson was beside himself with excitement with Daniels success, and drove to London, a rare event for him to leave the sanctuary of his beloved study, to congratulate his favorite pupil. They went to dinner at a popular steakhouse and clinked their bottles of beer in celebration.

"I knew it the moment I read it, that this was the one that would make it into the big-time."

Daniel simply smiled politely and drank his beer.

"I thought you'd be more excited." Masterson pushed his menu away and leaned over the table. "Is something wrong?"

Daniel looked around the crowded restaurant and mulled the right words. "No, it's just...I didn't think it would be like this. I thought it make a bigger impact...you know, change things."

"What would make a bigger impact?" Masterson asked in confusion.

He shrugged wordlessly. He wondered why he had such a tough time articulating his thoughts, when he could so successfully express them on paper. It didn't make any sense. He wanted to say that he had hoped that writing a best-selling novel would make a bigger difference in his life. A positive difference. But if anything, all it did was make things more complicated. But he didn't want to sound as if he were complaining about his success, and be misinterpreted, so he held his tongue.

"So, what would you like, boys?" A pretty waitress approached them with her notepad in hand. They both ordered the special; a steak, medium rare with baked potatoes and steamed asparagus. When she bustled off, Masterson pulled two thick cigars from his jacket pocket.

"I was saving these Cuban's for a special occasion and this is as good an occasion as it gets." He handed one across the table. Daniel took it and lit it up, though he hated the pungent taste and smell of cigars. It was then that he realized, as the world appeared to move in slow motion around him and the words that Masterson spoke blurred inaudibly, that he would have to work even harder to find whatever it was that eluded him. To find what would fill the emptiness that plagued him every day.

* * * * *

Daniel honed his craft and developed a unique, polished writing style that distinctly set him apart from other writers. He wrote five consecutive novels in the upcoming years and all of them went straight to the top of the bestsellers lists. *The Home*, *Diary of a Madman*, *The Redemption of Jimmy Vine*, *Narrow Escape* and *Embodiment of Evil* enamored the public and critics alike. He swept almost every literary award out there, and became a major contender against literary icons. Since *The Devils Moon* film was the surprising smash hit of 1976, earning an Oscar nomination for supporting actor, Larson Giles, screenplays were in the process of being developed for *Embodiment of Evil* and *The Redemption of Jimmy Vine*.

He decided to take a year off from writing novels and devoted all his energy into finishing his dissertation. At this point, he could afford to slow down his pace a bit. Once it was completed and presented, and he was no longer a student, he accepted a part-time teaching position at The University of Toronto within the English department. He moved to a trendy, expensively furnished condo near the campus and started teaching Restoration and Eighteenth Century Literature, Shakespeare, Medieval and Renaissance Literature and Creative Writing. When he wasn't teaching or marking papers, he worked on his ninth novel, titled *The Holy Fires*, about a priest who questions his faith after witnessing a brutal murder.

In 1978, he learned that he was in the running for the Booker Prize, the worlds most prestigious literary award for his seventh novel *The Redemption of Jimmy Vine*. He didn't attend the fall ceremony but learned that he had lost to popular British writer, Mary-Lynne Bonds. Her book, *When Angels Cry*, about a young girl living with her alcoholic, abusive parents garnered the top prize.

He was bitterly disappointed at the loss. It drove him into a miserable funk mood for several months on end, though he had little to be disappointed about. Financially, he was set and paid off his mother's loans and took over her monthly bills. Even when he had paid off his hefty student loans, he still had plenty of money to burn. He went out and bought a brand new BMW, plush leather furniture, and an extensive leather-bound collection of literary classics similar to what Miss Temple had in her office in Steinem. He hired a carpenter to build solid oak book cases to hold his first edition books, and made his spare room into an impressive library that he spent a fair amount of time in.

His teaching salary greatly paled in comparison to what he made writing, and though he could afford to write full-time, he liked the idea of being part of the academic community. He wanted to belong to something, but still needed a sense of control where he could distance himself at will.

He was often frustrated by the bureaucratic and administrative aspects of teaching, but thoroughly enjoyed the creative exchange of ideas with students and fellow teachers with mutual interests. He put up distinct barriers, though; only discussing work or art-related issues and declined to go out with other faculty members socially, where he would need to converse on a more personal level. He kept to himself; using his free time only to write and read, and rarely left his home, which was a five-minute walk to campus. He was familiar and comfortable within this solid academic environment; the structure, rigorous routine and high standards suited his driven, solitary personality.

He hadn't spoken to Rachel in over a year, since she read one of his books and called to tell him her thoughts on it. Their conversation had not ended on a pleasant note and he hadn't bothered to contact her since. She was busy herself these days. Her discussion with her grandmother that one afternoon had inspired her to what she had always aspired to do. She mustered enough courage to make her career dreams a reality. Dreams came at a price though.

She had to borrow a substantial amount of money from her parents and promised to pay them pack in full, with interest. She started her own music studio near downtown Toronto that she fittingly called 'Sweet Melodies'.

She hired three other instructors that were 'Royal Conservatory' trained to teach piano, flute, violin, guitar and theory and also hired out musicians for weddings, funerals and special occasions. Initially, it was touch and go, but eventually the idea took hold and the business started to thrive. Piano lessons for young children was the most popular service, becoming their primary source of income. Eventually they didn't even have to advertise because parents talked, and word-of-mouth was the best advertisement anyway. Within five years she paid off her delighted parents and built a second studio on the other side of Toronto. Business was booming, and with time she discovered the sharp entrepreneurial spirit that she never knew she possessed.

Though she was busy, Rachel often thought of Daniel. She had boyfriends come and go but never once considered actually marrying any one of them.

Her parents provided a strong example of what a solid, loving marriage should be like and she wouldn't settle for anything less than that. She wouldn't commit long-term until she fell in love, when there were no hesitations, and the only person she had ever felt that passionately about was Daniel. She couldn't even imagine being with anyone but him, but had reluctantly accepted the fact that it was not meant to be.

Though they were both far too busy with their demanding careers to be concerned about the lack in their personal lives; in quieter moments, when their thoughts turned inward, each pondered what could have been.

* * * * *

They arrived at St. Evans Memorial at seven- thirty that morning and pulled into a parking space. They had actually made pretty good time though Daniel scarcely remembered the bulk of the time spent on the road. He was so absorbed in his recollections that he hadn't even noticed how fast he been driving. Now that he was thrust back into the present, he recalled his mother's unstable medical condition and felt a sharp stab of trepidation.

The sun was attempting to peek out behind dismal clouds, but it was still fairly dark. A dewy sheer mist had enveloped the town of Tarlington following the rain. As he stared at the large medical building blanketed in fog, he was struck by how ominous a hospital appeared. In that moment, it looked like a place of death.

"You didn't actually kill your father…did you?" Rachel asked quietly, staring pointedly at the looming hospital.

He followed her gaze. "All I know is, a part of him died right before my eyes that night. The part that mattered anyway."

"What do you mean by that?"

He shrugged, indicating that he would not elaborate. She knew that pushing him would only seal his lips even tighter.

She unbuckled her seatbelt and turned to him. "Promise me something. Promise me that when we leave here tonight, you'll finish telling me what happened between you and your father the night he died."

Daniel sighed and agreed, recalling that that was his purpose in the first place anyway. But as always, that night laid in his memory like a bare, gaping hole that he was terrified to tread upon. He didn't know what might happen if he did. He wasn't ready to be exposed yet, or ready to face the torrent that would follow when he did. He put his fingers through his hair in agitation and got out of the car.

As they walked into the Emergency department, he astonished her by reaching for her hand. As they walked through the automatic doors together he involuntarily shivered and muttered gravely, "I don't have a good feeling about this."

Part Three

Chapter Eleven

When they walked into the hospital, Daniel noticed his family seated in the sickly green painted waiting room, directly across from the admitting desk.

They looked like a sullen, dejected bunch; obviously they hadn't received good news if they had gotten any news at all. He consciously had to force one foot in front of the other towards them, willing himself not to turn around and run before they saw him. Rachel sensed his apprehension and pulled him along gently. Kate saw them first and rushed over to them, her face completely washed of any color.

"I'm so glad you came!" she cried out and wrapped her arms around his neck forcefully. She shuddered against his shoulder and he lowered his head, using her hair and body to shield himself from the others view.

Kate looked terrible. Her once beautiful long locks were now drastically cropped to chin-level, totally without its lively luster or curl. She had gained a bit of weight and wore shapeless blue jeans and a rumpled over-sized sweater that did nothing for her figure. Her eyes were puffy and red, her nose an even brighter shade of red and her dry, bloodless lips quivered nervously.

"Is she all right?" he asked.

"No." She pulled back and pressed her trembling fingertips to her lips. "She's in surgery but they said her odds weren't good. They told us not to get our hopes up."

She was trying desperately to restrain herself and he gave her a lot of credit for that. Under such dire circumstances, one was apt to succumb to emotion, especially if a person was as sensitive as Kate, but she was trying hard to hold it together.

Rachel slipped in between them and gave Kate a big hug. "It was so nice of you to come," Kate gushed and clutched her tight. He was in constant amazement at how affectionate and consoling women could be, how they always knew what to say and do in situations like this. It was like they were bred for this nurturing stuff. He was stuck for words at the best of times.

After they pulled apart, and dabbed their eyes, Kate grabbed both their hands and led them into the waiting room. "Come see the others."

Daniel was shocked to discover that he barely recognized his own sisters.

Evie and Maddy, or 'Eve and Madelline' as Kate told him they liked to be called now, had changed considerably. They sat beside one another, as close as their seats would allow. Two tired-looking men were slumped beside them, Daniel assumed that they were their husbands. They had both married young, right out of high school and had children right away. Maddy had three kids and Evie had two. They weren't little girls anymore, they were young women now; Evie was twenty-four and Maddy was twenty-seven. They were very similar in appearance. Both had thin straight hair that fell down their back, parted in the middle, strong jaw lines and gorgeous deep blue eyes. Evie had a splash of freckles across her nose and cheeks that was the only distinguishable feature between them. There were three years between them, and just one year between he and Kate. As children, he and Kate had been inseparable and it was obvious, by the way they sat so close to one another, that these two were as thick as thieves. Kate and he bore no resemblance to them, and it was strange to think of those foreign-looking women as his sisters. They shared the same blood but that was all.

"Look who's here, everyone!" Kate exclaimed in a loud voice in the waiting room doorway. She squeezed their hands and added quietly. "I know Mom would be pleased that you both came."

Evie and Maddy exchanged a quick glance to one another, folded their arms across their chests and stared coldly at their older brother. He gave them a polite nod and sat down on a plastic white chair that squeaked under his weight. Rachel said 'hello' to everyone and sat beside him. He tried to ignore the hostile looks shot in his direction from his estranged siblings and looked at the clock in despair.

The painful waiting process would now begin.

* * * * *

When the doctor finally came in an hour later, Daniel had nearly bit all of his fingernails down. Dr. Clarkson walked in with his clipboard and they all stood up anxiously to hear his news. He was a short man, roughly five-foot-five and his sweaty hair matted unpleasantly to his head giving him a young, frazzled appearance. He didn't look much older than them, he was probably in the late-thirties range. It bothered Daniel to think of someone so young and inexperienced operating on his mother, and wished that they had of taken her into the city hospital instead.

Dr. Clarkson cleared his throat. "I'm afraid I don't have good news."

"Oh," Kate gasped and put her hands to her cheeks. Maddy and Evie huddled close to one another and clasped one anothers hands. Daniel walked out of waiting room before he could hear what else the young physician who looked fresh out of basic anatomy class, had to say.

He put his hands in his pockets, leaned against the wall near the drinking fountain and stared at the many posted signs that related to health cards and flu symptoms. The admitting clerk was at the typewriter, her back turned to him, and it sounded like she was typing like a madman. He could hear the quiet, constant clicks of the machine. He could also hear the drone of the doctors voice behind him and the sudden gut-wrenching wails from his family that followed.

He continued to stare at the young clerk, who didn't notice him, who continued with her typing. She was going about her job as usual, as if nothing were out of the ordinary. As if people weren't sick, dying or mourning under the same roof as her. As if lives weren't being changed in mere seconds around her. What kind of person works in a hospital anyway, he thought grimly. How can anyone shut out the sickness, death and pain that prevailed here, and go about their job as if it were any other day.

The more he watched the frantic typist, the more angry he became with her, as if it were her fault that he was here this morning with the many antagonistic women in his life, hearing news of his mother's death. Young Dr. Clarkson suddenly came up beside him and looked as if he were about to say something but Daniel freed him from the anguished search for the right words.

"She's dead isn't she."

"I'm afraid so. I'm sorry, but we did everything we could," he said gently.

Daniel wished that he could say the same.

* * * * *

Kate wanted to make all the arrangements and that was fine by everyone else. Maddy and Evie were inconsolable, and left together with their husbands straggling behind. They were all going to meet at Kate's later in the afternoon, after they had gotten some much needed rest and composed themselves. Daniel couldn't imagine napping, but he had only had three hours sleep the night before and his energy was waning. It seemed like yesterday was weeks ago, so much had changed in a matter of hours.

"You'll stay at my house of course," Kate declared whilst wiping her nose with a tissue. Her husband worked at the same tire plant that their Uncle Steve had once worked at, Frank had just gotten off the night shift and was on his way. She had called him to tell him the dreadful news and he was driving to the hospital as they spoke.

"No, that's nice of you to offer but we wouldn't want to impose." Daniel thrust up his hands. "If I remember correctly, there's a bed and breakfast just outside of Aldon, 'Cozy Cots' I think it's called and we'll go there if there is a room available."

"Over my dead body!" Kate exclaimed and after realizing what she had said, her eyes teared up. "I mean, that doesn't make any sense. We have a spare room and the kids would love to see you. You're family, how could we possibly make you rent a room somewhere!"

"Really Kate, it would make me more comfortable. I appreciate the offer but respectfully decline. Don't take it personal." His words were firm and she threw her hands up in exasperation. Rachel was in the bathroom and was not around to defuse the situation.

"Don't take it personal. That's funny. Don't take it personal!" she repeated in a loud, fervent voice. She put her hands to her face, sat down on one of the chairs and sobbed hard. Letting out all of the pent-up emotion she had tried hard to suppress, by habit, in front of her younger siblings. Fortunately, they were alone in the waiting room, and only the unaffected typist was about to hear.

"You don't know what it's been like," she wept. "After Dad died, everything changed. It was like we lost you and Dad all in the same day. It was so hard on Mom."

Daniel turned away and bit the insides of his cheeks.

"She would never tell you how much she missed you or how proud she was of you. Sometimes, you were all she ever talked about and it drove the girls up the wall. But in her eyes, you could do no wrong."

"Kate, I don't want to hear it," he exhaled and put his hands through his hair in frustration. He could see Rachel coming down the hall towards them.

"I don't care if you do or not. You need to know how much you hurt her when you didn't call or visit. She always let on that it didn't bother her but we all knew it did. That's why Madelline and Eve are so mad at you, you might have noticed that the two of them have no use for you at all. But they didn't grow up with you like I did, didn't know you like I once did. I don't resent you, you're my little brother and I love you, but there is one thing that gets to me. You never appreciated the wonderful woman that gave you all the opportunities that you have now." Kate stared hard at his back and added coldly. "You never thanked her once for all the sacrifices that she made for you."

Daniel swallowed hard and licked his lips. "I never meant to hurt her Kate. It was just…too painful to talk to her, to be around any of you. It hurt too much because…you all reminded me of him." His revelation startled him, as if the words had slipped out of his mouth unconsciously.

"I miss him, too, Daniel," she whispered and his breath caught in his throat. "We all miss him, but you can't…"

"Everything okay?" Rachel appeared in the doorway.

"We'll be at your place around five," Daniel stated shortly and left the waiting room without so much as a backwards glance.

* * * * *

They drove in complete silence to the tiny bed and breakfast three miles south of Aldon. Rachel wanted to ask him to finish telling him about his father's death but knew that it wasn't the right time to bring it up. She felt funny knowing that not once on the drive up, had she considered that Maria could actually die. She knew that her condition was serious by the tone of Kate's voice on the phone, but it was hard to believe that someone as young as Maria could have a fatal heart attack. It was unreal.

It was known to most that Maria had a few medical concerns, but none were considered life-threatening, and were well monitored by her physician. She had high blood pressure, diabetes and chronic back pain from a fall off a ladder in her youth. Kate was a registered nurse, worked days at the nursing home in Aldon, and had been giving her mother her daily insulin injections because Maria's fear of needles prevented her from doing it herself.

And because she and Kate were good friends, and had kept in touch since meeting one another at Daniel's graduation, Rachel was fairly certain that she knew more about Maria's health then her own son did. Nonetheless, her sudden death was still a shock.

Rachel looked over to Daniel who remained stoic and unreadable. She wanted to reach out to him, but wasn't sure how, and doubted he would willingly accept her attempt to comfort anyway. She was right.

* * * * *

Cozy Cots was a charming rustic two story log cabin, with only four rooms, set back into the bush, on a slight hill. They weren't going to enjoy the 'cozy' atmosphere though. At the front desk, Daniel rented a room for two nights. He tried to hand the cash to the stout, middle-aged proprietor, but the man was busy eyeing his messy signature on the check-in sheet.

"Bradley. Are you related to Maria Bradley?" he asked.

Daniel stiffened. "I'm her son."

"Really? So you're the writer, she always talked about you." He smiled warmly. "Your mother is quite the woman, I have to say. My son, Jeremy, whose eighteen now, had a real problem way back in school. Couldn't read or write or nothing, just couldn't quite grasp it and his fifth grade teacher wanted to hold him back. Your mom had this tutorial reading program up at the library a few nights a week back then, and we signed him up for that and within a few months his grades sky-rocketed. Whatever she did with him really clicked and he actually started reading and doing homework on his own, voluntarily! He passed, went on to sixth grade and has just been going strong academically ever since. He's off studying agriculture at Guelph now, wants to farm and he surely wouldn't be there if it weren't for her. We've always thought that Maria was one class act. Just a wonderful woman all around, you tell her I said that and that George, Myrtle and Jeremy say 'hello'," George said with a floppy grin. Daniel stared at him vacantly. He didn't want to cause this man, who obviously cared for his mother and thought very highly of her, any pain by telling him the truth. That he couldn't tell her the good news about Jeremy because she was lying motionless on a cold steel slab in the morgue. That her days running children's programs at the library were over.

She was gone. He couldn't induce that much pain and grief. Not in this kind man, and not within himself.

"I'll tell her." He took his room key from George's hands and walked away. As he walked back to the car, he thought about how strange it was that his mother had a life of her own that he had never known, or thought to ask about. There were probably many children whose lives she had enhanced through her many literary programs. They were her gift of love. And wasn't she the one who had ignited his own passion for reading. She, who had read to him before bed each night when he was a little boy, and lovingly taught him not only how to read and write but the importance of acquiring such knowledge.

As he hauled his luggage out of his vehicle and took it into the cottage, he remembered the love that his mother had for books and how she wanted to share not only with her own children, but with the entire community. He thought of the success that he had achieved, and knew that although she was immensely proud of him, it was what she had always aspired for herself. He was living her dream, and didn't even have the sense to enjoy it, share it or attribute it to her.

And now it was too late.

* * * * *

It wasn't until he stood before their door, attempting to unlock it with his key that Daniel realized that they hadn't paid for two separate rooms, that they would be rooming together. But it didn't really bother him if it didn't bother Rachel. They were adults, and he wasn't in the mood to be concerned about silly sleeping arrangements. Once inside the small room, he dropped his suitcase to the floor and sat tiredly down on the edge of the bed. It was just after eight o'clock in the morning but he felt like he been up for a week.

"I just can't believe it. I can't believe she's gone." Rachel put her hands to her temples and walked to the end of the room. Daniel flopped down on his back and stared at the ceiling, willing himself to fall asleep. Sleep, he thought, would be a nice escape right now.

"I hadn't talked to her in over a year. That's awful isn't it." Rachel sat down on the plush floral patterned chair in the corner.

"I hadn't talked to her in months, Rachel, and I'm her son for Christ's sake!" Daniel spat feeling anger well up in his chest.

"What are you thinking right now? What's going through your mind?" she asked airily and her tone reminded him of the endless shower of questions Miss Temple used to unload on him when he was young. He wasn't in the mood for that sappy psychological crap right now.

"Rachel, I'm not in a conversational mood," he growled.

"Tell me what you and Kate were talking about when I came back from the bathroom. I could sense the tension between you two, I know it was about something serious," she inquired, ignoring his malicious tone.

"I'm going out." he stood up abruptly.

"Where are you going?" she asked in surprise.

"Anywhere but here." He stomped to the door, grabbed the door handle and stopped. "I'm sorry. I don't mean to take this out on you. I just can't…talk about my family. Not right now."

"Don't leave." She came up behind him. "Stay here. We don't have to talk, I promise I won't ask you any more questions."

He opened the door. "I'm sorry, I just need to be alone for a while. I won't be long."

"I don't think you *should* be alone Daniel. Not right now, not when you're upset like this."

"I won't be long," he repeated, stepped out and closed the door behind him.

They both stared at the closed door for a long time before moving.

* * * * *

He drove to the liquor store, beside the sole coffee shop in town, but it wasn't open until nine o'clock. He had a half hour to kill. He decided to get a coffee and tour his hometown, to see how much had changed in twenty years. He doubted much had. Aldon was a quiet retirement community populated primarily by retired farmers and blue collar folk. The biggest event in town was Thursday night bingo for the seniors, the annual Tractor Pull and the monthly Ladies Auxiliary Bazaar and Bake-off. There was one public elementary school that held one hundred kids but the high school was shut down ten years earlier, now students were bused to Tarlington High.

All that the town had to offer was visible from the main street. It was pretty much indistinguishable from any other small town in North America. There were two gas stations, a ball park, arena, funeral home, drug store, a nursing home, one restaurant, "Smitty's' that recycled their specials every other day, a grocery store, post office and a two story public library that only opened for two hour time blocks due to lack of government funding. There were two churches on opposite sides of the street, one United and the other Catholic. There was a Presbyterian and Baptist church in Tarlington that several Aldon residents went to, though the majority of the population were Catholic.

Employment was scarce in this area, other than the tire plant and "Carling Construction', there were few opportunities for young people to earn their way. Many went away to college and trade school after high school and never returned. One could hardly blame them.

There was a weekly newspaper, aptly titled 'Aldon News' that mostly followed the seniors activities, town council meetings and local sports teams. Once in a while they would do a write-up on Daniel, the writer who had published yet another best-seller and feature a picture of Maria smiling candidly with his book in her hands. His mother had sent him those clippings and at the time he had been embarrassed by them and threw them out. Now, in hindsight, he regretted doing so. He would have to get a copy of those articles from Mr. Jefferson, the aging newspaper reporter.

He walked into the noisy coffee shop and felt all eyes on him at once. The conversation immediately subsided. Someone dropped a spoon somewhere in the room and it clattered loudly to the floor. It appeared as if everyone had frozen stiff at the sight of a new face, and he remembered that small-town folk were known for being a curious, close-knit bunch. Here, he stuck out like a sore thumb with his slick hairstyle, designer slacks and a BMW parked out front. He was once one of them, he was born and raised in this area, but it didn't matter though. It was brutally obvious that he wasn't one of them anymore.

He went to the counter and ordered a large black coffee from a pimple-faced teenager who looked all of sixteen. He could hear the muffled disconnected discussions around him;

"That's the Bradley boy isn't it?"

"Maria's boy. Danny is his name. He's a big-shot writer in Toronto now. Remember they did an article on him last year?"

"Look at the clothes he's wearing, whose he trying to impress!"

"Went to some uppity private school in Rowland when he was a kid. Hasn't been back since."

"Do you remember her husband, Joe? It's been almost twenty years since he died, if you can believe it."

"I read Isolation, his first book. Gruesome thing, I couldn't even finish it. Where do people get ideas like that? It's terrible I tell you. Kids shouldn't be allowed to read such filth. I won't be reading any more of his books, you can be sure of that"

"Probably thinks he's too good for this town. I wonder what he's back for, he hasn't visited his mother in years. Poor thing, after all she did for him."

"Farm accident I heard. Some equipment fell on his head when he was working on it and it crushed him. Terrible way to die."

"I heard his sister Madeline and her husband were trying for another. She's such a pretty girl but those kids of hers are a handful. I wonder why she wants another one."

"I wonder how Maria is doing. I saw her last week in the post office and she looked kind of rough. She's living with her daughter Kate and her *husband Frank down on the tenth line."*

It was funny that his whole, thirty-two year existence could be broken down by a complete stranger into fragmented, uninformed gossip. Apparently, everyone in the Sussell County seemed to know the barest facts of his life. That he was Maria and Joe's boy; his father died a strange and tragic death, he went to an uppity private school somewhere and was now a big-shot writer in Toronto who neglects his mother. At least the facts were correct. That was essentially his life in a nutshell, and it was rather depressing when it was blatantly laid out like that.

But the idle gossip was to be expected and didn't really bother him until he heard two men sitting at a table behind him talking quietly. He heard the name 'Joe' and it sparked his attention as the girl behind the counter handed him his coffee. The men were speaking softly but he could clearly hear each word that they were saying.

"Crazy as a loon I'll tell you what. He came into the co-op that day, ranting about prices and injustice of this and that for decent hardworking family men. Couldn't pay his bill and pitched a fit, right then and there in front of Bergman and everyone. It took three of us to throw his sorry ass out, and he's one tough bugger, so it took us a good long while. He was still screaming outside when we shut the doors on his face and he went to Bergmans truck and started kicking the shit out of it. We all went running out and wouldn't you know it but he wanted to take us all on, the crazy bastard. I never saw anything like it. Two days later he's dead, some accident they said. I don't think it was no accident though." a stubbled, greasy looking fellow in overalls whispered to his buddy, leaning over his cooled eggs. "I think he went off the deep end for good and killed himself. He was way in over his head at the bank, Lucy Talsbury later told me. She was working as a teller then. He had to pay for his boys schooling and had a real bad crop that year. If I recall correctly, we had a real wet April that year. I heard that there were troubles going on at home, which didn't surprise no one either. I think he cracked under the pressure and offed himself, which ain't no big pity. No one would miss a miserable old bastard like him. I couldn't stand the man myself. I always thought that there was something off about 'im"

"Here's your change, sir." The teenager held out the coins to Daniel but he was too busy glaring intensely at the counter, and ignored her outstretched hand. She was taken back by his sudden flushed face, and the thick chord of veins that enlarged at a rapid speed on his neck. He looked as if he were a balloon, ready to burst. Daniel swung around, eyes blazing and approached the two men who were unaware that he was so close.

"I didn't really know the man." The man across from the gossiper shrugged. "Saw him about town and at the co-op, but that was about..." He stopped mid-sentence and looked up at Daniel's glowering face.

"You got something to say about my father?" Daniel placed his hand gruffly on the big-mouths shoulder and gripped his collar. "'Cause it certainly sounds like you do."

"Look fella, I don't know what your problem is but I wasn't..." the man stumbled on his words as Daniel one-handedly forced him out of his chair.

The chair thumped to the floor behind him and the noise echoed in the silent restaurant. Everyone was watching. Two middle-aged men from opposite sides of the room stood up as if they were going to intervene, but merely stared at Daniels size in leery indecision.

"If you have something to say about my father, I'd like to hear it!" Daniel kept his death grip on him, and when the man didn't speak he shook him roughly with both arms.

"Why don't you have anything to say *now*, you spineless piece of shit!" he hollered, mere inches from his face, spittle flying from his lips. He had an overwhelming urge to bash this puny man to the ground, beating him to a bloody, unrecognizable pulp. But memories of the two other times in his life that he had lost control of himself and reacted violently flashed before his eyes. The time that he had fought Justin. And the time he had confronted his father. His gut churned as he remembered the blood that night, so very much blood, and the sickening defeated look in his father's eyes.

He let go of the trembling man's collar and stepped back. He slowly walked backwards to the front door, eyes cemented on his would-be opponent, not caring about the many pairs of eyes that watched him with fascination. He left the coffee shop, but stood stationary in front of its doors, not knowing where to go next.

"Crazy as they come. Just like his father," someone quipped when he walked away, breaking the unusual silence in the restaurant. Everyone instantly broke out into loud, gleeful conversation. They hadn't had so much excitement in years.

* * * * *

Rachel had just come out of the shower, and was dressing when Daniel walked in the room. She didn't ask where he had gone. If he wanted her to know, he'd tell her.

She noticed the paper and plastic bags in his hands and asked. "What do you have there?"

"Vodka and orange juice. Your favorite right?" He put the bottles on the wooden dresser, produced two white paper cups from the plastic bag and uncapped the refreshments.

"It's just after nine o'clock in the morning, Daniel. It's a little early to be drinking," she chastised with a frown, tossing the towel she had used on the bed.

"Orange juice is a morning drink. I'm just jazzing it up a bit," he reasoned, pouring his own cup half full of liquor.

"Daniel." She placed her hands on her hips. "Getting drunk isn't going to make things easier."

"I'm not getting drunk." He turned around and handed her a cup. "I just need to relax and this will calm me down."

She pushed the cup away. "I'm not drinking with you."

"Rachel," he groaned. She walked to the other end of the room. "I'm not asking you to get pissed up with me. I'm asking for you to…" He pondered for the right words. "To just be a friend. To sit back and let things happen without analyzing and questioning me. If you want to help…" He offered the drink again with an extended hand. "Then just have a drink with me. That's all I ask."

"Daniel." She bit her lip in frustration. "This isn't going to help you. Every time something new or unpleasant happens in your life, you try to run from it and escape into your isolated, familiar little world. Usually you hide in your writing and your career but you can't go anywhere right now. You have to face things, you have to face the reality of your life. I won't let you find another way to hide."

"I'm going to have to face my mother's death every day of my life from here on out, Rachel." He slammed her cup on the dresser. "She's gone and I can't hide from that. I want to have a couple drinks to dull the shock of the news, that's all. Now you can either join me or judge me like you always do." He drained his own cup in one, swift gulp.

"I'm saying this as your friend, all this misery you've been putting yourself through, it has to end sometime, Daniel. Or it's going to kill you."

Daniel turned his back towards her and poured himself another stiff drink.

Before he put the cup to his lips he said quietly. "You asked me if I killed my father and I did. No matter what anyone says different, I know what I did and I have to live with that. And now I have to live with the fact that I never had the guts to tell my mother the truth about what happened the night he died." He drank the contents and squeezed the cup until it broke into soft pieces in his hand.

"It all comes back to that night doesn't it. What happened, Daniel?" Rachel stepped closer to him. "Tell me what *really* happened that night."

He sighed in resignation, walked to the bed with the vodka bottle in his hand and plopped down on the edge.

"Daniel..."

He was ready to, now. Ready to tell the truth. "It started over dinner the Friday night before I went back to school. My mother made a roast, my favorite, and we were having a nice, quiet meal until my father walked into the kitchen..."

Chapter Twelve

Daniel looked up from his gravy lathered mashed potatoes when he heard the screen door slam shut. His father who was usually moderately drunk at this time of the day marched into the kitchen, looking like a man on a mission. He approached the table and put his large, menacing hands on the back of Katie's chair. His blood-shot eyes flashed lethally at each one of them and they stiffened in his presence. He was tensed too. He appeared to Daniel like a vicious cobra poised to strike. The only questions was, who his next victim was going to be.

"I saw your brother Steve in town not an hour ago," Joe growled at Maria, who looked away from his dreadful, reptilian eyes. "He told me about your little arrangement. Nice to know what my wife's been up to these days, since she don't tell me shit."

Maria placed her palms delicately on the table and said to her children, "Take your plates to your rooms and finish your supper there. Don't come out until I come and get you. Your father and I need to talk alone for a few minutes."

"Mommy, I don't want to!" Evie wailed, but Katie immediately grabbed her arm and pulled her out of the room, despite her protests.

"Mommy and Daddy need to talk in private Evie, they won't be long. We'll just go upstairs for a bit." Her voice was strained and almost unrecognizable.

Daniel picked up his plate and hurried out of the kitchen, too, but stopped around the corner. There was no way he was going to leave his mom completely alone when his father was like this. He placed his back against the wall, closed his eyes and waited for the fury.

"How much did you borrow from him, damnit!" Joe exclaimed loudly and slammed the kitchen table with the palm of his hands.

"Just a few hundred. Just to see us through. We were in overdraft and the bank was calling every day. Danny's school needed their bill paid this week, and I didn't know what to do," she explained in a high-pitched squeal that disturbed Daniel because of its desperation. His mother shouldn't have to plead like that, not to her own husband.

"We don't need charity for Christ's sake!' Joe swiped at the chair in front of him and knocked it over. "Not from your family, of all people."

"Steve offered and he's doing well at the plant. He could afford it on his salary and said we didn't have to rush to pay him back. He was just happy that he could help." She stood up, hands nervously gripping her apron.

"Yeah, I bet he was only too glad that he could fucking help. That's just what I need, all your in-laws to know we're having money problems. They'd love that wouldn't they, another reason to hate me. To prove that you could have done better." He paced the kitchen floor like a wild, caged animal. "Well it was *your* idea to send the boy off to school in the first place, knowing full well how much it cost. His bloody education is sending us to the poorhouse woman; with the cost of his uniform, room and board, books, phone bills and gas to drive him there and back. And whose fault is that! It's not mine, is it!" He lunged forward, grabbed her by the arms and shook her. "Is it! Is it!"

"No!" she screamed, and tried to push him away.

"That's right! It's *your* fault! All of it!" he hollered, and punched her hard in the face with his right hand.

She whimpered and fell back onto the chair. She touched her lip meekly and gasped at the blood on her fingertips. Daniel couldn't take any more, he dropped his plate and hurried into the kitchen, eyes glued on his cowering mother. Joe turned his way.

"You want in on this, boy! You really should be part of the discussion anyway, because it's all about what you and that damned school are doing to this family!" He lifted one side of the kitchen table up, tossed it on its side and slammed it back down. All the plates, food and glasses smashed to the floor, Maria cried out in surprise. Daniel backed away from the mess and a cold shimmer of fear raced up his spine. His father didn't say another word, merely looked them over with steely eyes, as if challenging them to make a sound or gesture.

Neither one moved, so he fumed off, like a tornado leaving its devastation.

Daniel rushed over to his mother, stepping over broken glass, cutlery and remnants of a beautiful home-cooked meal to look at her swollen, split lip.

"Are you all right?" He crouched before her. She nodded and turned away, tears brimming her skittish eyes.

"He's not always like this," she said softly. "It's just a stressful time. He can't help feeling frustrated."

"He's mad at me, Mom, he has no right taking it out on you." He stood up, got a cloth from a drawer, dampened it with cold water under the faucet and handed it to her.

"He doesn't mean to hurt anyone, he's not like that. He'll be sick with guilt now, and he'll apologize later, he always does." She bit her lip, knowing she had said too much.

"So this isn't the first time he's hit you." Daniel's fear did a swift one-eighty, and a furious rage swept over him at the thought of this kind of violence being a regular occurrence in his home when he wasn't there.

"No." She put up her hands and gripped Daniel's collar. "No, he's never done this before. He's never hit me, I swear!" But her voice although frantic, was hollow and insincere. He closed his eyes, shook his head and stood up slowly.

"Get the girls and leave. Go to Uncle Steve's or Aunt Ruth's. Go anywhere, just get out. I'll handle it from here." His voice sounded alien to him, it was controlled and authoritative but there was nothing even remotely controlled about how he felt. His body was bursting with an intense adrenaline laced energy, that left him feeling insanely powerful and restless. A dangerous combination under any circumstances.

"Daniel, no. Don't do this." Maria stood up and a trickle of blood ran down from her lip and pooled in the cleft of her chin. She had never seen Daniel so angry; he had always been quick-tempered, like his father, but he had never gotten this upset before. The sight of her son's face red with uncontrollable fury scared her more than anything Joe had ever said or done.

"Go, Mom."

"I won't let you do this," she said, and tears drenched her stricken face.

"And I won't let him hit you or anyone in this family again! Now go!" When she didn't move he screamed at her, and felt the urge to shake her himself. "GO!"

She left, fear and panic motivating each step, and it was then that he decided what he had to do. He watched the girls leave through the living room window, turned around and walked through the kitchen without even noticing or feeling the crunching of glass and broken plates under his sock feet.

He went to the front closet and found what he was looking for.

* * * * *

He walked to the shed, knowing that's where his father would be. He carried a wooden baseball bat in his left hand, liking the solid weight of it in his grasp. He knew there would be a confrontation and he wasn't going in there unprepared. The man he was about to quarrel with was not the same man who had raised him; who had patiently taught him how to play baseball and to drive the truck and tractor. This was not the quiet man he loved with all his heart and respected with all his soul. That man was gone. He didn't know who this man was, but he wasn't going to allow him to destroy his family.

* * * * *

"You're a real piece of work," Joe laughed coarsely when he cautiously entered the shed, bat in hand. Joe was sitting across the dirt-covered room, in front of his messy workbench, sitting on an upside down pail. The light was dim in there but Daniel could see that he was holding a smoldering Matinee cigarette in one hand and a Budweiser in the other. He was leaning forward, face passive, elbows on his knees looking almost comfortable and relaxed. Not looking like a man who had just barged into his own house, screaming bloody murder and destroying everything in his path. Daniel didn't understand his mood swings, and there was no way that he was going back to school when he was so unstable. In his mind, he was now the man in the house and had to take control of the situation. He was trying to do the right thing and all he meant to do was to exchange words. That's all he meant to do. To sort everything out once and for all.

He approached his father, the bat hanging lifelessly in his hand.

"You gonna hit me with that?" Joe scoffed when he got closer, and took a drag from his cigarette.

"I told the girls to leave. They won't be coming back tonight, I thought you should know," Daniel replied flatly, his heart feeling like it was going to thrash out of his chest. It was then that he realized how ridiculous the bat was, that it merely amplified the intensity of the situation instead of giving him protection and a sense of confidence.

"You told them to leave," Joe repeated, sniffed and took a long drink of his beer. He completely drained it and with one swift movement, threw it against the far wall, smashing it to smithereens. "You've been home, what, a week after being away for almost a year and already you think you run the place. I knew that school would change ya. You're gonna turn out like every other arrogant asshole I know in a suit." Joe horked and spit a good chunk of phlegm to the left of him.

"I don't think I run anything. I just saw how scared Mom was, how scared everyone was and I thought they should leave until you cooled off," Daniel reasoned but there was a distinct edge in his tone.

"You think I should cool off." Joe smirked. "My *son* thinks I should cool off." Although he was grinning, the smile did not reach his eyes. Daniel brought the bat up, hackles rising in him like a dog that sensed danger.

"Well what the fuck do you know!" Joe shouted, his voice echoing obscenely within the small building. Outside, Daniel could hear thunder rumbling and it was terribly ironic to him, that a storm was brewing outside the thin, crumbling walls of the shed.

"I don't know anything." Daniel backed up a step.

"Well, then why am I paying through the balls for your fancy education if you don't know nothing!" Joe stood up and flicked his cigarette to the floor.

"Look, I just came out here..."

"You just came out here to tell me what you think, and I don't give a rats ass *what* you think. Unlike everyone else you know, I don't care how smart you are." He stepped towards him. "I own this land that you're standing on boy, I own everything here. The house you live in, the food you eat and the clothes you wear. Where do you think it all comes from! It comes from *me* and the work and sweat I put into this place. But none of you care though, you don't care as long as you get what you want and your lives run smoothly. Do I get any respect or thanks for the sacrifices I make? No! Not from you or from anyone in this family!" Joe barked. "Do I get a say in anything? No, because no one cares what a dumb hick farmer thinks." He stopped in place, his eyes glazing over. He looked down at the floor, chest heaving. "I'm a small fish in a big aquarium, son, and when you're this small, you get eaten by all the big sharks and sons-a-bitches swimming around. You'll even get nipped by the other fishes, the ones you thought you could trust."

"Dad..."

"Just go. Go to your mom and sisters and tell them what a jerk I am. Call me every name in the book, persuade your mom to leave if you want. Tell all your aunts that they were right about me. That I'm poor, stupid mean drunk that ain't good for nothin'. Tell'em what they want to hear. " Joe turned around and waved his hand dismissively. "'Cause I really don't give a shit any more."

Daniel dropped the bat and rushed forward. "I didn't come out to fight you, and I don't want Mom to leave. I just...I don't know what to do." his voice cracked.

"Be the hero." Joe reached for his cigarette pack on the workbench, sat back down on the pail and shoved one in his mouth. "Tell em' you scared me good."

"It's not like that." Daniel shook his head.

"Make yourself useful then." He lit up the cigarette, and gracefully snapped the zippo shut. "Go inside and get me a cold beer."

"All right." Daniel swung around to run inside but his father's booming voice behind him stopped him dead.

"If you really want to do this school thing, it's all right with me. It's not about the money, I want you to know that. It never was about the money."

Daniel slowly turned back around, jaw dropped.

"It's not what I wanted for you, but I've come to think that every man has his own course in life. If this is yours, then I can deal with it, under one condition. You go all the way with it. You stick it out and give it *everything* you have. No son of mine is going to be second-rate." His voice shook with intensity. "Ain't no one in that school better than you, no matter where they come from or how much money they got. You're just as bright as any of them, if not brighter and you let'em know it. You show'em what you're made of, do your best and that'll be enough for me." He took a deep drag. "Now go get me that beer."

Daniel could barely move, his knees felt weak and unsteady. He froze, feeling the powerful significance of the moment. His father had never talked to him like that, and he was totally thrown off guard. Joe leaned forward woefully, lowered his head and clasped his hands as if he were deep in thought. Daniel took that as a cue to leave, though he didn't want to. He found his balance and ran. Outside, gentle beads of rain coursed down. It dampened his shirt and moistened his hair. He went up the steps, swung the back screen door open, and raced inside the house, stumbling over the mess on the floor to the refrigerator. Jumbles of incoherent thoughts rambled through his frazzled brain as he opened the door. Bottles clanked and rattled noisily. He reached for the chilled beer on the top shelf.

It was then that he heard the gun shot.

* * * * *

He would never remember running back out to the shed, but he must have, because within seconds he was out there again with a scream in his throat.

Neighbors would have heard the gun shot but attributed it the oncoming storm, mistaking it for thunder. But Daniel knew what that sound was, it was his father's double-barrel shotgun, the same gun Joe had used to put Sam out of his misery earlier that year. Apparently, he was trying to do the same thing for himself.

The sight before Daniel was as grisly and horrifying as death can ever look.

Joe Bradley was slumped on his side on the floor, with thick red blood pooling rapidly around what was left of his face. Half of his head had literally disintegrated in the blast, and remnants of it were gruesomely splattered across the sheds floor and walls.

"NOOO!" Daniel screeched painfully.

He dropped the bottle of beer, bolted to his father's side, knelt and gawked in horror at his corpse. There was no question whether he was dead or not. The fact that his brain was no longer intact concluded that question rather quickly.

"No, Dad, no! Nooo!" Daniel achingly cried out, clutching his father's lifeless hand to his tear-streaked face. "Why! Why did you do this!"

He sobbed, and squeezed his hand as hard as he could as if to awaken him.

All of his limbs shook violently, and a physical animal pain ripped through his chest and left him breathless and immobile. After a few moments, he leaned to his side and vomited on the floor in disgust and shock. He screamed and cried in that position for over two hours, holding unto his father's hand in utter agony while the storm raged loudly outside. When the rain died down, and the thunder rolled away, he kissed his father's limp fingers and sluggishly went inside the house to call his mother.

* * * * *

"Oh, my God," Rachel whispered and put her hands to her open mouth.

"I remember each second of that day as if it were yesterday. I relive it every day, and some nights in my dreams. How his face looked with half of it gone, with everything spattered all over the place and all that blood. So much gore and blood, I can't believe how much blood there is in a person."

He shook his head. "I go over what would have happened if I went traveling with Harold that week, like he asked me to, instead of going home. If I had of just said or done something different all that time that my father and I were together. If I hadn't gone out to the shed at all that night to talk to him or if I had of refused to get the beer that he asked for. After hearing that little speech he gave, which was his way of saying good-bye... I should have known! If I had of done *anything* different, maybe he wouldn't have done what he did. Maybe he'd still be alive."

He felt like a small weight had been physically ripped off his back, now that he was talking about a subject that had been bottled up for so long. But talking about it didn't change anything. His father still didn't have a pulse.

"You can't think that way, Daniel," Rachel admonished. "You can't take responsibility for what he did. That was his choice, he made the decision to take his life. You were just a teenage boy, you were just a kid when this happened."

Daniel ignored her. "It's the whole 'what if' thing. What if I hadn't gone to private school, if I had of adamantly refused to go in the first place then they wouldn't of had to worry about paying for it and he'd still be alive probably. It all came down to my education. My father resented the fact that I wasn't going to become a farmer, like him, when that was all that he had ever wanted for me. And if that wasn't bad enough, he had to pay tooth and nail for my expensive schooling, digging himself in the hole for something that he didn't even want. He already thought we all thought that he couldn't provide well enough for us, so when Mom went and borrowed money from my uncle, it was like a permanent slap against his pride and self-respect. Everything went spiraling down from there."

"Daniel listen to yourself. You're *digging* for reasons to blame yourself and you had no control over any of that." She got up from her chair, crawled on the bed and settled in beside him. She snatched the vodka bottle from his hands and placed it on the nightstand. "Come here." She held out her hands to him. "I want to hold you." She reached over and hugged him, startling him with her assertiveness but eventually he sank into her arms.

"That explains so much. So very much. You really should have told me sooner," she whispered into his neck.

He closed his eyes, and allowed himself to enjoy her affection for a moment.

"You were just a kid, Daniel. You have to remember that. You were just a kid," she repeated but he knew that his age meant little in the grand scheme of things. The only thing that mattered was the fact that his father was dead.

And to him, it didn't matter who physically pulled the trigger.

* * * * *

They slept in the small double bed together that night, their back and buttocks leaned comfortably against one another in the sweltering heat.

Neither one minded their closeness, it wasn't really the time for awkwardness. They had slept together so many times, and were so absorbed in their thoughts, that each found the others presence comforting.

Because Daniel was mildly drunk, he slept fitfully and spent most of the night staring at the alarm clock and listening to the repetitive communications between crickets and other chatty forest critters. He thought about that long ago day, when his father had impulsively picked up his shotgun, and pictured himself doing something different that would have changed the course of events.

He thought about his father's final words to him, and analyzed what they had meant. Joe had labeled himself as a 'poor, stupid, mean drunk' but Daniel had never once thought of him that way. Joe was not dumb, merely stuck in the ways of the past and too stubborn to adapt to change. He was a good man. Daniel believed that and knew that he had never meant to hurt anyone. That was why he had killed himself; because he couldn't stand to see the pain that he was causing in his family, or endure any longer the pain within himself.

Daniel closed his eyes. It was only in those harrowing moments before Joe took his life, that he had begun to truly understand the man he called his father. He had never known how complex this simple man had been. And because he had contributed so greatly to his misery, he would never forgive himself.

* * * * *

In the morning, they woke early and had a quiet breakfast downstairs. Daniel planned to visit Kate after breakfast to find out what was going on with the funeral arrangements but Rachel had a different idea on how to spend the morning.

"I want to make a stop before we go to Kate's."

"Where do you want to go?" Daniel asked, while pushing a greasy, unappetizing slab of sausage around his plate with a fork.

"Your parents' house. I want to see where you grew up, Daniel, where all this happened."

He dropped his cutlery.

Chapter Thirteen

His apprehension over seeing his parents' farm and confronting the very essence of his past, dissolved the moment he turned in their driveway. The house had been empty since his mother had moved to Kate's five years ago, immediately after Steve married and moved to Tarlington. It was obvious that no one had been coming down to maintain it, for its condition was appalling. The burnt lawn and dry flower beds were completely covered with thick, imposing weeds and dandelions, and the bushes were terribly overgrown and out of control. The white paint on the house had chipped and faded and the windows were streaked with dirt and grime.

Maria would be mortified. She had always strived to keep her house looking as orderly as possible, even when her children were young and she was terribly busy and over-worked. Daniel noticed Kate's black Ford truck parked at the end of the drive and pulled up behind it.

"I thought one of the girls would try to keep this place up," Daniel commented sharply as he turned off the engine.

"They're a bit busy, Daniel. They all work, and have a family and house of their own to take care of," Rachel reasoned as she unbuckled her seatbelt.

"That's no excuse for them to let Mom and Dad's place go all to shit. If they had of told me they weren't doing it, I'd hire someone myself to come in and take care of it," he replied and climbed stiffly out of the vehicle. He had a raging headache, and a rolling stomach from the previous days binge and wanted nothing more than to sleep half the day away. But he had already burned a bridge by not showing up at Kate's yesterday, so he had to make a good appearance today. The front door opened and Kate, herself, appeared on the porch. He was a little annoyed that she was even here. He was hoping to have the place to himself for a bit to ease his way down memory lane.

"I had a feeling you'd come out here this morning." She forced a weak smile and leaned her belly against the shabby, unstable wooden railing. She looked pale, her hair was dull and wiry and it looked like she hadn't slept a wink.

"Look at this!" Daniel approached the flower bed in front of the house and kicked the dry, weed-covered soil in distaste. Maria had loved her flower beds and had spent many loving hours tending to it. What would she think of it now? "Who the hell is responsible for keeping this place up?"

"You are!" Kate answered rigidly. "You own it, don't you remember?"

"I own it, yes, but as you recall, Kate, I live in Toronto. Since I was footing the bill, I figured the least the rest of you could do was take care of it," he snapped, putting his hands on his hips.

"Right. So while Mom was living with me, and I was taking care of her and all of her numerous medical needs as well as taking care of my own three kids and husband, and working on top of that, I'm supposed to race over here and make sure this place is in tip-top condition. Come on, Daniel, give me a break."

"Well, you should have told me then!" he growled. "I would have sold the place! It's ridiculous to have it rotting away like this!"

"I've brought this house up many times with you over the phone and you *never* wanted to talk about it! You always changed the subject so I gave up trying!" she exclaimed.

She was right, he never liked talking about this place or about his parents period. Yet another thing to feel guilty about, he thought as his eyes roamed and scrutinized his childhood dwelling.

It felt strange to be home, everything was the same but still very different. Although it was deteriorating, it still felt like home to him mostly because he could sense his parents all around him. Memories flashed before his eyes; swinging on a large tractor tire hanging from a tree with his sisters, playing in the sandbox, teaching Sam how to sit and shake a paw on the freshly mowed lawn, and weeding the flower beds on hot summer days with his mother. These were all good memories, times he hadn't thought about in almost twenty years.

"I don't want to fight with you," he relented and looked up at Kate who was near tears. "I just don't like seeing it like this."

"I don't either," she murmured. "But this isn't the time to talk about it. Visitation is tonight, the funeral tomorrow morning. I came over to get some pictures of mom to place on her…on the coffin."

"Do you need any help with anything?" Rachel asked gently but Kate shook her head.

"It's all taken care of, thanks. Are you two going to be at the funeral?" she asked pointedly and he was angered that she thought so little of his character to even ask.

"Of course we'll be there," he muttered irritably

"Be at Collins Funeral Home tonight at seven then, for the vigil."

"We'll be there," he repeated, and walked around the house to get away from her patronizing looks and to see the building that had troubled his thoughts for nearly two decades.

* * * * *

The sky above him was blue and cloudless. He gazed up at it as he walked behind the house, trying to distract himself from the inevitable. It was a beautiful, warm summer day and much too bright and cheery to be thinking about death and family turmoil. But that was exactly what he was doing. He walked two feet from the shed and stood there uncomfortably until Rachel came up beside. They stared at it for a few awed moments before she asked softly. "This is where he did it?"

He nodded, and wondered suddenly why his father had always called it a shed. It was originally built by his grandfather to be a small prairie style barn to store hay, feed and farm machinery. It stood alone, two hundred feet from the other barn that once held livestock, against the backdrop of fluttering corn fields. It had a cathedral ceiling projecting over the hayloft, was fifty feet tall, thirty feet wide and was once a solid and structurally sound building. Time and weather had not been kind to it. It clearly needed extensive work and maintenance to restore it back to its prime condition. The weathered grey siding was rotting, there were numerous holes in the steel roof caused by heavy rain, and the whole thing looked like it could collapse at any second. The sad-looking building emanated the very depth of deprivation and neglect, reinforcing every emotion he knew his father had felt in his last moments here.

Daniel closed his eyes and remembered how big the interior of the shed had looked to him when he was young. It was one big play room as far as he was concerned. He recalled jumping from the hayloft to the bales ten feet below and getting screamed at by his father when he later discovered the broken bales. He would get a swift spanking for it, but it didn't dissuade him one bit because the next time he got the chance, not only would he do it again, but he'd encourage his sisters to do it, too. He remembered the prominent smells of hay, oil, gas and dirty farm machinery in there. And even to this day those smells reminded him of his father.

He once loved spending time in the shed; following his father around and helping him fix equipment, stacking hay into the loft or puttering around under the hood of his beloved Ford Truck. Sometimes they didn't even do anything in there. On rainy Saturday afternoons, they'd sit idly on upside down pails, with Sam at their feet, and take a 'few moments to themselves' as his father liked to call it. Sometimes, if Daniel was lucky, his father would talk about his grandfather. Joe was never much of a conversationalist, but somehow these moments would stir up his memories and loosen his tongue. He would describe to his son his own childhood days in a time long past. As he'd smoke, his quiet words would resound through the shed and fill Daniel with a sense of pride for the land he lived on, and the heritage he belonged to. His father would cease to be a mysterious, unreachable being, and become a person just like everyone else.

He loved those times with him. It was their special time together. Daniel tried hard to focus on those good memories of his father here, instead of the single horrible incident that occurred here in this building that would mar its existence forever.

Daniel pursed his lips, deep in thought, arms folded tightly. As much as it bothered him to see the shed again, it disturbed him more to see it in such decay. He either wanted it to be used and in working condition or to be completely demolished. Not rotting away like this.

"I need to talk to my Uncle Steve about what to do with this place. Everything is just falling apart, it's ridiculous," he muttered and turned around to walk back to the house.

"Daniel," Rachel placed her hand on his arm gently. "Maybe right now isn't the time to worry about this. There are other things to be concerned about."

She nodded towards Kate, who was walking towards them soberly.

"I'm going over to Madeline's, I just talked to her on the phone. Eve's there now and we're all invited down for lunch if you're interested," she called to them.

"We'll be there!" Rachel replied with a wave and Daniel gave her a stern look in return.

"Okay, see you there!" As Kate turned back and headed towards her truck, Daniel laid into Rachel.

"What'd you say that for! I don't want to go there! I wanted some time to myself today before we went to the funeral home!"

"This isn't the time for you to be alone, Daniel, you have to be with your family now. They need you and you need them. You're going to spend as much time as you can with them the next few days if I have any say about it," she said harshly and walked away from him.

Before he followed behind her, he cast one last pensive look at the lonely, rotting building that begged for attention.

* * * * *

Madeline Moloney and her husband Darryl lived in a busy cul-de-sac on the south side of Aldon. They rented a small, one story white-sided home that was essentially the size of Daniel's rec room. When he first walked in the front door, he grimaced at how cluttered and plain it was. Everywhere he looked there were unfolded laundry, dishes and toys. So many toys. You'd think they had ten kids instead of three. Their furniture was a sickly purple covered in stains, the thin walls were papered green that was falling off in some places and nothing even came close to matching. His own condo was tidy, spotless and lavishly furnished. It was pristinely cleaned from top to bottom once a week by two expensive house cleaners that he had prudishly chosen. The three things in his life that he insisted upon was cleanliness, routine and order. He knew he got that from his mother, who got that from her own mother. Obviously, Madeline hadn't pick up on the tidying genes. He walked towards the open kitchen and stepped painfully on what turned out to be a Leggo. He decided to tread carefully from then on.

Madeline declared that everyone should congregate outside since neither the kitchen or living room could hold all the couples and their children. He headed out the back door and tried to stay out of the childrens' way. They ignored him completely and raced about in their own little worlds. The women stayed in the kitchen, and busied themselves with preparing a cold lunch, while the men sat awkwardly together on lawn chairs watching the children run amok. Eve's husband couldn't get the day off and had to work at the insurance office in Tarlington, and Frank had to work as well, so that left only him and Darryl.

"So, you're a writer," Darryl commented after a long moment of silence and Daniel nodded wryly at his stiff attempt at conversation.

"Yes, I am."

"I read two of your books. *The Devil's Eye...*" He inhaled on the cigarette in his mouth.

"Moon. *The Devil's Moon*, you mean," he corrected him.

"Sorry, you're right. '*The Devil's Moon...*'" he emphasized it and exhaled a great cloud of smoke. "And *The Redemption of Jimmy Vine*. I heard they were making a movie based on that, is that true?"

"Well, their *trying* to make one. Their having trouble writing the screenplay and the studio is having problems finding the right director," he replied and sipped his glass of lemonade.

"Well, it's a good book. I liked it. I don't read much, but I thought I should read it since you know, you're family and all." He smiled wanly and Daniel smiled back. Darryl didn't look like an avid reader. He had a thick, long mullet cut that touched the back of his shoulders, which complimented his unruly moustache and side burns. He wore tight, holed blue jeans and a faded Jimi Hendrix t-shirt. His large, stubby hands looked dirty and rather unsightly; a permanent oil stained souvenir from his work as a mechanic at a body shop in Tarlington.

The conversation become stagnant, so Darryl started the long process of digging for, and lighting up another cigarette. Daniel looked over at the eight children playing and giggling merrily on the plastic slide and in the wooden sandbox. He envied them terribly. They didn't know yet or comprehend the fact that their grandmother was dead. The older ones, Kate's children would take it harder, when they were faced with the fact, but it was possible that the other ones would never even remember Maria. It was sad really, that these kids would never know or appreciate what a wonderful person their grandmother was. They were too young to even realize what they were missing. Yet here he was, near his middle thirties and hadn't fully realized it himself.

Maddy appeared at the back door and wiped her hands on her red apron. "Lunch is on!" She called out to her children to come inside and shot Daniel a strange, leery look before going back into the house. That look said it all. She didn't want him here. She was right, he didn't really belong here anyway, and wished Rachel hadn't made him come in the first place. They were his family, yes, but clearly in name only.

"Well, better get the kiddies some grub," Darryl grunted and stood up, probably grateful for a way out of their pathetic conversation. Everyone charged into the house to fill their plates but Daniel stayed behind to let the adults help the children with their meals. The kitchen was so small that not everyone could fit in there anyway.

Rachel came outside and sat down on a lawn chair beside him. They could hear the parents calling out, above the clatter, asking their kids if they wanted mustard or mayonnaise, plain or rippled chips, or juice or pop. The kids were still playing and screaming, it literally sounded like a zoo in there and Daniel was relieved for the slight reprieve.

"It's a lovely day isn't it," Rachel stated, looking up at the opaque sky.

He tilted his head and whispered sourly. "I want to go soon."

"Daniel! How can you say that! This is your family..."

"Yes, I've heard that speech before and I *know* their my family," he cut her off. "But I feel out of place here and want to go back to the bed and breakfast to relax. It's been a stressful few days. We'll see everyone tonight and all day at the funeral tomorrow anyway."

"I can't believe you." She shook her head with annoyance. "You haven't seen your family in how many years and now that your mothers died and you have to spend a *little* bit of time with them, all you do is bitch about it." She slapped her hands on her legs and stood up.

"Fine, whatever. I'm sick of arguing with you about it. Do you want to go now?"

"No, and keep your voice down," He shushed her, fearing that they could hear them through the open kitchen window. "We'll leave shortly after lunch."

"Just eat and run. Yeah, that's polite." She put her hands on her hips.

He seethed internally, her sarcasm was getting under his skin. Why couldn't she see his side and empathize, just once.

"Go on in, you two, there's lots of food," Eve proclaimed as she herded her kids out the screen door and balanced their plates of food in her hands.

While she attempted to get them seated long enough to eat, Daniel and Rachel went inside. By that time, most everyone had their plates filled with sandwiches, chips, potato salad and deviled eggs, and were heading out to the picnic table. Daniel picked up a paper plate and fork and warily eyed the kitchen around him.

"Looks good." Rachel reached over the old Formica metal table and picked up a slice of egg salad sandwich.

The kitchen was painted in a harsh, almost blinding mustard yellow. A 1950s Frigamatic fridge purred unhealthily in the corner beside a debilitated stove. Everything, from the utensils and plates to the tiled floor, looked cheap and used. It suddenly occurred to him that his sister could be in financial trouble. Looking around this place, it certainly appeared as if she was. He had never even thought of his sisters having money woes, but Madeline hadn't worked as a clerk at the drug store since the birth of her first child, and it wasn't as if Darryl would be raking in the cash as an unlicenced auto mechanic in a small town. A sick feeling rooted in his stomach at the thought of them struggling to pay their bills, when he was hoarding half of his wealth away and squandering the other half.

"You're not hungry?" Rachel asked.

"Not really. I feel kind of sick." He set down his own plate. "I think I'm going to sit on the couch for a few minutes."

"Daniel, you really should come outside. You can't hide in here, it won't look good."

"I'll be out in a few minutes," he promised as he walked into the living room, ignoring her advice. She stood, with one hand on her hip and glared disapprovingly at him. He moved some toy cars and a forgotten piece of cheese off the seat of the couch and plopped himself down. Surprisingly, it was soft and rather comfortable. He leaned his head back against the cushion, closed his eyes and listened to the distant sounds of children laughing and chattering outside. He heard the back screen door slam, and was pleased that Rachel had left him alone. A few minutes of silence was all he needed.

But that wasn't in the cards. Within seconds he distinctly felt like he was being watched and opened his eyes. Madeline's oldest son, Josh was staring boldly at him from the hallway. He had just come from the washroom and was curious to see who was sleeping on his couch.

"Hi." Daniel sat up straight. Josh was eight years old, he knew that much at least, and had straight blond hair cut incredibly short and bright blue eyes.

He was tall and gangly for his age; a mirror image of his mother with a sweet angelic baby face and pert nose. Josh scurried into the living room and sat on the floor across from him, in front of the chipped coffee table.

"You're Josh, right?"

He nodded seriously.

"I'm your Uncle Daniel."

"I know," he replied and reached under the table for something. "My mom told me about you. You write books."

"That's right."

"She won't let me read them though. She says their adult books, and I can only read them when I turn sixteen."

"Oh." Daniel smirked.

"I don't think she likes you much," Josh added and Daniel almost laughed at his keen observation. He didn't think his sister liked him much either.

Josh brought a plain box out from under the table and set it on the floor. "No one will play this with me. I got it for my birthday a few weeks ago, and

Mom and Dad don't know how to play and none of my friends do either."

"What is it?" Daniel leaned forward.

"A chess set." Josh looked up. "Do you know how to play chess?"

Daniel blinked rapidly, realizing he hadn't played since he had lost to Justin in the tournament so many years ago. "A little bit."

"Can you teach me?" he asked eagerly, eyes brightening.

"Sure," Daniel grinned. He settled himself on the shag carpet and grabbed the box to take out the board and pieces. It was a cheap plastic set, but it would do.

"Do you know the rules?"

"I don't know anything about chess," Josh answered unhappily. "You'll have to teach me everything."

"Okay. The ultimate goal of chess is to checkmate your opponent's king. Checkmate is when the king has no other moves to make and it's captured by his opponent. Each of the players begin the game with eight pawns and eight major pieces," he explained while he set the board on the table and set the pieces on it properly.

"There's one king, one queen, two rooks or some people call it castles, two bishops and two knights. Now there is a certain way to set up all the pieces and I can teach you that some other time, but for now you just have to know that the black pieces are set up directly across from their white counterparts."

Josh listened carefully, and watched every move he made.

"White always moves first, okay, so let's say that you're white. It's your turn. Now only the knight can hop its opponent's pieces. All the other ones have to move…" He looked up, sensing a movement at the other end of the room and saw Madeline staring at them from the doorway. She was carrying a couple dirty plates in her hands and had an odd, unreadable expression on her face.

"He's teaching me how to play chess, Mom!" Josh announced excitedly to her and she nodded.

"I can see that."

"Maybe he can teach you too so that you can play with me," he burst out and she frowned.

"I don't think we'll have time for him to teach me, honey. Daniel will be going back to Toronto soon, that's where he lives remember, so we probably won't be seeing him again for a while after tomorrow." She turned her back to them and went back into the kitchen where he could hear her toss the plates into the garbage.

Daniel gritted his teeth. If her purpose was to hurt him than she had succeeded. Her bitter words had stung.

"Is she right? Are you going back to Toronto?" Josh asked earnestly and Daniel turned his attention back to the chess set.

"Yeah, but not for a while. Alright, so the king can move in any direction. Horizontal, vertical and diagonal but the queen can only…"

* * * * *

"Checkmate," Daniel announced an hour later. Josh grabbed two fistfuls of pieces and thrust them at him.

"Set it up. Let's play again." His eyes twinkled vividly, his youthful energy and excitement was contagious.

"Alright." He looked down at his Rolex, remembering that not too long ago he had desperately wanted to leave. But that bleak feeling had passed, he felt like he could sit here all afternoon with Josh. Funny how ones perspective on a situation could change with the right kind of company.

He was thoroughly impressed with the kid. Josh was remarkably sharp for his age. He caught on quickly and asked intelligent questions. The game was a tough one to catch on to, but Josh was having no troubles at all with the basic concept. He took time between each move to think things through and didn't discourage easily. He was a bright boy.

Two hours later, Rachel came into the living room. She said quietly that she wanted to take a nap before supper and wanted to leave soon. He found it mildly amusing that after their argument earlier, she was the one that wanted to leave first. She sat down on the couch beside them, and they finished the game rapidly. When he had beat Josh for the third time, he started to put away the pieces.

"Do you have to leave now?" Josh asked forlornly.

"Yes, but I'll be seeing you again soon."

"Good, so we can play again sometime?"

Daniel nodded shyly. "Yeah."

"Thanks again for teaching me. It's a real good game." He scampered to his room and left Daniel staring off in wonder after him.

Rachel smiled sadly to herself upon witnessing the boys display of high aptitude. She whispered inaudibly. "Oh great. Another you."

Outside, they declared that they were leaving and said the customary farewells to their remaining family members. Eve had already left with her kids so that they could go down for naps, and Darryl and Madeline were languidly cleaning up toys that were scattered across their lawn. Kate was sipping lemonade on a lawn chair, looking fatigued and out of sorts.

When he and Rachel were walking down the drive-way towards the BMW they heard her racing behind and calling after them. They turned around to see what she wanted.

"I forgot to tell you," Kate said breathlessly and put her hands to her flushed cheeks. "I'm sure you figured as much, but you're a pallbearer tomorrow."

His shoulders sagged at the concept of carrying his mother's body in a box. For the last three hours, he had forgotten the reason why he was here but the heaviness of reality once again washed over him. "Who else is doing it?"

"Steve, Darryl, Gerald and Frank." She answered. Maria's brother and son-in-laws. She wasn't close to her other siblings, and most of them had moved away anyway, making it that much harder to keep in touch.

"That's an uneven number," he commented.

"It doesn't matter," Kate replied sharply, "Those were the important men in her life and that's whose going to be her pallbearers."

"Right." He looked down at the ground. "Fine."

"I'll see you tonight. Do you remember where the funeral home is?"

"Of course!" He walked around his car. "I remember more than you think, Kate."

"Good. Then I'll expect you there."

"Like I said, we'll be there." He unlocked his door and climbed into the suffocating stagnant air inside. Rachel and Kate continued to chat affably.

He turned the ignition, and waited for the air conditioner to kick in. An unpleasant shiver traced up his spine despite the raging heat of the afternoon. He thought about what he had to do in the next few days and felt physically nauseous because of it.

He was going to bury his mother.

She was dead and gone forever.

It didn't seem real. Of all the writing and research he had done on the subject of death, it was only now that he realized that the stark reality of it, and the wake it left behind couldn't be described with mere words.

Chapter Fourteen

He tugged uncomfortably at the confining striped black tie around his neck for the hundredth time the next morning. He had always considered a tie to be the largest, strangely accepted phenomenon known to man. How could a long, thick piece of colored cloth, wrapped and dangled from a man's neck make him appear stylish or more attractive. It didn't make sense to him. He was sure that a woman had invented the damn thing to torture men for all of the cruelties that they had been subjected to over time.

All these muddled thoughts dashed through his mind throughout the funeral service, as he focused on his physical discomforts instead of confronting the real reason that he was there.

The gleaming coffin at the front and center of the funeral home reminded him though. It was surrounded by lush, green flowers and had a picture of his smiling mother on it when she was in her early twenties. He couldn't bare to look at that picture. It wasn't just painful, it was excruciating to see her so youthful and glowing with a vivid radiance. She looked so beautiful in that picture, so full of life. He stared at his trembling hands on his lap and willed his mind to concentrate on something else. He needed to block out the hurt, the memories and the unmerciful guilt.

"We must remember that death *is* a part of life. It is a passage from this life to a new life, which was promised by Christ. This passage..." the sweating priest droned on but Daniel wasn't listening. He continued to squirm restlessly in his seat.

Five minutes later, Kate was called up by the priest to give the eulogy, and he watched her walk unsteadily to the podium, tissue in hand. He didn't want to hear her speak about his mother. He didn't want to see her cry or hear her reminisce. He just wanted to get out.

Kate leaned into the microphone, took a deep breath and spoke softly. "Anyone that knew my mother, would know how compassionate and kind she was. They would know much she loved her family and would see how much she selflessly gave to those around her. As far as I'm concerned, we are all blessed to have known her. She was a wonderful woman and left us much too soon." Her voice quivered.

"I'm not a good public speaker and cannot begin to articulate what my mother meant to me or how she impacted my life but I can tell you that she was my best friend and role model. She helped me through very tough times, and made sure I was alright even when she was troubled with her own problems. She was there whenever I needed her, no matter what, and always made me feel loved and wanted. As devastating as her loss is, I am comforted by the fact that she has left us for a far better place. We are all here for a purpose, and she achieved hers, by touching all of our lives in some special way. We say good-bye today but we will never forget, and we are forever changed by her goodness. Thank you all for coming here today, for joining us in the celebration of a beautiful life."

When she finished, her face was white and amassed with tears. She stumbled back to her chair where she collapsed into her husbands waiting arms.

Daniel swallowed hard and bit his lip hard to keep his lips from trembling uncontrollably. The entire room sounded as if it were sobbing, Kate's tears had caused a chain reaction, and he felt trapped beneath its weighty influence. The priest continued with the service, over the distracting noise of sobs and snivels, and then it was time. Time to carry his mother to her final resting place.

He stood up with the other men and walked towards the coffin.

* * * * *

Rachel watched him through her own tears, standing before the grave site with Steve and his wife under the intense, blazing sun. The priest had finished with his final prayers and the service was coming to a close. She looked around with wonder at the Aldon cemetery, which was located one mile east of town, and marveled at its natural beauty. It was clearly well tended to by someone with a green thumb and a passion for horticulture. It was literally a landscaper's dream with acres and acres of rolling green hills covered with lush, freshly mowed grass, exquisitely pruned evergreen shrubs and gloriously tall oak trees. Someone had lovingly placed fresh, colorful flowers of varying types in front of all the tombstones but the painstaking landscaping and thoughtfulness couldn't conceal the sense of death that prevailed here. The colorful and growing greenery didn't mask the fact that it was a cemetery. Home for the dead.

At the end of the service, most of the parishioners sobbed mutely with clutched Kleenexes as they walked back to their cars. Rachel stood up on tiptoes and scanned the area for Daniel. She couldn't find him, and turned to ask Steve if he had seen him leave. Steve was staring at the coffin, his right arm wrapped stiffly around his wife's thick waist.

"I'm so sorry, Steve."

"We were always close. Even when we were little. She was the youngest out of us all, just the baby." He raised his thick left hand, gripped his pudgy cheeks with his thumb and index finger and sobbed.

Rachel stepped away politely, feeling like she was intruding on his sorrow and looked around for Daniel again. She saw him in the distance, on the side of the highway, leaning against his BMW so that his back was turned to the crowd. How he got over there so fast, she couldn't even guess. She walked towards him, slowed down by her high heels that sank into the moist ground. Twice she thought she was going to trip and fall flat on her face but eventually she successfully made her way to the bottom of the hill, upright and unharmed.

"Daniel," she said as she walked around his car and approached him.

He was staring off into the distance, at either the forest on the other side of the highway or the ardent sun. She couldn't tell which. He looked wearied, his face pale, lips tightly drawn.

"Daniel. Are you okay?" She placed her hand on his shoulder. It was almost a full minute before he spoke.

"She's dead. It didn't seem real before but now…" He shook his head fervently. He didn't say anything for almost thirty seconds.

"I was a bad son," he said roughly. "Kate was right, I never even thanked her. After she fought for me to go to that school, scrimped and saved so that I could stay there, and sacrificed her marriage so that I could have a good education. She did all that for me…and I never even thanked her." a harsh, aching sob choked out of his throat and he blinked his eyes rapidly. She hated to see him in such agony, but in a sense, it was time that he finally realized that his choices and actions had consequences.

"There's nothing you can do about it now," she whispered as he stuffed his hands into his pockets in despair.

"You don't understand." He looked directly up at the sky. "No one understands."

"I want to." She stepped forward and wrapped her arms comfortably around his neck. He whispered into her hair.

"I never told her what she meant to me. I never told her that everything I am, everything I wanted to be was because of her. I loved her and she never knew that."

He sobbed mutely into her shoulder, his breathing coming in hoarse, violent gasps, his entire body shook. To her side, Rachel could see Kate rushing towards them, her own face as white as a sheet.

"Daniel," Kate croaked, placing her hand on his shoulder. He stood up to look at her. A primal sound escaped his throat as he pulled away from Rachel and threw his arms around his sister. Rachel could see Kate motioning to someone up the hill and turned to see Eve and Madelline staring at them with confused, anguished faces. Their husbands gestured for them to go on and it looked as if they were coming towards them, somewhat reluctantly.

Rachel stepped back, and allowed them space for what she assumed would be a private family moment. Eve and Madelline advanced on their older siblings, and Kate opened her arm out and allowed them into their awkward circle. The four of them were finally gathered. They were a strange unlikely group who seemed terribly uncomfortable so close to one another, but within seconds their barriers broke down and their mutual grief surfaced. Their cries were the sounds of powerful, pent-up and unleashed emotions that each had longed to express with one another for almost two decades. Their circle became smaller, as they gripped and held one another tightly and cried for the family that they had lost. They cried for many reasons, while other family members and friends watched and smiled sadly at the long-awaited reunion.

* * * * *

He sat idly on a hard church pew the next morning. It was the same pew and spot that he had sat in when he was a kid, on those long ago mornings when his mother brought he and Kate to mass. That was their special time together. Those memories were all he could think about any more.

He wasn't even sure Father Reilly was around, he could be waiting for nothing, but still he sat. His back started to ache from the uncomfortable pew, he began to shift his weight around painfully. He wondered why they didn't make these things more comfortable for people to sit on, and cursed when a sharp pain tore through his lower back. The weather was hazy and humid, the air thick and heavy. His brow soon moistened with sweat. But still he sat.

Father Reilly walked in moments later with a stack of music sheets in his hands. When his eyes met on Daniel's, they softened as if he had just seen a wounded animal. Daniel hated that look of sympathy and pity. People must think that that particular expression is comforting for one in mourning but in reality, it is more unsettling than anything.

Father placed the music sheets on the piano as Daniel walked up the aisle towards him. "Good morning, Daniel. I want to say again how very sorry I am about your mother. She was a wonderful woman, one that will be sorely missed in this community. My deepest sympathies," he said solemnly.

"Thank you, Father. I appreciate that," he said as they shook hands. "I was wondering if we could talk alone for a moment."

"Of course. Come with me." Father Reilly led him to a door on the right side of the sanctuary, hidden from view by the large pipe organ and down a long hall. At the end of it was his small office, a prim and orderly room, scarcely furnished. He sat in a wooden chair behind the bare desk, and Daniel sat on a faded green couch across from him. The room was drearily claustrophobic and he hoped the Father didn't spend much time in such a confining place.

Daniel rubbed his eyes while the priest settled into his chair. He decided to get right to the point. "It's been so long since I've been here, in any church for that matter. It's been a while since I thought about God or what I believe in. Since Mom died, it's all I can think about. How short everything is; what it all means and what I'm doing here. It sounds so philosophical and I don't want to get into a deep religious discussion with you about faith and the afterlife but…"

He trailed off and looked down at his sweaty hands. "Until now, I've never thought about my own mortality. I never looked at my life from a broad perspective. I've just been going day-to-day without thinking about where it's all leading up to."

"I have no idea where I'm headed, what anything means or what matters. I'm not going in the right direction, I can see that now and I want to make changes, but I don't know how." His voice faded. "If I died in a couple years, like my Mom and Dad who died very young, what would there be left for others to remember about me by? All I did was write a couple books, and that is all I have. All that will outlive me. I haven't done anything that really *means* anything, to me or to anyone else."

Father Reilly put his elbows up on his desk and clasped his chubby hands together. "You wouldn't believe how many people come and ask me what their life's purpose is, what their lives mean and what I think God wants from them. They usually come to me after a major event occurs in their life, like a death in the family or upon hearing news of a terminal illness. It is a tough question, one that a wiser man than I should be answering but this is what I think. I don't know what God wants from any of us, but I know what He doesn't want. This is my opinion, mind you, but I don't think He would want those he loves to pine and waste their lives away so meaninglessly. So many spend a good portion of their time on this earth worrying about money, their careers, their looks, their assets and the trivial matters of others.

"They grieve for loved ones, long dead when they are still very much alive. They ignore and take for granted the very things that matter most in their lives; like their health, their loved ones and their spirit. I could be wrong, but I think God only wishes for us to be happy, and to enjoy the many gifts that he has bestowed upon us. To me, one of the greatest sins against God is to waste one's life, to neglect the beauty that surrounds us every day and to wallow in unnecessary discontentment." He smiled wanly. "But that is only my opinion."

Daniel nodded, not knowing how to respond appropriately. Not sure if that answered his question or not.

"Did you know that the biggest source of stress in most peoples lives is worrying about things that they can't control? So much in our lives is beyond our grasp, so I'm advising you Daniel to let go of what you can't change. You weren't able to prevent your parents' deaths, therefore, you shouldn't let those events define who you are. It happened, and as despondent as you may be, you must eventually move on."

Daniels eyes narrowed at the mention of his parents' death. "What do you mean by that?"

Father Reilly sighed. "It's a small town, people talk. Your father was a troubled, troubled man. Your mother told me as much, and I also knew his extended family. I heard that you have taken his death quite hard, and are still struggling with it. I'm going to take this opportunity to tell you that there was nothing you could have done to have changed his fate. If he had his mind set on taking his own life, he would have done it sometime. It doesn't matter what transpired the day that he did it, the day before or the week before. Whatever happened between you and him that day would not have motivated him to do what he did. He would already have had thoughts of doing it or would have done it some other time. He was very disturbed."

"Stop it! I don't want to hear it," Daniel exclaimed. "I didn't come here to talk about my father."

"I think you did," Father Reilly challenged.

"You're wrong. It doesn't matter anyway…but he wouldn't have done it…even if he had thoughts of suicide before, he never would have acted on them until I…" Daniel stuttered, put his head in his hands and then raised it quickly with flashing eyes. "Don't tell me what you don't know anything about! You weren't there; you didn't see his face. You didn't see him…" He winced at the memory.

"Tell me what you saw. then," Father urged.

"I saw pain. A lot of pain. I think he thought I had betrayed him and that everyone had turned their back on him. When I walked in that shed that night, the way I did, I think he just decided to give up. What could be worse than having your own son turn against you."

"You don't know what he was thinking, Daniel. You…"

"And you don't either!" Daniel cut him off. "So don't talk to me about things you know nothing about." He bit his trembling lips.

"You can't go on living with this burden. The guilt is eating you alive." He was shocked at the violent change in Daniel's behavior. There was so much anger in him, so much self-directed fury.

Daniel looked up at the priest, and his eyes looked old and fatigued. "I don't know how to get past it." His normal, placid voice returned. "I don't even know if I should. Perhaps this is justice of a sort, punishment for what I did that day. All I want to do is just to forget it ever happened."

"You can't forget, Daniel, but you can forgive. Forgive your father for what he put you through and forgive yourself for what you consider to be wrong-doings. Pray for God's forgiveness, but more importantly, pray for your own. It's time you let go of that time in your life; you've paid the price for your sins ten-fold and it's time to move on. It's time to claim your life again, to find the happiness and peace that has eluded you. Give yourself permission to do that," Father Reilly said sternly.

"I don't know if I can," Daniel admitted.

"You will, Daniel. You'll get through this. Just being here with me today indicates that you're willing to try. That you want your life back."

"I do." He nodded to himself, eyes closed.

"Then it's time you did something about it," Father Reilly added softly, "Sometimes the greatest gift that God can give…is a second chance."

* * * * *

After Daniel left, Father Reilly reached into his desk drawer and pulled out his copy of Daniel's novel, *The Devils Moon*. It was one of his favorite fictional novels, for it superbly described the complexities of the human spirit, of the moral and ethical issues we struggle with on a daily basis. But more importantly, it was an uplifting story of redemption and courage.

Daniel was an exceptional writer, Reilly had read all of his books, and they were all wonderfully original but he noticed two common denominators within them all. The main character was always a male who had to face enormous personal challenges and appeared in constant inner turmoil and emotional conflict. This character was always introverted, flawed, and vulnerable yet morally strong despite of this. He would always rise to the occasion in the end and redeem himself, but the endings themselves were usually vague and much was left up to the reader's imagination. There was never any closure, no climatic moment that tied everything together or happy finish. His stories were realistic and left you wanting more. His characters were so remarkably complex and intriguing, and the pace so rapidly smooth, that it kept the reader interested and moved. He was a literary genius.

Reilly wondered if Daniel had noticed the similarities in all of his works, if he had planned that or if it was unintentional. He wondered if he noticed how similar his characters were to him, or if he had written himself into all of these novels unconsciously, while he worked through his own emotional dilemmas. He found it interesting that Daniel could write so aptly about emotional liberation and soul salvation when his own soul was still very much adrift.

Reilly sat back in his chair as he recalled a conversation he had almost twenty years ago, with Maria Bradley. He was not a remorseful man, he believed everything happened for a reason, but still kicked himself every time he thought about this discussion. It was the one true regret he had in his life. He could blame it on inexperience with dealing with these types of situations but the truth was, he had made a huge error in judgement.

Maria had come into the church one Sunday morning with Daniel and his sister and asked to speak to him alone.

He brought her to his office and asked her bluntly. "What is troubling you?"

"I don't know where to start." She had wiggled in her chair nervously. "I don't think it's right to speak disrespectfully of one's husband, I really don't, but I need to talk to someone about this. There is something wrong with Joe and I don't know what to do. He's changed somehow; he's not himself at all any more."

She put up her hands defensively. "But he's my husband and of course I still love him dearly."

"No one questions your devotion or commitment to your marriage vows, Mrs. Bradley." *He had reassured her.* "This conversation is completely confidential. Feel free to speak your mind."

"Okay." *She nodded and breathed in deeply.* "Joe, well, he's a complicated man. He's always been a quiet, moody person but he's never been mean or aggressive. Lately though, he yells all the time, exploding over literally nothing. It's not just with me but with the kids too. It frightens them...it frightens me. He hides in the shed and drinks most days and only does the bare minimum around the farm. We're just getting by financially, and it's getting pretty bad actually. I'm scared, I really don't see how we're going to afford Danny's school bills in the fall or even pay our basic bills."

She paused, lowered her head and said. "I thought once that nothing could be worse than living with my mother." *She looked up slowly and whispered.* "I was wrong."

She reached in her purse and produced a handkerchief. "I could endure it if it was just me but I see what all this tension is doing to the children. I resent him for it. I know that that's wrong to say but I do. I don't want a home like my mother's, where everyone is frightened and quiet and counting the days when their old enough to leave for good. I love my children too much for them to live like that." *She dabbed her moist eyes.*

"Why do you think your husband is acting this way? Why is he so angry? Think back to when he first started acting differently."

"It started when Danny left for private school," *she had answered without hesitation.* "We fought about him leaving a lot, and it was a sore subject between us for several months. I guess it still is. Joe wanted Danny to take over the farm and I want him to be educated and become a professional, like a doctor or a lawyer. Joe got so mad at me that he stopped sleeping in our bed and won't eat meals with the family anymore. He's totally withdrawn from all interaction with the family, and has even stopped speaking to all of his friends. Around March, he started drinking every day, all day. And then Sam died..." *Her voice cracked and she couldn't continue. He could tell that she was slightly embarrassed for feeling so emotional over the death of a dog.*

"Mrs. Bradley. Has your husband ever physically harmed you or your children?" *Father asked.*

"He's never hurt the children," *she whispered and looked shamefully down at her tissue. She was about to say something else but when she looked* up, he was looking blatantly down at his watch.

"I'm so sorry, I hate to cut this short but I have to get ready for mass. I have to go meet with the choir now." He stood up. "Can we set up another time for you to come in and talk?"

She started at him for a few seconds, as if she couldn't believe that he had interrupted her when she was revealing to him the most significant, private details of her life. But her flash of anger dissipated with a few blinks of her eyes and a stubborn set in her jaw.

"No, I'm afraid I can't do this again." She stood up as well and shoved her damp handkerchief back into her purse. "Thanks for your time, Father."

"Maria, please." He realized his mistake and quickly came around the desk and placed a comforting hand on her arm. "You need to unload this emotional burden. Obviously you're going through a rough time and need someone to talk to or you wouldn't have approached me," he stated, knowing that she was a proud, reserved woman who kept most things to herself. She wouldn't have come to him unless she had a serious concern.

She nodded, and turned her back on him. "You're right, Father, I do need to talk to someone but it can't be with you. No offense, I appreciate that you listened to me today but I won't be coming to you with this again. I shouldn't have come in the first place, it was a mistake. I don't think the church can help me with this." She looked him straight in the eye. "This is something my family and I will have to handle on our own."

"I'll always be here, Mrs. Bradley," he called out when she opened the door. "In case you change your mind. If you don't think I can help, the least I can do is listen."

"Thanks for the offer but that won't be necessary." She slipped out of his office, closed the door behind her and charged down the hall.

He sank back into his chair, and frantically scanned his brain for a way to fix the damage that he had done. But there was no fix. He had dismissed her, had become distracted in her time of personal revelation and ruined whatever chances he had had to help her. He had failed her and her family.

Maria had come to him to vent her frustrations and to find answers. To find reason out of chaos, to find a listening, empathetic ear, for verbal reinforcement of her faith. But she had left more empty and powerless then when she had come in.

That distressing conversation had weighted on his mind until the day he heard that her husband had died, and then haunted him fiercely from there after. When he saw Daniel in the church today, and he had asked to speak to him like his mother had, his heart had pounded with furious relief. For he now had a chance to rectify what he had done. He would do what he could to help Maria's boy and it would be his tiny redemption. Like a storyline straight out of Daniels books, he had been given the chance to make things right and he took it.

He could only pray that it made a difference.

Chapter Fifteen

They drove most of the way back to Toronto in silence. The radio played softly but neither one was listening to it. They were lost in their own thoughts, scarcely noticing the other cars passing or the green landscape disappearing behind them.

They stopped once at a coffee shop on the side of the highway because Daniel had wanted a cup of coffee. He had asked Rachel if she wanted to go inside and get an early lunch but she had declined. She just wanted to go home. When they reached the city limits, it felt to them both as if they had been away for months instead of days. So much had happened, so much had been said, so much had been examined. They were exhausted; physically, emotionally and mentally. A funeral was very draining, and dredging up the past and facing the overwhelming emotions that surfaced with it, seemed to expend more energy than actual physical exertion.

He pulled alongside the curb in front of her townhouse and parked. He wasn't ready for her to leave yet, although they had barely spoken since the day before, her presence was comforting and calming. He didn't want her to go. He was glad that she had come, despite his initial reluctance. The last few days would have been hell without her.

She reached for the door handle and was just about to get out when he grabbed her arm. He wasn't even sure of what he was about to say until the words came tumbling out of his mouth.

"Thank you for coming."

Her face went slack and her jaw dropped slightly, she was temporarily speechless at the surprising vulnerability in his tone.

"You're a good friend, Rachel, probably my only one. You're there even when I didn't know I needed you to be."

"You have a funny way of treating your friends, Daniel." She swiftly opened the car door, grabbed her luggage from the back and got out. She stood on the sidewalk for a second, leaned into the car and said softly, "I'm sorry about your mom." She wrenched herself out and slammed the door firmly, shaking the car with its force. He watched her race up the steps away from him and curbed the urge to follow her. She was everything he wanted, everything he needed. But she didn't need someone like him. Someone consumed with self-loathing and completely aware of his short-comings.

She deserved better.

Much better.

He put the car in drive, pulled away and joined the steady flow of traffic.

* * * * *

He used his key and let himself to his quiet, slightly darkened condo. He let the door swing open on its own, stood solidly in the doorway, and stared at his home. His open-concept bachelor pad suddenly looked preposterously enormous for just one person. On the main floor, there was the recreation room, living room, kitchen and one bathroom. Upstairs there were two bedrooms, his study and the bathroom. The place was three times the size of Madeline's house, he could easily house his entire family here.

The heavy shades were drawn, causing ominous, dark shadows. He flicked on the light switch and immediately noticed the hardwood and tiled floors gleaming with fresh polish. The pre-dominantly white kitchen on his left looked so new, it looked like it had never been used, and smelled freshly of lemon scented cleaning supplies.

Though his condo contained the best appliances, was decorated lavishly, and absurdly clean and tidy, it didn't look particularly cozy or warm. It looked cold and sterile to be perfectly honest. Like a display at a furniture store, it looked pretty but lacked personality.

There were no framed pictures of family members, friends or pets on the walls or displayed throughout. There was nothing that would reveal to someone his interests or tastes, only his library exhibited his passion for books and it was hidden from view. It was simply rooms with the necessary necessities and the odd luxury item that only the wealthy could afford. He hadn't even decorated the place, he had hired a professional decorator to come in and do it for him. He had no real personal investment in his dwelling; it was merely a place to eat, sleep and write on his typewriter.

This was his home, he spent most of his time here and yet it was void of any his characteristics. It was lifeless. As was he. It adequately defined him as a person; well-groomed and monetarily successful yet drab and empty under a cold exterior.

He never noticed this before, but now the flaws of his flawless home glared blatantly back at him. He walked in, closed the door behind him and

ISOLATION

dropped his suitcase carelessly.
He needed a drink.

* * * * *

He polished off two large glasses of bourbon on ice while he read the last few days newspapers on a stool at the kitchen nook. He cleaned and dried the glass and put it back in the cupboard. He then wiped the counter to get rid of the nasty water ring and decided to take a well-earned nap. He slept almost six hours curled up lazily on the couch and woke groggy and irritable at eight o'clock that night.

Annoyed at himself for sleeping that long, he jumped up, ordered a pepperoni pizza and had a shower. Once he was cleaned, shaven and dressed, the pizza arrived. He ate three slices of it hungrily at the nook, as he watched the reluctant sun go down through the bay window. He put the box of remaining pizza into the empty fridge, poured himself another glass of straight bourbon and went upstairs to his study.

It was time he started writing again.

He sat for a long time in front of the old typewriter, staring at the empty page, his fingers resting on the keys in anticipation. He had nothing. Not one line. He took a long drink, looked out the window to the dead, night sky and turned back to the taunting page before him.

He had yet to face a serious bout of writer's block, and certainly didn't want to have one now. It had always been a lingering fear of his, and probably was for most writers. What if one day the words didn't come? What if he wasn't able to produce ten good pages or more out of thin air each day? What if whatever he did churn out was utter crap and the critics panned it? What if he eventually had to wrestle and force each sentence out of his muddled brain until it either drove him mad or propelled him to quit. What then? Which scenario was worse? He drained the glass and let the liquor burn a path down to his stomach.

Twenty minutes later, he decided that it just wasn't going to happen and stood up. The creative juices weren't flowing and it wasn't right to force it.

There was nothing to be gained by staring at an empty page all night so he decided to have some more pizza and watch television before going to bed to read. He was halfway down the stairs when the phone rang. He raced down the seven steps and grabbed the phone around the corner in the kitchen.

"Hello?"

"Bradley, how have you been?" It was Masterson's booming voice.

Daniel wondered how he would have found out, way out in Rowland, that his mother had died.

"Fine, how have you been?"

"I have news. Are you free tomorrow?"

Obviously he hadn't heard of his mother's death, and Daniel wasn't about to tell him either. Masterson wasn't the type for affectionate gestures or clucks of sympathy. And he didn't want that anyway.

Daniel and he hadn't seen one another since celebrating the success of his third novel which was years ago. It was about time that they got caught up face-to-face.

"Is something wrong?"

"No, everything is fine. Great in fact, it's good news, m'boy." His voice amplified like an excited schoolgirl's. "You know where Pralling is?"

Pralling was a one-horse town, similar to Aldon that was an equal distance between Rowland and Toronto. They both would have a fair drive to get there. Daniel figured the man must have something *really* important to tell him to go all that lengths just to see him. Masterson was a notorious recluse, and rarely left the school for anything.

They agreed to meet there at one o'clock the next day, but Masterson refused to tell him anything more about his news. After he said 'good-bye', Daniel hung up the phone, and got himself a cold piece of pizza from the fridge. He decided to forego the fourth brandy, the previous ones weren't settling properly in his stomach, and retreated to the rec room to find a movie. He turned on a couple of lamps to obliterate the darkness and turned the dial on his twenty-seven inch television to find a good channel, but there was nothing on. He went into the caliginous kitchen, and didn't even bother to switch on the light. He poured himself a full glass of bourbon, sat on the stool and stared into nothingness.

It would be a long night.

* * * * *

The next day, after calling Rick and getting things back in order, he drove to 'The Dock', a run of the mill bar and grill in Pralling that specialized in wings and hamburgers. He had to stop twice on the way there to vomit on the gravel shoulder, and chewed on a couple dry aspirins the rest of the way to dull his throbbing headache. He couldn't remember ever feeling worse; each movement he made pained, not only in his head but throughout his joints and muscles as if he had run a lengthy marathon the day before. The nausea though, was beyond agony. He would have preferred pain, to the wretched wave-like sensations of his stomach contents tumbling and rolling within him.

When Daniel walked into the restaurant, Masterson was already at a table with a sparkle in his once faded blue eyes. They shook hands and Daniel was amazed to see that the old fella hadn't seemed to age in the last twenty years. He looked as old as he ever did.

"You okay? You look like shit," Masterson observed, eyes taking in his unshaven, pale face and blood-shot eyes.

"Good to see you too," he snorted, trying too hard to natural and congenial.

"So, why the big rush to see me? On the phone, you made it sound as if it were an emergency." Daniel draped his coat on the seat beside him and settled into the hard, wooden chair. The place was busy and the food on others tables looked promising, but the prominent combined smell of cigarette smoke and grease made his stomach rumble uneasily. He wouldn't be eating today.

Masterson smiled, reached into the leather suitcase on the floor beside him and gingerly placed a thick paperback novel on the table. The black and white picture on the cover of it was of a soldier in full gear, of what rank, army or country you couldn't tell because the young man was walking away from the camera. He had his rifle clutched firmly in his right hand and was walking confidently and purposefully into the blazing sunlight. The book was titled *The Killing Years. A Soldier's Story* by William.P.Masterson.

"You wrote this?" Daniel choked out and picked the book up.

"That I did. It's loosely based on my father's experiences in the war. When he died, he left me his journal, and it..." Masterson paused. "It inspired me to say the least. I had no idea my father was an aspiring writer. I didn't know that much about him actually. After the war he worked in a bank and refused to talk about those years. He was a very quiet, restrained man. Even when I studied history in university, and questioned him on what he saw and did when he was a soldier, he wouldn't tell me. We weren't all that close to be perfectly honest, and his indifference towards me was part of the problem. It wasn't until I read his journal that I got to know him as he really was, as a fully dimensional person. I learned about all the heroic acts he performed in the war, the friendships he made during that time and about all the death and blood that he witnessed. He even wrote of the undying love that he had for my mother throughout the chaos of those years. A love that he never expressed in front of me, I never saw them kiss even once. As stupid as it sounds, my father became real to me after his death. Unfortunately, by then it was too late to salvage our strained relationship but I thought that his story was worth telling."

Daniel flipped through the pages in amazement, it was over seven hundred pages long.

"It's sat in my desk drawer for decades."

A waitress with a bad complexion and fiery red hair approached their table. "What would you fellas like to drink?"

After they ordered, she bustled away and Daniel leaned forward. "If you had it written, why didn't you send it to a publisher?"

Masterson stroked his beard and hesitated before speaking. "I, like my father, had aspirations of becoming an author. I took it to the next level and studied English lit in university and there I wrote my first novel-length story. It took me over a year to write it and when it was done I gave it to my English professor to review. That took all the courage in the world because I respected him immensely and desperately needed his approval and support. He took me aside and told me exactly what he thought. He said that I wrote at an amateur level, that the plot and dialogue was weak if not non-existent. That I didn't have what it took, and he gave me a list of reasons why. To put it mildly, he hated my book and thought it was a heap of trash. He said I would make a great teacher, but that I shouldn't waste my time focusing on a writing career. As you can imagine, I was crushed."

"Looking back, I should have told the bastard to kiss my ass but I hadn't honed my sharp tongue then, and what little self-esteem I had, he trampled on. I can't believe how much power I gave him. I gave him the ability to destroy everything I had ever worked toward. He belittled my ambitions and skills and ultimately squashed all desire I had to write. After I wrote *this* book, I never even considered getting it published because I didn't think it or anything I ever wrote would be good enough for him or for anybody. I decided to give the manuscript to my family members when the time was right, and it would simply be a treasured document of our family history."

His expression changed, his eyes softened.

"But then I met you, and saw your talent and how you continuously pushed yourself to get better at your craft. How you threw yourself out to others mercy, writing what you wanted, not caring what the critics, or I, or anyone thought. It inspired me to do the same, Daniel. I sent it out six months ago, and received my first published copy in the mail yesterday morning." He reached across the table, took the book from Daniels hands and opened it to the second page. There was one simple line in italics; *'For Daniel. Who taught me how to take a risk again.'*

"This book is dedicated to you." He smiled, and it was strange to see his crinkled, sullen face light up like a child's.

"You didn't have to do that." Daniel flushed with embarrassment.

"You dedicated your first novel to me, and referred to me as your mentor, but if anything, you've been mine. You taught me more than you know. Because of you, I want to get back in the game again," Masterson added with grave seriousness. "You're a damned good writer, Daniel, and I just couldn't be more proud of you."

Daniel was moved by his strong words but found it ironic that he could inspire someone else to follow their passion, when he couldn't even inspire himself.

"Here ya go, boys." The waitress appeared and clumsily plunked their drinks on the table, ruining the intense gravity of the moment. They broke their eyes away from one another and grabbed their drinks with trembling hands.

Masterson raised his small glass of scotch on the rocks and Daniel raised his bottle of chilled beer. They clinked their beverages in the air, both glowing with emotional exuberance and took a drink.

* * * * *

Daniel looked down at Masterson's novel in his hand that night. He was three chapters in and though it was thickly descriptive on historical, political, and geographical information, it was a very interesting read. It was rather strange though to be reading his teachers work. All these years he'd been sending Masterson to review his own writing and had never once considered that he had desires to write himself. He wondered how he could be so blind to the people around him. There was so much happening under his nose, that he hadn't had the sense or inclination to notice. He suddenly felt like he was missing out. He had never felt that way before, but since his mother passed, he had become very aware of the lives of those around him.

He turned to the second page of Masterson's book, and traced his finger along his dedication. *'For Daniel. Who taught me how to take a risk again.'*

His heart pounded every time he read that line. Did he really mean that much to Masterson? Had he truly affected him so deeply? He found it enormously hard to believe. How could his writing inspire anyone? His books were mere outlets for his own frustrations. Something he discovered that he was good at and kept at like a boy who learns that he's a natural at a sport. The more you do something you enjoy, the better you got at it, it was as simple as that. To him, writing was like breathing. A natural process. His writing was the only shining light in his dark, chaotic life. It was what kept him going, what made him get out of bed each day.

He sat on the stool at the nook and poured himself another glass of bourbon from the near empty bottle. He knew he was drinking a lot, more than usual, but right now it felt like the right thing to do. He needed something to dull the nerves, something to ease away the emptiness of the dark nights. Something to help him forget.

He was swigging the bitter fluid back when the phone rang, he reached for it.

"Hello?"

"Daniel, it's me," Kate said and he rolled his eyes. He knew that she'd figure out that he was drinking by his voice, and didn't want to get the third degree about it. He would have to try hard not to slur his words or he'd be on the phone with her all night.

"You left so quickly yesterday, no one had the chance to say good-bye."

"I know. Something came up and Rachel had to get back for work," he lied.

"You should have come over before you left. There is so much that we need to talk about."

"Like what?" He reached across the counter, gripped the bourbon bottle and topped himself up.

"Have you been drinking?" she burst out and he winced.

"No, of course not. You woke me up, I was having a nap. I'm just not quite awake yet."

"You're having a nap at ten o'clock at night?" she asked in disbelief.

"I was in bed I mean. It's been a long week, Kate. Give me a break." He took a drink and glared at the fridge.

"We just never got a chance to really talk. I was hoping to spend some time with you alone, and with Eve and Madeline to just catch up on things. Some quality, family time together. You know."

"I know and I'm sorry."

"When I saw you crying at the funeral..." Kate's voice cracked and he closed his eyes, knowing that he was in for an onslaught of tears. "I have to admit that a part of me was happy. I was relieved to see you affected, to see you express emotion about something. And when we hugged, it was just like we were kids again. Best friends who spent every waking hour with one another and knew everything little thing about the other. Those were some of the happiest days of my life, Daniel, before you left for school and it was just the two of us without a care in the world. I can't tell you how much I miss that. You were my best friend." She started to cry then, the soft sobs echoed through the phone line and resonated in his ears.

"I miss those days, too," he admitted quietly and she started to cry harder.

"I know that you punish yourself every day because you think you made Dad do what he did, but you didn't! You hear me? You didn't! And I'm sick of you killing yourself over it. Nobody blames you, Daniel, nobody."

I do, he thought and clenched his fist.

"Suicide is a self-motivated act. Nobody could have made him do it, it was his own choice, he's dead and you're alive."

"You didn't..."

"You're alive!" she screamed, startling him. "You're alive, and your family needs you. So many people need you so you need to get over this and get your head on straight. You missed out on rectifying things with Mom, do you really want to make that mistake again?"

"Kate, you don't understand. I was the last person to see him *alive*. He blew his brains out two seconds after I left him that night. How can you expect me not to blame myself!" he burst out incredulously.

"You seem to forget why you had to go to the shed that night to see him in the first place. You obviously have forgotten what he did to Mom, what he did to all of us. Dad was no angel, he was very disturbed and angry and someone had to stand up to him. Someone had to stop him before it got any worse. You did, Daniel, you did something that night when all the rest of us were too afraid to. What happened after is not your fault."

They both absorbed this for a second. "Believe me, Daniel, I've had my own bouts of guilt over this issue but I've dealt with it. When I was seventeen, I went through a phase of what you might call depression. I called it a blue period. All I could think about was what Dad did and all the things that led up to that night. I couldn't eat or sleep and didn't want to do anything. Didn't even want to get out of bed in the morning, just wanted to lie there and cry all day. After a while, Mom decided something had to be done because I wasn't snapping out of it on my own and made me see a doctor. Dr. Simmons sent me to a therapist, Dr. Primers, who worked with me for a few years."

Daniel sat up straight, eyes wide. He had no idea about this, how come no one had ever told him? "Why didn't you ever tell me that?"

"Because you were never around, never called and it wasn't the sort of thing you just up and tell someone out of the blue. Oh, by the way, when I was seventeen all I could think about was slicing my wrists with a razor and ending it all."

"Jesus Christ, Kate!" Daniel cursed. He had a right to know that was going on, why didn't his mother tell him? *Because you never gave her the chance*, an inner voice answered bluntly.

"I was there every time that Dad went on a tirade and took it out on Mom and it got pretty bad…but I'm working hard to not allow that to affect me now. It has nothing to do with my present or future, it just made me stronger. You have to make peace with this, too, Daniel, you have to get out of your blue period and face the world again. You can't change what happened so you just have to learn to live with it and move on."

"I know. I know." He nodded and swallowed hard but his throat remained dry. "How…how bad did it get?" He wasn't sure why he asked, but a part of him needed to know.

"I haven't thought about it in so long, Daniel." Kate sighed and he could hear the tension building within her. "I'll never forget the first time he hit her. I was absolutely terrified. He had come home late that night and Mom had given his dinner to Sam because it had dried out from sitting on the stove so long. He was hungry and drunk, and mean as a bear. From upstairs I could hear him call her every name in the book, and then he grabbed her and slammed her up against the wall. She must have hit her head or something because once he let go of her she slid lifelessly to the floor. And he left her lying on the kitchen floor like that, and went to the shed, like the coward that he was. I could see her feet from where I was standing, and she laid there for almost a minute. Then she got up and finished doing dishes, but I could hear her sniffing so I know she was crying. I was too scared to go down to see if she was alright. I just gripped the banister for dear life, too afraid to move or cry or make a sound. I'll never forget that feeling, that helplessness, that complete and utter fear of something that I didn't understand. I just couldn't believe that my father could do that. I was in denial for a while, thinking that it was our fault that he was acting like that, and took the blame for all his rages. But the truth was, it was all him. He was in the wrong, and I'm not going to waste another second of my life grieving for the mistakes that he made. And you shouldn't either, Daniel."

There was a moment of strained silence until Kate questioned shortly. "I don't want to end this but Amanda is calling me from upstairs and I gotta go. But before I do, I just have to ask. What's going on with you and Rachel? Everyone has asked me about it, are you two together again?"

He looked out the large kitchen window and shrugged. "I don't really know what's going on, Kate, nothing I guess." He didn't want to talk about Rachel, he was too upset right now to worry about his love life.

"Daniel, Daniel, Daniel," she murmured. "Did it ever occur to you to call her? Ask her out and court her a little bit?"

His shoulders sagged, he clutched the phone tighter.

"You know as well as I do that she would come back to you if you asked her," Kate said with disdain. "If you want her in your life, you have to tell her that. She's not a mind-reader, you know. You have to tell her how you feel."

"It's more complicated than that." He shook his head. "Look, I don't want to talk about this right now."

"She's waited around twenty years for you Daniel, and it doesn't get any less complicated than that. How many girls would actually do that? Doesn't the fact that she came back with you this week, and helped you through this tell you how she feels? This is a woman who would be there for you in a second and would do anything for you if you only gave her an inch of encouragement and respect."

"I respect her," he said defensively.

"If you really respected her, you'd tell her how you feel about her instead of letting her hang on the sidelines all the time. She loves you, Daniel, she always has and she deserves better than this. I know you feel the same way about her, but you're too stubborn and stupid to see it."

"She's a good friend of mine and I don't want to see her hurt any more. It's time you made a final decision about her. If it's really over, then tell her that and let her go. I know it's not my place…" She hesitated. "But I love you both, and I want you to be happy. I just don't think it's right, the way you two have gone on all these years."

"Don't hold back, Kate, tell me what you really think," he said sarcastically but instantly regretted his bitter tone. She was right about him and Rachel.

Kate was always right.

"Look, I have to go. Amanda is going nutty upstairs, and I don't know where in the world Frank is."

"Kate…" Daniel called out before she hung up.

"Yes?"

"I miss you. I really do." Tears brimmed his eyes and his face flushed. "I …I don't think I can get through this alone."

"That's the thing, you don't have to," she soothed. "You have a family here that loves you and needs you, they want to be with you, Daniel. If only you'd let them in."

"I'm going to come back home." He nodded, the words sounding right on his tongue. "I'm not teaching over the summer. I can come back and spend time with you all and renovate the house and…"

"Sleep on it, Daniel," Kate cut him off gently. "Dr. Primers told me to take baby steps. It will take time, change takes time."

"I want to make things better, Kate. I want you to believe that," he said firmly and he could almost hear her smile.

"I really got to go. I'll talk to you later."

"I'll call you this week," he promised, and for the first time truly meant it.

"Okay." She hung up the phone and he listened to the dead dial tone for almost a full minute before hanging up as well. He visualized his sister at seventeen, lying on her plaid comforter in bed in the middle of the day contemplating suicide and it made his blood turn ice cold. He didn't even know about it. Here she was suffering, and he was off at school without a second's thought about his family, of the people he had left behind.

He stood up suddenly, so abruptly that the stool knocked over behind him.

He reached for the half-empty glass in front of him. He brought it to his lips and was just about to take a drink when a surreal vision of a young Katie picking up a sharp razor blade flashed in front of his eyes. He gagged, spun around and threw the glass savagely against the wall. It smashed powerfully into tiny bits and the sound was so richly satisfying that he reached for the bourbon bottle and hollered as he wheeled it against the wall as well. The glass pieces burst across the room as the brown, watery liquor spread across the floor at lightening speed.

All feeling left his legs, he dropped to his knees and dug his palms into his eyes. An animal wail escaped his lips at lifes injustices, at how history consistently repeated itself despite all efforts to the contrary. He had seen with his own eyes how his father's actions had destroyed his family, and yet here he was, making the same mistakes that he had.

He didn't want to be like him, turning out like his father had always been his greatest, darkest fear. But he was more like him now then ever. He could change though. There was still time. He stood up, sniffed a few times and looked down at the kitchen counter. Masterson's book was wide open to the second page, and that single line transfixed him once again. *'For Daniel. Who taught me how to take a risk again.'*

The thing was, he had never taken a real risk in his life. Not about anything that mattered anyway. But he was ready to. And he didn't want to wait another minute, he was afraid that he might change his mind if he did. He had to do it tonight. He slammed the book shut, and rushed through the spilled bourbon and broken glass to the door.

* * * * *

He had drunk three glasses of straight bourbon earlier and although he wasn't near drunk, he had consumed too much to drive legally. It would be over an hour's walk to Rachel's townhouse and it was already ten-thirty, but he was wide awake and had never felt more sober in his life. He wouldn't walk anyway, he would run. Not only would it be faster but the increased blood circulation and oxygen intake from increased exertion would make him think better. And he needed to get his thoughts together. He pulled on his running shoes and a light jacket from the closet and set about his way at a swift, jogging pace on the darkened sidewalks. As he stared off into the cloudy night sky, with the cool wind ripping through his hair, he felt an awareness that he had never experienced before. He felt awake for the first time in a long, long time, and suddenly everything seemed very clear. He needed to tell her to her face how he really felt about her and to make right at least one thing out of his life.

While he formed the words he wanted to say in his mind, his heart began to pound unbearably, just like when he was fourteen, at the height of his crush for her. In the years since, he had never gotten excited when she was around. He never felt anything about anything, but now he was overwhelmed with the intensity of emotions that channeled through his body at rapid speed.

How is it possible, he thought, that the reality of death could literally wake one back to life. How the face of death in a loved one, could immediately ignite ones understanding of life's value, and make everything so very clear.

* * * * *

It began to rain then, not hard but steadily, and plump cool drops plopped on his brow and streaked down his face. He welcomed it. He was overheating and starting to sweat but wasn't tiring in the least. He felt like he could run all night. He breathed in through his nose and exhaled through his mouth, and could almost feel all of his organs, muscles and joints working in perfect unison. He felt like a machine, a powerful mechanism until Rachel's townhouse came into view.

He felt the first twinge of nervousness but wasn't about to back down and turn around. He had come this far and he was going all the way. He jogged over, leaped up her steps and stood before her door. He was panting but his chest heaved more with excitement then from actual oxygen deprivation.

With a deep breath, he rang the door bell and closed his eyes in anticipation.

The door opened swiftly and a tall, handsome male with sharp eyes and jet-black hair stood in front of him. He was wearing only a t-shirt and boxer shorts and it was clear that he had just woken up.

"Can I help you?" he asked drearily.

"Oh." Daniel checked the number on the door to make sure he had the right place. It was number thirty-four. That *was* Rachel's townhouse number.

"Does Rachel Sheldon still live here?" His gut churned, realizing who the man was. He was too late. He should have known. A girl like Rachel wouldn't stay single forever.

"Yeah, she's inside. Can I tell her whose here?"

"No. Never mind. I didn't realize how late it was. She's probably sleeping. I'll come back another time." He started backing down the steps.

"She's right here, just wait a second. She's coming down the stairs." The man held up his hand to stop him but Daniel was already halfway down the steps.

He couldn't believe he had brazenly ran all the way over here in the rain in the middle of the night only to be humiliated. He cursed himself for being so stupid. He was so disgusted with himself and distracted that he caught his heel on the slick step and stumbled slightly, almost falling down. He grabbed for the railing for balance and pulled himself up awkwardly.

"Daniel?" Rachel appeared in the doorway, wrapping a white terry-cloth robe around herself modestly. "It's almost midnight! What are you doing here?"

"Nothing." He pulled himself upright. "I just made a mistake."

"Why don't you come in for a second, it's raining!" she called out.

"I have to go." He wouldn't even turn around and continued down the steps.

"Don't make me come down after you!" she threatened, worried that he was drunk. "Daniel, please, just come in and talk for a moment. You can meet my brother, Robbie, the one that went to Western when you were a student there. He's over for a visit from Ottawa, I'll introduce you." She stepped tentatively out into the rain in her matching white slippers.

"Your brother," he repeated, and raised his head, immensely relieved.

"Yes, my brother." She nodded and folded her arms. He smiled slightly and raced up the steps towards her, stopping one step below her so that they were eye level. She always looked self-assured and stylish, even when she had just woken up. She was never self-conscious about the way she looked and he loved that about her. The cool wind caught in her hair and breezed through it, her eyes fluttered within its intensity. The rain matted down hair and coursed down her face in sexy striations. She looked as perfect as a painting, so utterly perfect, and he was momentarily mesmerized by her untainted beauty.

"Come inside," she whispered.

"No." He reached out and grabbed her arm to keep her from going. "I need to talk to you alone."

"What are you doing here, Daniel?" She shook her head dismally.

"I came all this way tonight to tell you..."

"You need a friend tonight don't you. You need a listening ear and a bed to sleep in but in the morning you'll be gone as always right? Well I'm not here just to fill a void every time you feel lonely Daniel. You can't just use me every time you feel like it," she snapped, eyes flashing.

"That's not it. I came to tell you that I'm sorry. I've been such an idiot all these years, I've treated you terribly and I can't tell you how sorry I am for that," he said sincerely.

"Yes, you have been somewhat of an ass," she agreed with a nod, indicating that he shouldn't stop there.

"But most of all, I'm here to tell you exactly how I feel for you because I don't want to let another word go unsaid. I couldn't stand it if something happened to you, and I never took the chance to tell you how much you mean to me. I don't deserve you, I really don't and I'm not sure why you put up with me all these years. But I'm glad you did because I love you, Rachel." His hand slid down her arm and squeezed hers. "I always have, but it's taken me a long time to...to see things clearly. I want to be with you and only you."

She gripped his strong, wet hand and considered his words, those wonderful words that she had waited almost twenty years to hear. There was a time when she would have melted completely upon hearing that, but that time had passed.

"You know how I feel about you, I've always been quite honest about that but I've changed, Daniel. As much as care for you, I won't put myself through your crap anymore. You said once before that you couldn't give me what I wanted in a relationship. What makes you think that you can now?"

"I can fill your head with explanations and promises but those are just words, Rachel. And actions speak louder than words." He leaned forward and brushed his lips against hers. "Give me a chance, and I'll prove to you that things have changed."

She loved the taste of his mouth on hers but still she hesitated, her mind and common sense for once dominating over her impulsive heart. "I don't know, Daniel, I really don't. I'm too old to play mind games and deal with your many issues. It's too complicated, I'm sorry but that's the truth. You're still not ready for the commitment that I'm looking for, especially now after the death of your mother and all those unresolved family problems. You're in an emotional place right now, this is not the time for you to start a relationship."

"I'm ready. I want this, Rachel, I really want us to work." He wiped the flailing hair from her eyes, cupped her chin with both hands and kissed her full on the mouth. It was a long, gentle kiss and she was pleasantly surprised by it, for he was never one to initiate affection. She succumbed to its seductive power and easily could have stayed kissing like that all night long.

When they pulled apart, he gazed into her eyes, his hands still on her face and whispered, "I love you."

"Daniel." She hesitated. "I'm not just going to jump into this blindly again. Like you say, actions speak louder than words and if you want me then you need to prove to me that you've changed."

"What do you want me to do?" he asked desperately, looking like a man on the verge of drowning.

She pursed her lips and eventually said with a frown. "I don't know. We can go out for dinner sometime. Talk things out, see how that goes and go from there."

"That's all I can ask for." He wrapped his arms easily around her waist and hugged her to him as the wind and rain swirled wildly around them.

"I don't want to lose you," he murmured. They stayed locked in place for almost a full minute, not minding the elements around them one bit. When they finally pulled apart, he looked up and saw Robbie peaking out discreetly behind the curtains of the front window. Rachel caught his gaze and looked back. Robbie quickly snapped the curtain shut.

"I better go."

She smirked, "Do you want a ride home?"

"I'd rather run but thanks anyway." He stepped back from her. "I'll call you."

"Go home and get out of the rain, you fool." She smiled playfully and raced back inside, completely drenched. Before she closed the door, she waved good-bye and he stood there in the pouring rain, waving back at her incredulously. Why she put up with him, he'd never know, but he was luckiest man in the world. He started for home.

He ran through the downpour, feeling like a man just waking from a heavily drugged sleep. The world around him seemed to shed its dullness and looked new, bright and boundless again.

He still had a long way to go, he knew that, and many obstacles to climb but for the first time ever, things didn't look so bleak. He didn't feel lost any more. He didn't quite know where he was going yet, but for some reason he suddenly knew that whatever happened, he would be just fine. He had the desire now, to face instead of hide, from the challenges that life inevitably brings. He just hoped the feeling would last.

He pumped his glistening wet arms faster, lifted his knees high and ran hard the rest of the way home; enjoying the invigorating rush of his heart pounding ferociously in his chest and the blood pumping through his veins.

He felt alive.

He *was* alive. And there was so much to do.

Epilogue
Two Years Later

The ultimate journey does not require travel, only an open mind.
-Jill Migchels

The school bell rang and the students grabbed their materials and fled for the freedom of the classroom door. Daniel gripped the white chalk in his powdered right hand and called out to the class. "I want that report on my desk on Monday! No excuses, no extensions!"

They groaned in unison and he smiled good-naturedly. He told them as they passed his desk to have a good weekend.

"Mr. Bradley." One of his students, Drake Watson approached him nervously.

"Yes, Drake."

Drake was one of his favorite students, not because he was one of the brightest but because he worked hard, probably harder then anyone in any of his classes. He liked ambition, and red-haired, freckle-faced Drake had plenty of it. He had come from an impoverished area in downtown Toronto, and had worked hard all through high school to get a full scholarship. He wanted to be a high school teacher, and his easy, genuine manner with people combined with his insatiable desire to learn, proved that he would be an asset to any school that hired him.

"I'm having problems with that assignment that's due on Monday. I just don't understand poetry well and I really don't get William Blake's work. I was hoping that you'd help me a little bit," Drake admitted, eyes downcast at the prospect of failing an assignment that he desperately needed to pass to keep his average up.

"Sure, but I don't have time today." He looked at his watch, it was almost four o'clock. "I have a meeting with the dean in five minutes, can we get together tomorrow morning? I was planning to come in and catch up on some marking anyway, we could go over it then."

"That would be great." Drake exhaled with relief.

"Alright, I'll meet you here at ten. Don't be late," he warned with a smile and Drake laughed.

As he walked out of the classroom, he called out, "Thanks professor!"

Daniel hated being called that, or 'Mr. Bradley'. It sounded old to him but none of the students had caught on to calling him by his first name. He reached for his suitcase and raced out of the room, closing the door behind him. Two years ago he would have refused to tutor the boy, claiming he was too busy, and would have passed him off to a teachers assistant or the resource center who would have assisted him. Though he was still busy, even more so now, he had come to believe that these interactions with his students made him a better teacher. A better communicator. And the feedback that he had received in recent months in regards to his lectures, fueled that belief.

The dean had found him earlier that day in the hall, and had requested to see him after class. It had sounded important. He knew he wasn't in trouble but feared that the program that he was in the midst of developing might be in jeopardy. He and two full-time English lit professors were currently coordinating a creative writing program that they hoped to implement next year. It would be a year long graduate course where the students would have the opportunity to specialize in areas like fiction, non-fiction, drama, and poetry. They would bring in weekly guest speakers that were published writers, who would give them helpful insight into getting their work published. They, the instructors, would also assist the students in preparing their manuscripts to be sent away.

Daniel was very excited about the program, was spear-heading it himself and felt it was a big step for the English department. But there were many steps to getting a program like this into full-swing and they were still in the preliminary planning stage.

He traveled to the administration building, walked through the maze of offices and desks, past the receptionist who nodded him on, and eventually knocked on the dean's heavy wood door.

"Daniel." Dean Cornell opened the door with a smile. "Come in. Sit down."

He indicated to the leather chairs across from his desk and they both sat down. Bill Cornell was in his early fifties; an affable, thin man with a closely trimmed beard and an attachment to tailor made black suits and silk black ties. He was a relaxed and assured, intensely bright and witty and very popular amongst his faculty and students.

"How are things with the creative writing program going?"

"Good. But if you wanted to talk about that, I should have brought Timmers and Langley in as well. Their just as involved in it as I am, and

Timmers has even booked Laura Jewel to be our first guest speaker." Laura Jewel was an up and coming Canadian author whose recent novel, *The Devil Speaks,* toppled the competition on the bestsellers lists the previous year.

"Laura Jewel. Very good," Cornell murmured and stroked his beard. "But that's not why I brought you in here today."

"What's wrong?"

"Nothing. It's good news in fact. I was at the right place at the right time and learned some news that I probably shouldn't be passing on, but I am."

"I want to be the first to tell you that you're nominated once again for the Booker Prize. For *Existence*. I'm sure you'll be getting a call later today or early tomorrow about it."

"Are you serious?" Daniel gasped, he had written *Existence* within a five month period, immediately after his mother had passed. He had scraped the other novel he was working on because of its dark, rather depressing subject matter that only intensified his grieving process. He wrote instead a light, captivating tale about three brilliantly gifted siblings who are estranged and reunite after their parents' tragic death. The storyline paralleled his own life in many ways, and it was also his first stab at a happy ending. The book turned out to be a roaring success, much to his surprise, since it had taken so little time to write.

Cornell stood up and reached his hand across the desk. "Selfish me, I wanted to be the first to congratulate you."

Daniel stood up, grabbed his hand and pumped it enthusiastically. "Thank you, sir."

"With this nomination and promising writing program that you're launching, you're doing an enormous amount of good for the name of this school, Darriel. You're making us all very proud, young man. Very proud," he said earnestly.

Daniel's cheeks started to pain, he was smiling so hard.

* * * * *

He unlocked the door to his condo and walked in to the mildly darkened kitchen. As he headed to the stairs, he noticed the dirty dishes lying on the counters and newspapers strewn about, yet didn't feel the irrepressible urge to clean it up. The clutter looked fine. His place looked lived in now, and rather cozy since he had begun restraining his compulsive habits. It took almost two years, but he could finally walk into a room without scrutinizing it for dust or dirt. He now felt comfortable within his own surroundings.

Much had changed in the last little while and the new, more natural décor reflected that.

He bounded up the carpeted steps in wide strides and raced into his bedroom to change, but the sight before him stopped him quickly.

"Rachel? What are you doing home so early?" He turned on the light switch and walked in. She was sitting on the edge of the bed in the dark, fully dressed, staring off into space. "Are you okay?"

"I don't know," she whispered, and he could see that she was shaking.

"What's wrong?" His euphoria instantly vanished, his limbs numbed. He sat down beside her and put his arm around her shoulders. "Tell me, what is it?"

"I'm afraid you'll get mad." She closed her eyes and swallowed.

"I won't be mad, just tell me what's gotten you so upset."

She inhaled. "I'm pregnant."

The words took a few seconds to register and when it did, it struck him hard. "Pregnant?" His arm slipped off of her.

"I knew you'd be mad. You've never wanted children and I was trying so hard to be careful, but sometimes no matter what you do, it just happens."

He barely heard her, he was thinking of the child that she bore inside of her.

His child.

He was going to be a father.

He had never actually said that he didn't want a family, the subject simply never came up. Having children had never even entered his mind.

"I don't want to give it up or get rid of it. I won't," she blurted out ardently, eyes blazing, body tensed for a fight.

"I would never ask you to." He squeezed her hands. "I want it. I want this baby."

"You do?" Her jaw dropped.

"I do. This is great news." He leaned forward and hugged her into him.

"But I thought…"

"You were wrong. It is possible for Rachel Sheldon to be wrong sometimes you know," he joked. "You'll make a wonderful mother, Rachel, you really will."

"After all these years, you still find a way to surprise me, Bradley." She smiled through watery eyes. When they pulled apart, they talked a while about her pregnancy and then he remembered his other news.

"I have more good news. I found out today that I'm in the running for another Booker Prize," he said excitedly.

"For *Existence*?" she gasped, wiping her eyes.

"Yep." He stood up and started untying his tie.

"Oh, you must be so excited," she gushed. "That's a lot to take in one day."

"I'm going to call Masterson and tell him tonight. Hopefully we can get together in the next few weeks for dinner, we'll have to work out a night when all three of us are free."

Masterson had since retired from teaching and was now a full-time writer.

He was incredibly ambitious for his age and had already produced two more novels since his first soldier's story. He wrote tales of war and heroism until political tyranny and though he hadn't garnered any awards or acclaim, he couldn't have cared less. He was doing what he wanted, and to him that was more than enough. They tried to get together with him once a month for dinner.

"That would be nice," she nodded.

"I'm going to call Kate tonight and tell her all of our good news. When we go down for our visit this weekend, we should take the whole family out for dinner to celebrate."

They had been going to Aldon for a visit one weekend per month for the last two years, after he had spent the summer of 1980 renovating his parents' home for Madeline's growing family to move into. That summer had been a touching, intense time for the Bradley family. Feelings surfaced, issues were vocalized, tears were shed but a peace was finally settled among his siblings. They buried the past that summer, as they scrubbed the Bradley house clean of shadows, resentments and lurking memories. They all wanted to move on, but more importantly, they wanted to strengthen their family ties again. He was grateful that Eve and Madeline were willing to give him a chance, and he worked hard to re-establish a relationship with them.

And on one lone, dark night in August, when the moon was high, he set flame to the isolated shed that was no longer of use to anyone. He watched it burn brightly, overwhelmed with powerful varying emotions, and forced images into his mind of better times spent here. When nature's insatiable beast finally burned it down to mere ashes, he turned his back on the ruin once and for all. It was over. History was not meant to be forgotten, but it was not meant to be repeated either. It was time to write a new chapter for his life.

When he returned to Toronto; after heavy persuasion on the subject from Kate, he started seeing a respected psychiatrist. It was a slow, painful process but eventually he was able to start expressing his guilt-ridden angst towards his father and himself, and also began to verbalize the remorse he felt for not reaching out to his mother when she was alive. He started to articulate what he should have said to her, and confronted the excruciating emotions that accompanied those revelations. He even quit writing for six months so that he could sort out his own thoughts and inner dialogue without getting distracted.

He still had things to work on; issues with his parents that still troubled him in the late night hours but he started to think of himself as a 'work in progress' too. The healing process had just begun and he reminded himself that he had time. He had his whole life to restore what was still broken. He was just through obsessing over the past. It was time to move on.

"Well, I'll go start dinner," Rachel grunted as she pushed herself off the bed.

"No." He turned around. "Let's go out. We have too much to celebrate to stay home tonight."

"Really?" Her eyes brightened, Daniel still rarely liked to go out. His literary success made him a minor celebrity and everywhere he went, people noticed him and asked for an autograph. He hated the attention.

"Really." He stepped forward and placed his hands on her bent elbows.

"It's a new chapter for us, Rachel, and everything is going to change now."

Things had *needed* to change, he couldn't even think of the place that he was in two years earlier. He never wanted to sink that low again, never wanted to feel that lonely and isolated, where he didn't want to live in his own skin. Now that he knew what was out there, he could never go back to that bleak kind of emptiness again.

Once they were ready to go, he serenely walked his wife to their car, opened the door for her and watched her get into the BMW. On the way to the restaurant, he thought about the tiny life growing inside of her; of the child she would bear that they would shape and mold together. A child that would be everything he wasn't. A child free of everything that had repressed him; who would have the gift of choices, of knowing that they could be and do anything that they wanted to. He would be for this baby, everything that his mother had been for him, everything his father wanted to be, and continue their great legacy. He would surround this baby, with the family that he was beginning to know again, and fill its life with all that he had missed out on for so long.

He was going to be someone's father.

And as he reached over to hold Rachel's hand, a warm, unexpected smile spread across his face.